D0959087

THE LEMON

THE LEMON

S. E. BOYD

Viking

VIKING
An imprint of Penguin Random House LLC
penguinrandomhouse.com

LIBRARY OF CONGRESS CATALOGING-IN-PUBLICATION DATA

Names: Boyd, S. E., author.
Title: The lemon : a novel / S. E. Boyd.
Description: [New York] : Viking, [2022]
Identifiers: LCCN 2022012113 (print) | LCCN 2022012114 (ebook) |
ISBN 9780593490440 (hardcover) | ISBN 9780593490457 (ebook)
Subjects: LCGFT: Humorous fiction. | Novels.
Classification: LCC PS3602.O9329 L46 2022 (print) |
LCC PS3602.O9329 (ebook) | DDC 813/.6—dc23/eng/20220318
LC record available at https://lccn.loc.gov/2022012113
LC ebook record available at https://lccn.loc.gov/2022012114

Printed in the United States of America
1st Printing

BOOK DESIGN BY LUCIA BERNARD

To Raoul's,

Our own French Restaurant with the French Name

JOHN DOE

BELFAST, NORTHERN IRELAND

Sunday, June 30, 2019, 8:44 p.m.

It started with the potted herring. The herring was from Ardglass, they pointed out. And there was potato apple bread from Armagh, eaten in the home of an ex-IRA bomb maker with one arm ("Not a top bomb maker," joked a producer). Then a beef pasty supper with a former Ulster Defence Association man. Not to be confused with the former Ulster Freedom Fighters man with whom John Doe shared an Ulster fry, or the Real IRA man who'd given him a fifteens cake, and something called champ, which seemed like it was just mashed potatoes and onions, but one didn't want to be rude.

Doe had also sat across from a former officer commanding of the Irish National Liberation Army and shared a vegetable roll, which, true to the backward logic of Northern Ireland, was basically a circular meat loaf that included very few vegetables. They'd done home visits in places like the Falls and the Shankill, in shitty little flats with big, beautiful sectarian murals. And once Doe had spoken with enough twitchy-eyed "ex"-militants to understand that the current state of politics in Northern Ireland was actually some sort of invisible-fence rodeo, likely to turn into Pamplona-style goring as soon as the bulls realized the fence wasn't real, he started in on the restaurants and bars.

There was a conversation with the chef at Deanes at Queens over lamb rump, ham hock, brie fritters, and cockles, plus wheaten bread served with Abernethy Butter. A fancy meal and B-roll of the River Lagan at OX. John Long's for fish and chips. Pints in a pub called Duke of York, which was blown up during the Troubles and rebuilt. And an interview with a locally born action-movie celebrity in one of the snugs inside the Crown Liquor Saloon, with its ornate stained glass and Italian woodworking.

At each stop, the makeup artist would make sure Doe was properly disheveled, and the sound guy would make sure his levels were excellent, and the first AD would run back through the outline and questions and possible conversation angles. The camera operators would make sure to get close-ups of the little details Doe liked—the places where you could see one mural had been painted on top of another, the contents of someone's bookshelf, the stray dogs (wherever they were, Doe wanted to capture images of the dogs).

When the camera was on, Doe was gracious and generous and thoughtful and giving but unafraid to ask hard questions, ensuring they were delivered with respect and enough runway. He could go on like this for hours at a time, and the way they filmed, that's what he did. But when the camera was off, Doe retreated back to a corner to smoke Raptor-brand cigarettes, which he had shipped in from Canada, with his PA and/or the director of photography, or to read, or to listen to Brian Eno's *Music for Airports* with over-the-ear, noise-canceling headphones.

Once filming had wrapped, and he'd carefully extricated himself from committing to any sort of social engagement with the locally born action-movie celebrity, who'd kept asking all the women on set if they "liked to get wet," Doe walked back to his hotel alone. He was recognized a few times, but mostly after the fact. One man wearing a red-and-white sweatshirt with George Best's face stenciled on the back asked him for a selfie and he complied. He watched a teenage couple kiss with an impressive amount of tongue, and a freckled boy, who would later be identified as twelve, drive by in a luxury car, which would later be identified as stolen.

Doe got to his hotel at nine p.m. In the lobby, he saw a blonde woman wearing a Barbour Acorn waxed cotton jacket sketching something on a napkin and drinking a gin and tonic. As she got up, she made eye contact with Doe.

"John."

"Lara."

He watched her walk out the door, then texted his friend Paolo and told him to meet him at a local pub called the Christmas at ten thirty.

The hotel he was staying at was called bandit, intentionally lower-case, for whatever e. e. cummings–fetishizing reason the external marketing agency hired to help with the name had come up with. The hotel's theme seemed to be loosely based on the idea that the lower part of Northern Ireland used to be known as Bandit Country, though clearly this external marketing agency failed to dig deeper into the meaning or they might've discovered that this was because the Armagh area had been a safe haven for the IRA. Either way, murals of County Armagh (created by local Catholic street artists!) adorned the walls, and the restaurant, Orchard (apparently Armagh is also known for orchards!), only used farm goods from Armagh.

The rooftop bar was made to look like an abandoned rural shed surrounded by a high hedge that contained the "secret" entrance to the bar. Inside, you sat on reclaimed tractor parts and ordered craft cocktails made by bartenders wearing aprons sewn by Armagh artisans. The cocktail names played off small towns in the county (the Darkley and Stormy, for example) and the list was woven through with straw. Doe was staying at bandit because bandit was new and "boutique," and new, boutique hotels had the best suites, and it was well-known that John Doe loved himself a great hotel suite.

His suite at bandit was actually three separate rooms, each showcasing a different part of the same mural of Lough Neagh. There was a sitting room with a long, comfortable weathered leather couch, a library room filled with first editions from Northern Irish authors, a bedroom with a big blue leather headboard, and a bathroom featuring a claw-foot tub apparently reclaimed from a farmhouse once owned by the Earl of Shaftesbury.

Doe had reached a level of fame at which people assumed he needed things customized to his liking, and thus Doe made demands that things be customized to his liking. In his contract, it was stipulated that Doe needed a suite, and it was preferable that that suite had a California king–size bed (Doe liked to sleep across a bed with no pillow) and a bathtub (preferably claw-foot, though that wasn't a deal breaker). He needed a box of Ecru #9 Embassy 96 lb. stationery cards with corresponding envelopes, alongside a Baronfig Squire rollerball pen, so he could write letters longhand, or at least entertain the romantic notion of writing letters longhand. And he needed a bowl of local citrus.

It was 9:09 p.m. when Doe got back to his room and found said bowl of artisanal citrus waiting for him. He was informed via a small handwritten card that the citrus, so rare in Ireland, was from a farm in Bannfoot, a small village in the townland of Derryinver, within, of course, County Armagh. After taking off his coat, he rolled up his sleeves and retrieved his knife bag. From it, he got out a cutting board and his R. Murphy Jackson Cannon bar knife. Created by a 150-year-old knife maker in Massachusetts, in collaboration with a Boston bartender Doe had worked for a long time ago, the bar knife was made from high-carbon stainless steel with a square tip to notch citrus and remove seeds. The handle was made of a durable tropical hardwood known as cocobolo. In total, Doe owned about a hundred of these knives, and he brought one with him wherever he went (though, much to the frustration of the network's sponsorship wrangler, he refused to publicize this fact).

At 9:13 p.m., he picked up several lemons and placed them next to the cutting board. He took one, felt along its mottled skin, and, barely looking, placed it down on the board and chopped off the ends. Then, with a cut side facing down, he halved it, flipped each half onto its back like an upside-down turtle, and made a clean slice through the middle without cutting all the way to the rind. Then he flipped it back over, made five clean, even cuts all the way through each half, picked the lemon slices off the board with his knife, and moved them to the side.

Once he'd cut through six lemons, John Doe picked up the final slice and carried it with him into the closet in the front hall. In the closet, he found his old, weathered leather belt, looped it around his neck, popped the lemon slice in his mouth, and unbuttoned his pants.

When he stopped breathing, the clock on the bedside table next to a note from the manager regarding the origin of the locally bottled spring water said 9:26.

PART I

THE MAN

1.

CHARLIE McCREE

BELFAST, NORTHERN IRELAND

Monday, July 1, 2019, 8:13 a.m.

Charles Ulysses McCree—aka Smilin' Charlie McCree—whistled down the hall of the top floor of bandit in a long-shot bid to conceal the fact that he was barely holding himself together. The pathways connecting his brain to his arms and legs and feet and fingers had been disrupted. Some of his extremities ached, while others were numb. There was no rhyme or reason to it. Not that he could see, anyway. Before Charlie came to work this morning, he had dropped a mug of tea in his kitchen. One moment he was holding it, the next he was not, and fucked if he knew what had transpired in the interim. Perhaps he was dreaming; perhaps a sinkhole had opened in his brain. But while some existing neural pathways had been severed, new ones had formed. His hair hurt, for example. So did his fingernails. Dead things brought to life by a record-breaking two-day blitz upon the City of Belfast.

His eyes may have lost the ability to focus properly, but he was still able to discern the form of a housekeeper as she emerged from the dark fog of the hallway before him. Her name tag read "Kitty." Presented with this information, Charlie attempted to pass himself off not only as a human being, but as a human being who sings.

" 'Oh Kitty, my darling, remember,' " he intoned. " 'That the doom will be mine if I stay.' "

"Fuck off with ya, Charlie," she said, brushing past.

The weekend had been bloody sensational. The festivities started in the dark among the mannequins at the Filthy Quarter on Dublin Road, as they always did, because the decor allowed the lads to simulate intercourse with insensate objects, a cherished pastime. Having achieved a suitable level of intoxication, Charlie and his mates then set out to sup from every pub in the center of the city—the Garrick, White's, McHugh's, the Bullitt Hotel bar, the John Hewitt—moving haphazardly from one to the next, becoming louder and more damaged, bouncing off lorries and light poles and Proddies and Papes, mounting bold charges and beating craven retreats, and in time covering a significant swath of the city, like a robotic vacuum cleaner that generates mess instead of sucking it up.

Friday yielded to Saturday and, after an interlude of impromptu public sleep, Charlie and the lads hit the daylight like an enemy beachhead and fought well into the afternoon. As the hours passed and his mates began to show signs of wear, Charlie only gathered force. He was a hard man to keep pace with. Alcohol amplified his essential Charlie-ness and turned it into a matter of public concern. There was no hostility to it, however. Only joy. Only lust for living. At one point, Charlie acquired a bridal veil, presumably from a hen party in which he had temporarily embedded himself. This accoutrement, he was later informed, inspired him to attempt to kiss a police officer on the mouth while speaking in a womanly voice and to steal a multitude of orange parking cones, which the lads subsequently used as megaphones to inform the masses about the many arcane toilet procedures favored by Her Majesty, the queen.

By late afternoon on Saturday, time had slipped from its skein and morale ebbed. By nine p.m., most of Charlie's mates had fallen away. Some had been decked, over women or for slights intended or unwitting. Others were sickened. One simply lost heart and skulked off. No matter: Charlie just replaced them with new friends. It was easy. When Charlie attained a certain state, he ceased to be a normal human trapped in body and status, limited by personal and moral inhibitions and the strictures of a class-based society. He became magnetic, magnificent. Charlie in his cups ascended to the rarified air. He became Prince Charlie of Belfast, friend to man and woman, leader in song, and the city lined up behind him.

And then came the hard light of Monday morning and Charlie did what any self-respecting man would do: he got up, pulled a strange bridal veil out of his pants, threw up, and went to work.

He had taken the job at bandit after his band, which fused Irish rebel music with ska, had been banished from most of the city's clubs for what he was certain was a mix of political reasons and personal jealousies. As Charlie temporarily paused his ascension to global stardom, he, like so many others who dreamed of artistic immortality, turned to the hospitality business. But unlike some of his fellow artistes, Charlie loved it. He was a good talker, charming and presentable and not a bad-looking guy, all of which helped.

But he also had a hidden genius. Charlie could convey a sense of Belfast authenticity, while at the same time not laying it on so thick that the foreigners who stayed at bandit felt excluded or ill at ease. This was a delicate dance, to be certain. Success in hospitality in Belfast was the product of relentless calibration. The sort of rich foreign tourist who stayed at bandit wanted an authentic Belfast experience. But they preferred it come at a safe remove. They didn't want to be made to feel guilty or uncomfortable while getting it. Charlie's genius was in walking that line. He could tell hair-raising stories. Sure, sometimes he took factual liberties, but he was so engaging that no one ever questioned him. And no matter how dark the tale, Charlie always took care to end it on a grace note: people can behave in terrible ways, but goodness prevails with faith and good works, and the visitors who come to this place are brave, and their attention means a great deal to his people. *Though we have suffered,* he implied with his every utterance, *fear not, we do not fancy ourselves superior to you.*

His friend Seamus accused him of running some kind of rank, Troubles-themed minstrel show—and, sure, there was an element of performance to it—but Charlie wasn't doing it out of cynicism. Perish the thought. He was the world's greatest optimist. He just wanted to make people happy. He just wanted to connect. To enter their lives and live on in their memories. That's why he loved performing music, after all. He could have been a hard man about dealing with these tourists as they walked around sticking their fingers in the wounds of his city, but his favored approach came as a great relief to his guests, particularly the Irish Americans, and for it they tipped him lavishly.

CHARLIE CONTINUED DOWN the hallway, listing slightly, performing a quick check of his vital systems. In the seconds since being cursed by Kitty the housekeeper, something had gone wrong with his foot. It felt abraded, like the top of the inside of his shoe had been lined with sandpaper. Charlie couldn't figure out what it was, but it hurt. Then it hit him: the tea. The scalding liquid must have landed on his foot. It had just taken a couple of hours for the signal to arrive at his brain, like a lorry through a checkpoint. *Jesus fuck*, he thought, *I am the most bombed-out individual in the most bombed-out city in Ireland*.

When he'd arrived at work an hour earlier, it was with the fearful conviction that his body would at any moment void in all directions in front of a mass of horrified guests, like a great green fountain of sick. He needed to mobilize. He picked up a phone and pretended a guest was speaking to him.

"Yes sir," he said. "Two pillows. Fluffy ones. Right away, sir."

He'd then obtained two pillows from a room behind the desk and set out on his travels, even though the pillows were incredibly fucking hard for him to carry in his present condition. He wandered down hallways, into stairwells, and throughout the facility for some thirty minutes before he found himself on the top floor, passing a suite whose door was slightly ajar, from which a faint mewling sound was heard.

What is this, then? Charlie wondered. He first knocked gently. "Hello? This is Charlie from the front desk?"

When no one came, Charlie gently pushed the door until it stopped against something soft and heavy. Charlie craned his neck around and that's when he saw them: two men by the closet. One was on his knees. Charlie took measure of the man. He didn't look like he should be on his knees. There was something about his skin, his hair, his clothing. He was preternaturally neat and composed. He looked like he'd never been on his knees in his life. And yet he was. That was interesting.

The other man was hanging from the closet rod with a belt around his neck, boxer briefs and jeans around his ankles, and a lemon wedge in his mouth. Charlie had delivered those lemons to this room himself and written a little note explaining that they came from a farm in

Bannfoot, a small village in the townland of Derryinver, within the County Armagh. *Quite a turn for that humble fruit,* Charlie thought. *Sure, life is nothing but surprises.*

Charlie was ready to turn and walk right back down the hallway. The protocol in situations such as these was to see little, say less, and then wait until the local police were summoned by an odor. But before he fled back to the front desk, Charlie noticed something: a Patek Philippe Nautilus on the kneeling man's wrist. It must have cost twenty thousand quid. And there was a Rolex Daytona on the dead man's wrist, probably worth about the same. Charlie had read about these items on the internet. These were very nice items, he'd learned: items that indicated the presence of real money. Which meant that humble Charlie had suddenly found himself in the intimate company of both death and money. Which was quite interesting when you really thought about it.

The man bowed his head, closed his eyes, and took a breath. He stood up, smoothing his shirt and pants. His movement caused a slight breeze that found its way to Charlie's crooked nose. *Yer man smells fucking great,* Charlie thought. *Jesus, what a brilliant-smelling man. What kind of life produces that kind of smell?* he wondered. *What kind of money?*

The man took another breath and composed himself.

Intoxicated by the rich musk, Charlie leaned slightly into the door. It creaked.

The man looked up and saw Charlie. And so shaken was he that he simply stared as if trying to figure out whether Charlie was real.

"May I?"

Paolo nodded. "Can you help me?" he said quietly, his eyes brimming with tears.

Fascinating, Charlie thought. *How thrilling was life! Endless surprises! A man of this caliber wanting help from the likes of yer man Smilin' Charlie.*

Charlie had always assumed that the rich just knew how to handle situations like this on their own, that they had people on call to lavish favors upon those who could keep their mouths shut and to shoot the rest. But here was this great man, asking Charlie McCree for help. The universe had shifted. Almost undetectably so. But it had. For once, Charlie was not the subordinate. He was an equal. Even more than that: he was sort of frankly pretty fucking superior when you really thought about it.

"This," the man said. "This is a very important man. And a good man." He swallowed. "I don't know what to do."

A good man, Charlie thought. *It's so rare in life that one encounters a good man. We all fall, we all sin, none of us is perfect. Not even yer man with the Rolex, evidently. But we cannot let our sins define us, nor should we try to define others by their sins. It was Jesus himself who said it. And Jesus was a good man too. Well, half a man, anyway. Or a third of a man? Which part was the ghost?* He could never get the math right. Whatever the percentages, Charlie just wanted to be on the side of goodness.

Also, by now he'd noticed the dead man's evident penis. And there was only one thing to do when a man came upon such a scene. "You need to make it so it looks like yer man . . ." Charlie gripped his throat and stuck out his tongue. "Instead of . . ." Charlie released his throat and gestured to the man's crotch. "Otherwise, there will simply be no end to the laughter."

The man swallowed and glanced down at the dead man. He couldn't get a word out. Charlie's proposal expanded, filling the air. The man mustered a small nod.

"I will do everything in my power to help you, sir," Charlie said to the man's watch. "I am at your disposal."

"Have you had any experience with this before, working in the hotel?"

"Oh, loads," Charlie said.

He hadn't, but what was experience, really?

"Okay, so, what do we do?" the man said.

"Well, for starters, sir, take out the lemon."

"Right, okay," the man said. He leaned over and, with visible distaste, carefully removed the lemon. He looked for a trash bin to throw it in.

"No, sir," Charlie said.

The man stared at him blankly.

"Evidence, sir."

Do the very rich not watch television?

The man understood.

"Right," he said. "So, what? We throw it out the window?"

This man was testing Charlie's patience.

"If we throw it out the window, sir, it could hit someone, and if they collect it and call the police, the police might take it to the lab for testing," Charlie said. "Trust me, I am from Belfast."

Charlie put the pillows down and grabbed the plastic liner from the small bin by the desk.

"Just give it to me," he continued. "I'll take care of it." Charlie gestured for the man to drop it in the bag. He did, and Charlie carefully tied the bag up and placed it in his pocket. "We've an incinerator downstairs," he explained. "Now the pants, sir."

The man nodded and got on his knees, and he carefully pulled up the dead man's boxer briefs, then his black jeans. This was difficult, as rigor mortis had set in. As he struggled to pack the man's unit back in behind the button fly, Charlie could see it was all becoming real for the other man now, the finality of it. Charlie had observed this before, the initial wave of panic giving way to acceptance that the unnatural stillness that had overtaken the person in question was, in fact, death.

He was deeply moved, and thus offered a silent intercession for the soul of the dead man, and for the living one as well. And in that silence, there was the click of a camera phone.

The man turned around and saw Charlie standing there, holding the phone. Charlie didn't even know why he'd done it. *What a silly thing to do!* he thought. *Taking a photo at a moment like this.* He smiled and slipped the phone back into his pocket. The man stared at him. There was a look of fear on his face. No doubt it was the fear stirred in every man when he comes face-to-face with the only true thing in life: that death will have us all. Charlie, hoping to distract the poor man from his sorrows, filled the silence with action.

"We're not out of the woods yet," he said, employing an idiom he'd heard on television. "Now, here's what we're going to do." Jesus, Charlie loved giving orders to a man wearing a watch like that. "I'm going to leave this room," he said. "I'm going to go have a wee nap in the stairwell. And then I'm going to return to the desk and I'm going to tell my manager that a man has taken his own life here. I'm going to say you were here when I walked in, and that I stayed a moment because you were upset and I didn't know what to do. And that is all I am going to say. Do you understand?"

The man kept staring at him, unsure.

"This is Belfast," Charlie said. "I wouldn't last long here if I didn't know how to keep a secret."

"Okay," Paolo said. He took a breath. "Thank you."

Charlie stuck out his hand. He was pleased to find it fully operational. He squeezed the kneeling man's hand and found it both muscular and soft. *Money,* he thought. *It was money that made your hands like that.*

"Well, best of luck, sir," he said.

"Thank you . . . ?"

Charlie straightened his posture.

"The name is Charles Ulysses McCree," said Charlie. "But my friends call me Charlie."

"Thank you, Charlie."

"My pleasure, Mr. . . . ?"

"Cabrini. Paolo."

There it was.

"The famous chef, is it?"

"Yeah."

"My pleasure, Chef."

"Paolo, please."

Charlie maintained his grip on Paolo's hand. They looked at each other, eye to eye, man to man, and Charlie's whole being hummed. In spite of himself, he saw in this hastily improvised union the seeds of a partnership, and from those seeds he foresaw the sprouting of alternate futures: a future in which Charlie coolly and unselfconsciously worked side-by-side with this man, and other such men, solving thorny problems and advancing his own interests by protecting theirs, until one day, he simply became one of them. But Charlie already felt himself changing. This situation had alerted him to a capability within himself he didn't know existed. It had expanded him somehow. What an adventure, this existence! All his life had been defined by borders, by limits. Many of the people he'd grown up with loved those borders. They took great comfort in them. But not Charlie. Charlie had no interest in containment. He regarded the man, his mind aswarm with possibility. Here it was: the future, and only days before his thirty-seventh birthday.

"Oh," said Paolo. "Let me just— For your trouble."

Paolo removed his wallet from his back pocket and opened it. He riffled through a mass of receipts and ticket stubs. His face turned red.

He riffled more. He looked embarrassed. *Poor devil*, Charlie thought. He was flattered that such a great man felt so comfortable being vulnerable with him like this. But then the man removed a single note, a tenner, and handed it to Charlie using an arm from which dangled a watch that cost more than Charlie would make that year.

"I'm sorry," Paolo said. "I don't . . . I usually have cash."

"Quite all right, sir," Charlie said. Three seconds passed and neither man moved.

"And, look, if you're ever in New York," Paolo said, "I want you to look me up. You can come to my restaurant and be my guest. It's the least I can do, Charlie. I'd love to host you. I really would."

The coldness disappeared. "I'd like that a great deal, Paolo," Charlie said. "Good luck."

He turned, opened the door, stepped out, closed it, and walked back down the hallway, refreshed and aglow. Charlie's brain was firing away now, clean and clear, his eyes seeing, his limbs working in concert, and his foot hurting only a little. *What a top man*, he thought as he strode down gray-blue carpet toward the elevators and into the future, feeling the lemon in his pocket with every step.

2.

CHEF PAOLO CABRINI

BELFAST, NORTHERN IRELAND

Monday, July 1, 2019, 9:01 a.m.

There were three chefs in the world more famous than Paolo Cabrini, all of whom were French and two of whom were dead. Paolo had cooked for five presidents, four kings, three prime ministers, two chancellors, and One Direction, which he learned was a pop band. He spoke six languages fluently, personally oversaw a staff of two hundred, and had once both officiated and cooked for a billionaire friend's wedding on an active volcano.

Paolo had been in kitchens for forty years, and kitchens were cauldrons of crisis, and yet he'd always thrived. Other chefs used to call him the Iceman (until he discovered that was also the nickname of a notorious mob assassin) for the way nothing fazed him. One (less famous) chef who'd worked with Paolo put it best: "If the pilot dies, Paolo is the one you want to land the plane."

And yet, as he lay weeping in a giant, empty claw-foot tub once owned by the Earl of Shaftesbury twenty feet from where his best friend had just died, running back through his CV didn't help. He just kept thinking about the click.

Paolo had heard it just as he was struggling to pull up Doe's boxers. Which meant that that black-haired Irishman had a picture that made it look like Paolo was touching his dead and arguably even more famous best friend's privates. And, for his silence in the matter, Paolo had given this man, what? Ten pounds. He smacked himself on the forehead. Stupid!

Maybe he could go downstairs and take out money from the cash machine in the lobby. But how much? Five hundred pounds? A thousand? Ten thousand? Would a lot more money make it look like a bribe? What was the legality of all of this? If this picture came out, would he be arrested? Charged with a crime?

He'd only agreed to the man's plan because he wanted Doe to have dignity in his death. He wanted his friend to be remembered for all the truly remarkable, world-changing things he'd done. The way he'd touched millions of people all over this planet. For his cynicism about the things you should be cynical about, and his unfettered curiosity and earnestness about the other stuff. For his passing to not become a punch line.

Paolo remembered when the wife of a line producer on Doe's show died a few years before, leaving the man to raise a six-year-old boy by himself. The producer told him that Doe stayed at their shitty Brooklyn apartment for two months, sleeping on the couch, cooking for them, and playing with the boy for hours on end while the producer grieved. One day, the producer walked by the kitchen while Doe was making the boy breakfast and heard Doe telling him in urgent tones that life wasn't all sadness and loss. It could be beautiful, and exciting, and hilarious—you just had to stay open, and to do that you had to be strong, and you had to be brave, and you had to be kind.

"Little buddy," he said, "there are just so many adventures to be had."

The producer told Paolo that, upon hearing that, he'd sobbed loudly in the hall. Doe never mentioned a thing.

Thinking that he was doing all of this for that man momentarily steeled Paolo. That sort of man should not be found dead self-pleasuring. That sort of man deserved to die a hero. And so Paolo got out of the tub. As he took the dress shirt he'd meticulously folded and placed beside the tub's ornate claw feet and began to put it back on, he tried to figure out his next step.

He realized, with some amount of trepidation, he needed to call Nia Greene.

Paolo picked up his cell phone and found her number. But then he realized that though he needed to call Nia, he also needed to lie to Nia so as not to implicate her in any of this shit. And Nia was not a person you lied to. She would eat his craven heart with a glass of Châteauneuf-du-Pape. He put down his phone by the tub and walked over to the bathroom sink. Paolo looked at himself briefly in the mirror, carefully avoiding his own eyes, then walked back to the tub and regarded the phone.

Call.

Just call.

Just hit the button.

Call.

In the distance he thought he heard the faint whine of a siren.

3.

NIA GREENE

NEW YORK, NY

Monday, July 1, 2019, 4:07 a.m.

It was a Tuesday in the year 2000 when Nia Greene discovered her boss had been weighing his own feces.

She was, at the time, a junior agent at AAE—Artists Are Everything—a mid-tier talent agency in Los Angeles, working under Ken Buber, a feared agency head. Nia had served as Buber's assistant for two years, dealing with his tantrums, his paranoia, his exacting nutritional requirements, and his cruel errands. She'd been hit by four water bottles, a waffle, and a chair. Only the latter occasioned a meeting with an HR person, who subtly employed the language of healing to threaten Nia to keep her mouth shut.

The job was challenging on all fronts. Nia had been made to literally scream her enthusiasm for her job in front of colleagues. She was forced to multitask to the nth degree—dealing with the intricacies of the business, managing the relentless day-to-day, and coping with the unique psychology of each client. As an assistant she was completely powerless, but she was also the person people had to talk to when they wanted their money, which made her an irresistible target for the pissed-off talent. If a client managed to bypass her and scream directly at her boss, her boss would be out five seconds later loudly threatening disembowelment and termination. All the while, Nia was forced to fend off the other assistants' ceaseless attempts to sabotage her and get her job. It was savage, exhausting, and not a little exciting, and Nia had survived it all and become an agent.

More specifically, she became an agent who one day rushed into Ken Buber's private bathroom after a client's aging Saint Bernard emptied itself onto his carpet in the middle of a meeting. Nia intended to get toilet paper or tissues to sop up the mess. But when she slid open the door, something else caught her eye: a custom toilet with a little plateau in the center, and on that little plateau, a little digital scale. Nia looked to the right, and there was a notepad and a pencil on a small table. The notepad contained two columns of figures in Ken Buber's handwriting. *What the fuck?* she thought, before a small, rough hand belonging to a mute and reddened Buber violently pulled her out of the bathroom.

But it was too late. Nia had seen the scale and Buber knew it, and she knew that he knew it, which was wonderful, and the natural order was suddenly altered. You could see each of them in that moment calculating what they had gained and lost. He wondered: *What will I have to give her to keep her quiet about my scale? What damage can she do? What would people say if they knew?* And she in turn wondered: *What can I get in exchange for my silence? What damage can he do, knowing that I know about the scale? What damage can* I *do?* It was all good fun and it happened on Tuesday, July 18, 2000.

Nia Greene remembered because that was the day she met and

signed John Doe, the day that she embarked on the greatest adventure of her life—an adventure that ended at 4:07 a.m. New York time, on July 1, 2019, the moment Paolo Cabrini called from Belfast to tell her that John had killed himself.

LOVE IS ALL well and good, but if there's one thing Nia Greene knew about weathering a crisis, it was that if you're not a master compartmentalizer, you're dead. You needed to cultivate a kind of functional sociopathy in this business that allowed you to turn off normal human feeling and dedicate yourself wholly to achieving a desired result. That was how you succeeded. So that's what Nia did when she got the call from Paolo Cabrini.

"Paolo," Nia said, after absorbing the initial shock wave of grief, "I'm going to be an asshole to you, but it's not because I don't care. Do you understand?"

"I understand," he said.

"Tell me what happened."

"He hanged himself. With a belt. In a closet here."

"*Here* as in . . . ?"

"At the hotel."

"Who found him?"

"I did. This morning."

"When's the last time you saw him?"

"We were supposed to meet last night and he didn't show up. I figured, you know, he was just . . ."

"Being John."

Paolo took a deep breath. "Yeah. We always meet for breakfast, so this morning I went to his room and found him. In the closet."

"How did you get into his room?"

"He always gives me a key."

"Was there a note?"

"No."

"Did he seem off to you at all the last few days?"

"No. Well, maybe. I don't know."

"In the room, did you see anything unusual? No one else had been in there? Nothing seemed strange?"

"No," he said. "Nothing strange."

"Belfast can be a pretty touchy town. He didn't piss anyone off or anything?"

"No."

"Any signs of struggle in the room?"

"No."

"So," she said, almost to herself. "Suicide."

Paolo paused. "Yes. Definitely."

"Okay. Am I the first person you told?"

The line went quiet again.

"Paolo?"

"Yes, Nia. You are."

Nia let that hang in the air for a moment before responding.

"Paolo, are you sure you're telling me everything?"

Nia heard breathing on the line, interrupted by the odd sob. A breeze rustled the leaves through an open window. A clock ticked.

"Are you telling me everything?" she asked again, more softly this time.

More breathing.

"No," Paolo finally said.

Nia leaned back and sighed. She rubbed her eyes. "Was it what I think it was?"

"Yes," Paolo said.

"Fuck."

"How did you know?"

"Because I know everything about him, Paolo," she said.

"Right."

"Is he still . . . the way you found him?"

"No, I couldn't leave him like that."

"Okay."

Since she was a kid, Nia had had this gift. It wasn't quite composure, though it was related to it. And it wasn't quite instinct, though it was related to that too. While some kids, when caught doing something, would instinctively lie or fess up, Nia's mind would go past both lie and truth to the second, and third, and fourth links in a chain reaction. When she got to the end of the line of one story, she did the same for the other. Then she evaluated the potential outcomes and made her decision. She did it so fast that no one else was aware of it. It had served her well.

Nia was now weighing all potential causes of death equally, as though she was the one with the power to decide which was real. In a way, she was, and she would. *Let's game it out,* she thought.

Start with the true story: Nia saw no upside to the true story, save for the virtue of it being true. If he'd merely been caught performing autoerotic asphyxiation they could have made a case for him destigmatizing a kink. They could have maybe traded on his self-acceptance and authenticity and come out of it if not ahead then certainly not too far behind. But no. If this got out, it would be like the scale on Ken Buber's toilet: once seen, never unseen. It would undo John's legacy, taint his work, and probably sink his books and shows. He'd become a punch line. Another celebrity jerk-off mishap. That would be the image that first came to mind when people spoke the name John Doe. Nia refused to let this happen.

So what about an alternative cause of death? Foul play? Nah. Doe could be prickly, but he was savvy enough not to get accidentally tangled up with dangerous people. And while his personal life could be messy, he was always disciplined when he was on a shoot. He didn't go clubbing. He didn't trawl for women. His hard-drug days were over. Nia ruled this one out.

Which brought her to suicide. What if John Doe was a great man who, after a long and secret and heroic battle with depression, succumbed to despair and killed himself? A man who carried within him not only a tenacious curiosity about the world and a zeal for life but also a profound darkness that eventually consumed him? That wouldn't eclipse his legacy—it would color it, maybe deepen it. People who read his books and watched his show would realize what a gift it was that he lasted as long as he did, in spite of it all, to live the way he did and bring you this message of joy and quest and optimism. They'd realize that he loved life not because it was loveable, but because it was so fragile. You would see on the screen and in those pages a man chasing life, but also heroically evading despair. You would see the heroic battle. At least for a time.

Without question, there would be an explosion of awareness for mental health issues and a flood of donations for suicide prevention organizations. A whole cottage industry would crop up, and they'd cry from the rooftops, *If it could happen to this guy, it could happen to anyone. So take care of yourselves, and take care of one another.*

Years ago, she had asked Doe what his wishes were for the disposition of his remains. They were working on their wills together. He told her, "Light my corpse on fire, load it into a catapult, and shoot it at any acapella group that does Prince covers." But he didn't put it in writing, and she couldn't help but think he wouldn't mind if his death actually helped some people who were having a hard time. He was not without his demons either. He was fond of quoting a lyric by a country singer named John Moreland when he talked about his past: "Well these angels in my eardrums, they can't tell bad from good."

In a way, Nia was keeping a scorecard: suicide versus accidental death, and the result was decisive. John Doe had committed suicide.

"Okay, here's what we're gonna do," she told Paolo. "You tell the front desk. They'll call the police. But don't talk to anyone else. And if you have to talk to someone else, you know what to say. Keep it simple."

"Okay."

"Otherwise, don't talk to anyone. Everything comes through me until I say otherwise."

"Okay."

Nia took a breath. She heard Paolo breathing on the other end of the line.

"Are you okay?" she asked.

"No," he said. "Are you?"

"No," she said. "I love you, buddy. With all my heart."

"I love you too."

"I've got to get to work."

She hung up.

Nia gave herself exactly five minutes to think about her years with John Doe. She actually set a timer. A mourning timer. In that time, she briefly allowed herself the luxury of grief. And then the timer went off and she got to work.

IT WAS 4:22 A.M. This was good. Reporters in New York and LA would all be asleep. There was still time. The problem was the UK. It was the start of business there, and reporters would be doing morning rounds, calling sources, calling cops. It was going to break. Realistically, Nia had only a couple of hours to define John Doe's legacy forever, so it was imperative that the first story be the right story.

Stage two: After compartmentalization, the key to being a good agent or a publicist—and Nia served as both for John—is relationships. Everyone says this, of course, to the point where it's been bled of all meaning. But Nia saw it a little differently. It wasn't relationships per se—not like normal people define relationships. It was something more akin to ritualistic gift-giving between hunter-gatherer bands. She'd studied this in college when she was considering going to grad school for anthropology. When one group visited another, they would always come bearing gifts. I'd come visit and give you an obsidian dagger, say. And when you came to visit me, you'd give me something of equivalent value, and so on and so forth.

These exchanges kept the relationship alive—the obligation to give and the expectation of receiving in kind. That held people together, gave them a reason to see each other, created trust, and laid the groundwork for alliances and friendships. If someone didn't reciprocate a gift, there could be hostility. If someone responded to a gift by giving something of five times more value, that could wreck the relationship too. Balance was everything. In Hollywood, a lot of people didn't get this. They understood cashing in a favor—they practically got off on it—but they didn't understand the obligation of giving in the first place, especially if they weren't asked. Nia Greene did. She had given out a lot of obsidian daggers in her career, unbidden. And it was time to collect.

Her first call, then, was to the managing director of the BBC, Colin Vester. Nia had met him when he was a rising star at the network. A great reporter, a talented producer. She had reached out to him in 2004 because she liked his work and figured he was going places. She'd thought that if she invested in him then, it could really pay off when he reached the next level. So she'd offered him the chance to do a weeklong ride-along with John Doe as he and his producers traveled the UK looking for places to shoot the show. Doe was a big star by that point; she'd granted unfettered access, Doe had given good quote, and the segment had come out great. Nia had stayed in touch with Vester after that and made sure to occasionally broker a drink between him and John as Vester climbed the corporate ladder.

He picked up on the third ring.

"Nia Greene, so nice to hear from you. How's our lad?"

"Are you in your office, Colin?"

"Yeah."

"Are you alone?"

"There's no one here but me."

"Colin, I want to tell you something, but I need to know that I can trust you, and you won't tell anyone until I say so."

"Start to tell me, and we can touch base as we go. Fair?"

"I need an embargo."

Vester sighed. "Okay. But I'm taking notes."

"Okay," Nia said. "John is dead."

She heard him exhale.

"Fuck. What happened?"

"They found his body hanging in a closet in a hotel in Belfast."

"Suicide?"

"Yes."

"The police ruled it a suicide?"

"Not yet, but it was."

"Couldn't be foul play?"

"No."

"I hate to ask this, Nia, but I have to. Do *you* think he committed suicide?"

"Yes."

"Okay. You understand I'll have to verify with the police."

"Of course."

"Okay. Nia, I'd like to run with this story."

"Not right now."

"You do know this is going to get out, probably by this afternoon."

"I know. And I want you to have it. I just have a couple of conditions."

"Go ahead."

"I need you to send your best reporter to the precinct to see if there's a police report. They can get the report, but I need them to try to get the police not to talk to any other press. I need some time. I'm the only way to confirm the reports, and I need to keep it that way."

"My Belfast bureau chief is keen, and she's owed a couple favors by some higher-ups at the PSNI."

"That's all I ask. I'm going to send over the names of some people you can speak to in the meantime. Some of John's famous friends. Once I get my shit together over here, I'll text you the go-ahead and you can have the scoop. It'll be a real story."

"I can't wait long, Nia," he said. "This is going to get out."

"I know."

"Okay," he said. "I'll ring Belfast."

"Okay. I'll be in touch."

"Nia?"

"Yeah."

"Did you find him?"

"No."

"Who found him?"

"I can't say."

"It'll be in the police report," he said.

"I know. And when you find it, you can call him. I'll set it up."

"So it's a he?"

"Fuck off, Colin."

"Sorry."

"Keep me posted and I'll do the same."

"Right . . . Nia? You all right?"

"I'm glad to be busy."

Nia hung up. *That should put a plug in it at least for a moment,* she thought, *unless the hotel leaks.* But she was betting on the hotel being discreet, wanting a couple of hours to get its own story straight before the news broke. It was 4:32 a.m. in New York, 1:32 a.m. in LA, 9:32 a.m. in London and Belfast. She could probably hold the Brits until lunchtime in New York. In the meantime, Nia needed to line up coverage at outlets she knew would handle the story sensitively. *The Washington Post, The New York Times,* the networks. The BBC story would be a solid foundation, but she needed good stories from domestic outlets. She needed something positive for people to tweet about and for websites to aggregate. Websites aggregating other websites was a form of inbreeding and usually yielded the same result: a newborn truth with one foot, no brain, and a hand growing out of its cheek. But they could be made useful.

The gravest danger to her narrative was any lingering uncertainty about the cause of death. Nia needed confirmation from the Belfast police, which, if forthcoming, would shore up their story and prevent runaway speculation. But that might take a while. If there was any doubt about how Doe died, two alternate explanations might come out: that it was foul play or that something salacious had happened. Maybe a disgruntled production assistant from Doe's show would see an opportunity to score some attention and turn up with some half-remembered anecdote that gets traction. Or some jealous chef or bartender who thought he should have had Doe's career would start telling some lascivious story from Doe's coke days. Or one of the musicians Doe dated, panicked about her declining star power, would see a chance to get back into the public eye with a tell-all. Whatever it was, it could build and attach itself to him permanently. Those people were all dangerous, and they could tarnish his legacy.

She checked her phone. What next? She leaned back in her chair and thought through her moves. She'd need a list of sources that journalists could get on the phone quickly once the news broke, and she needed to brief them first without it seeming like she was trying to control the story. She needed to refine the narrative a bit more. She'd have to scan his books for money quotes. She'd reach out to reporters at *The New York Times* and *Variety* with some notes and contacts, to help them write a story worth doing and ease the sting of being scooped by foreign press. She wanted the good stories out first so social media could respond to those. She did not want the gossip writer out first, or the aggregator, or the internet content producer whose stridency was always directly correlated to their terror of talking to other humans on the phone. She hated those people. Hated hated hated them. *Please god*, she prayed to all available deities and other governing forces of the universe. *Please don't let one of those people get their hands on this story.*

4.

KATIE HORATIO

NEW YORK, NY

Monday, July 1, 2019, 7:02 a.m.

Katie Horatio always thought it was weird the cockroaches ran from her when she turned on the lights. *Why do they run? Don't they know?* If anything, she should be running from them. Her name—Kathryn Horatio—may have been on the sub-sub-sublease along with her six roommates in this damp, $4,050-per-month two-bedroom Tomb-for-Youth, but the roaches were here first. They were both alphas and elders, and for that they earned Katie's unqualified submission.

Katie turned off the light in the kitchen and, emboldened by darkness, the roaches commenced dribbling out of their hiding places to resume their positions. She padded softly past three unconscious roommates strewn around the living room as though they had been murdered, their bodies wound in sheets and dropped from a helicopter. The air was sour. She entered the bathroom, where her clothes for the day hung from the shower bar. She selected two oversize, heavy-gauge sweaters that smelled vaguely of bog. It felt like a two-sweater day. She looked in the mirror. Her face was a picture of exhaustion and fear, but also sex and hatred. Katie was a writer. On the internet.

It's not that Katie really minded sharing with the roaches. She was happy to make any reasonable concessions to them in the service of comity. All she asked was that she never had to kill any of them. Cockroaches were like fried wontons full of gunk. Katie knew this intuitively before she moved into the Tomb-for-Youth, but she established it empirically her first morning there, when she committed the critical error of walking into the kitchen without first making a lot of noise and turning on the light. She stepped right on one of them, and her foot slipped a bit in the wonton. From there a nightmare scenario unfurled in her mind: stepping on one cockroach and slipping right onto another, then another, gathering momentum, skating panicked across the kitchen floor before smashing through the window and falling to the overgrown patio below, her body like a mangled pomegranate. This chain of events had imprinted itself on her consciousness like a prophecy. She never stopped thinking about it.

As she studied herself in the mirror, a roommate entered the bathroom and plopped down on the toilet without saying a word. Katie rethought the outfit situation and pulled a hoodie over her two sweaters. Then she threw on a pair of jeans and a pair of polar fleece pants. Fleece, she imagined, can cushion a blow more effectively than denim.

Walking like a child in a homemade robot costume, Katie exited her apartment and descended the slippery, bowed stairs. She wrenched open the heavy front door and stepped out into the light of Avenue B. She began perspiring immediately because it was eighty-seven degrees outside.

Katie Horatio walked to work every day. She did this very carefully, each step advanced with the utmost care, her eyes sweeping from left to right and her head pivoting up and down, scanning for danger—for falling pianos and carelessly discarded banana peels, careening e-bikes and plummeting air conditioners, rapists and murderers, and patches of ice and wet trash. Two months earlier, she had downloaded an app on her phone that allowed her to report unsafe conditions directly to the city. So far, she had filed hundreds of such complaints. Some of her friends called her a hypochondriac, but those friends had health insurance so they could enjoy the luxury of pejoratives. Katie was not crazy. She simply responded to data. And the data was terrifying. *The New York Times* reported that something like fourteen thousand buildings in the city constituted a threat to pedestrians. In the last month, a fifty-one-year-old man had been killed when something ironically called a coping stone fell on his head from the top of a fourteen-story building. Soon after, a famous architect was killed when a chunk of facade dislodged from a Seventh Avenue building and landed on her. In Queens, a sheet of plywood came loose from a construction site during a windstorm, took to the air, and ended its journey by shearing the head off an old woman. Katie imagined a wicked god celebrating this kill with his friends like a teenager who had skipped a rock across a pond and hit a duck in the face.

At various points during her morning commute, Katie's lizard brain would alert her to the presence of something on the sidewalk ahead. She would step around this stimulus without looking at it. In New York, some streets are lined with gold, she had learned, but most are lined with things that came out of people in moments of anguish.

A rogue skateboard shot past her on the sidewalk, practically sending her into a protective crouch. It had come from a group of teens who spent their days filming one another trying and failing to execute rudimentary skateboard tricks. She'd been observing them for two years, and for all the practice, they never got any better.

"Why aren't you good at this yet?" Katie snapped.

"Why aren't you sucking on my balls, grandma?" one of them replied.

Pedestrian deaths were up. Bicycle deaths were up. Twelve people tripped and hit their heads on curbs or stoops and just died. And that's not to mention Katie's true nightmare: falling through one of the city's innumerable brittle metal cellar doors. Three people had died this way just this year, and dozens had been injured. Katie had actually seen it happen once. The man was dressed respectably and wearing glasses, and the doors had simply given out under his weight. First he was there, then he was gone, and his screams, like all screams, went unanswered.

There are so many ways to die in New York, she thought, and most of them are humiliating.

Katie had a job. She worked at a digital media company called SWVLL, pronounced "swivel," whose purpose at this point was to issue an undifferentiated outflow of daily content in the hopes that a viable business plan would eventually reveal itself. In the mid-aughts, SWVLL had started as an email newsletter, sending out hipster catnip e-blasts detailing where you could find Nooka watches and inexpensive belt buckles shaped like Nintendo controllers, before pivoting into the blogosphere in the late aughts, posting gaudy traffic numbers with chestnuts such as "50 Reasons Hot Dogs ARE Sandwiches" and "Every State Ranked by Their Body Mass Index."

These days, as social media came to control content flow, and with traffic at an eighth of what it was at its peak, SWVLL was in the throes of a pivot death spiral. No one there knew what exactly it was they were supposed to be making—snackable posts? funny videos? influencer events? something to do with TikTok?—and as a result, the job was chaotic and reactive. The site had become like an exhausted peddler going from town to town with a trunk of random objects asking people, *Do you like this digital clock? No? How about this gibbon skeleton?*

Katie entered the lobby of her building, walked quickly past the elevators to the back stairs, and ascended, holding tight to the railing. Like all of her coworkers at SWVLL, she was a contractor. This, their CEO said, "sparked optimal agility." But really, it was a way to avoid paying for health insurance. When a coworker had the temerity to complain about this in a town hall meeting, the CEO said he preferred his team be lean and hungry. He likened it to fasting: a "hack" that he said he performed regularly to center himself and unleash his creativity. There was also some muddled reference to a managerial practice embraced by the US military. Whatever the philosophy behind the decision, the complainant's position was later eliminated.

As Katie mounted the stairs, she took stock of her life. She hadn't gone to a top school, just a pretty good school, but she'd done well there. She'd gone for psychology, as much to understand herself as others. But somewhere during her sophomore year she'd discovered a small but real yen for writing. It seemed to come from nowhere, like a goiter. She liked having control over her own expression. She liked how writing for publication was a way to be public without leaving your room. She wasn't great at it, but she was definitely pretty good. She worked hard, read omnivorously, and wrote every day. By the spring semester, she'd won an essay award.

This earned her an invitation to write for the school newspaper. They were workaday assignments—a dozen earnest students camping on the quad to foster empathy for the area's homeless, controversial menu changes in the dining halls—but she felt she put a little something extra into them to elevate the material. Where others would interview one person, she'd interview four. She was good at picking up on telling details: the scuffed shoes of the security guard trying to organize a union; the crooked tie of the school finance chief who had come under fire for his views on divestment. She was adept with ledes and kickers alike, sucking people in and sending them home satisfied. She even landed a book review in the local paper.

People noticed. Her friends suddenly seemed to admire her. Her classmates listened when she spoke. By senior year, a future had come into focus. A cool professor who claimed to have "dabbled a bit" in journalism took her aside and told her she had a real gift, and it would be a shame if she didn't pursue a life in belles lettres. That's actually what he called it. Katie was thrilled, and she studiously and earnestly gave it her best girl Friday.

The problem was, she thought that would be enough. It wasn't. Her peers—the ones who attended top schools and could afford unpaid internships—went to work for *The New York Times* and *Vanity Fair.* Bereft of connections or educational pedigree, Katie landed here, at SWVLL: a place governed by what appeared to be a reverse alchemical process that took each piece of gold she crafted, converted it into a mug of pig diarrhea, and then threw it into the face of the world under her name. In a way, Katie was defaming her own reputation just by showing up for work every day. Before long, she was unemployable anywhere else.

No matter what Katie tried to do to address this state of affairs, nothing made it better. Everything made it worse, but in a way she hadn't foreseen. Her editors, terrified of the Thursday performance meeting featuring a spreadsheet projected onto the wall with any stagnant or decreased numbers bolded and highlighted in bloodred, were made to sing for their supper, and thus chased anything that put them in the black. The skill Katie possessed as an actual competent writer who cared about words paradoxically made her worse at her job. The best SWVLL writers were fast-moving, self-promoting sociopaths who could churn out SEO-compatible content and shout its merits as loudly as possible to their inexplicably gigantic social media feeds. Those were the good soldiers in the fight, sacrificing their good names to momentarily keep a dying website from bleeding out in exchange for a fist bump and shot of flavored alcohol from whatever liquor company was sponsoring their mandated company happy hour that week.

Life had become disorienting. Cause had been divorced from effect. Katie had expected the adult world to be harder, meaner, and more competent. She thought she could cope with that. But it wasn't harder, meaner, and more competent. It was just dumb. She couldn't figure out how to operate in it. She struggled, stagnated. Her star fell, and with it her self-esteem. Her friends stopped asking about work. Her parents invited her to move home. Before long, she had become obsessed with the precarity of her existence and started wearing three pairs of pants just to go to the corner bodega to try to steal some milk. Belles lettres indeed. That cool professor had since died in a motorcycle accident, but he still came to her in dreams, begging teary-eyed for forgiveness. But it was too late.

The SWVLL office took up a full floor and had exposed brick walls and heavy wooden beams. This, combined with rows of employees huddled shoulder to shoulder, conveyed an air of sweatshop chic. The company founder sat in the dead center of the room, his large, dark, expensive hairstyle bobbing up and down. He'd selected this spot, as he so frequently reminded the staff, to demonstrate his commitment to transparency, egalitarianism, and open communication—though it was just as likely that he wanted everyone to be able to hear him as he talked about money, arranged foreign sexual adventures, and made reservations to restaurants that, as far as his staffers were concerned, may as well have been located on Venus. In 2017 alone he'd seen *Hamilton* seven times, and still referenced it often and at length, as though the grand march of human culture had ended with its debut on Broadway.

The open office plan did what open office plans do: it created a cone of silence and drove all personal communication underground to text, to WhatsApp, to chat, to Mercer Street behind the building. But never to Slack. To disclose something personal on Slack, the staff suspected, was to speak in the presence of an informer.

Katie sighed. The weekend had been inauspicious. On Saturday, she threw up in an Uber. She'd accompanied a man she'd met online to a gallery opening where she drank too much complimentary wine. Later, as they had sex on his couch, he attempted a series of moves that he'd clearly gotten from half a lifetime of watching porn, but his execution was wanting. The effect was neither erotic nor exciting, delivered, as much of it was, with a faltering voice and with small, soft hands. It simply defied plausibility. There are limits to the human imagination, after all. At least that's what she had announced to her date—"There are limits to the human imagination!"—before she'd wriggled out from under him, mid-coitus, got up, applied her three protective layers of clothing, loaded four bottles of his wine into her backpack, and left him there on his nice leather sofa, blinking and naked like an albino salamander.

Katie had spirited the stolen bottles of wine to her friend Chloe's apartment, and there they drank all of them. The night felt like a triumph, a win snatched from the jaws of perpetual defeat. They laughed. They danced. Katie got drunk enough that an Uber home suddenly seemed like a reasonable splurge. Five minutes later, she got in, and within five seconds she had vomited. The rest was a flurry of noise and movement.

She'd awoken at home the next day to a notification on her phone that she had been charged a $150 cleaning fee. Katie tried to dispute it. She told the person on the other end of the customer service chat that it never happened, that it was a scam, that she would report it to the authorities, that she *certainly did not vomit in the Uber.* The person, or bot or whatever it was, responded by producing a video of Katie vomiting in the Uber. She had thought that Uber cameras were there to keep people from attacking their drivers. But it turns out they were there mostly to nail you if you threw up in the car. Katie resolved that should she ever manage to somehow crack the ranks of the lower-middle class, she would throw up only in regular taxis and always pay in cash.

Katie had no savings. She spent five dollars a day on food. The fine had cost her thirty days' worth of meals. She had not yet eaten that Monday morning. She had probably sweated off a pound just walking to work. She went to the kitchen area. The office had complimentary hot drinks to scald flesh and dry snacks to lodge in windpipes, but an emergency was an emergency. Katie grabbed an armful of tiny bags of organic pretzels and commenced the humiliating daily ritual of wandering around the office looking for a desk.

The founder of SWVLL had recently imposed a policy of "hot-desking," which was supposed to foster additional transparency, egalitarianism, and open communication across departments. In reality, it just wasted time and further disoriented and demoralized his workforce. After circling the office space twice, Katie realized with a wave of rising dread that the only vacant desks were in a ring around him, like a morale Chernobyl. She sighed, dumped her pretzels on the desk next to his, and sat down.

"What up, my dude?" he asked.

"Hey, River," she said, removing her laptop from her bag and organizing her pretzels with all the dignity she could muster.

He was looking at her, so she looked at him too. As usual, he was a spectacle. The clothes that J. Barton "River" Middlebury III wore were like children's clothes, only larger and infinitely more expensive: sweatpants, a hoodie, a bright orange flat-billed cap that may as well have had a propeller on top, and a pair of gigantic neon high-tops. Sometimes he rode a longboard to work. Sometimes he rode it *at* work, a sight that flooded Katie's mind with fantasies of murder. But the longboard was nowhere to be found today. Otherwise he just looked like a Romney.

"Yo, Shady Katie, can I talk to you a sec?" he said.

"Uh, sure," she said. "Conference room, or . . . ?"

"Right here is fine."

"Okay."

"So, listen, I gotta put you on probation," he said, in a stage whisper.

"Okay."

"Your content hasn't been performing. I thought we had something with 'What Condiment Is Your Personality?' but it just didn't connect in a meaningful way with our users."

"Right."

He leaned forward and took a deep breath. "Look, Horatio," he said. "I want you to stay here. I want this to be your forever home, bro, because I think you're a fucking superstar and a shit-hot writer capable of creating fire content. But we're just not seeing the kind of engagement we need to justify your salary."

"I'm not on salary."

He leaned back. "I mean, we can talk fucking semantics all day—but do we want to do that sort of petty semantic bullshit? Is that how we want to spend our time? Because we can, if you want. I can get petty as fuck, Horatio. Ask anyone."

"No, River, we don't want to get petty."

"Good. We need to move forward with positive intention." He leaned forward again and tented his hands between his knees. "I'm giving you a week to level up. Okay?"

"Okay."

"Otherwise, we're going to have to both mutually agree that you aren't a good fit here and off-board you, and you're going to have to continue your journey elsewhere."

"Okay."

An earnest look fell across his face, and he placed his pale little paws on her knees and gave a squeeze.

"Be young, scrappy, and hungry—just like my man."

"Okay," she said.

"Don't throw away your shot."

"I won't."

Katie lifted her feet off the ground, gripped her desk-for-the-day, and rotated her chair away from River. She placed her feet back on the floor, opened her laptop, and stared blankly. Her mind was a wasteland. She didn't have a single idea for a post. Not even a notion. At previous moments of peak frustration, she fantasized about posting something like "22 Things You Didn't Know about Chipotle That Also Disprove the Holocaust," or "Ten Legendary Toys from Your Childhood That Prove Gender Is a Biological Fact" just to put a quick end to the torment. But she couldn't imagine having the energy to do such a thing now. Instead, she opened all fourteen bags of pretzels, dumped them out on her desk, and began numbly inserting them into her mouth while she waited for the end.

AN HOUR LATER, at 10:19 a.m., a sound rippled through the silent office: a gasp, then another gasp. A "holy shit." A "whoa." Whatever it was was noteworthy enough for some people to respond verbally, audibly, which had never happened before. There was a frantic tapping of laptop keys that sounded like rainfall. Reawakened to the world around her, Katie opened Slack. Messages were cascading down in the #Fire-Ideas channel, riddled with sad emojis and reaction-to-tragedy GIFs from reality television shows. Katie eventually found the headline on BBC.com. It was written by a man named Colin Vester. *God, the Brits have such smart names,* she thought. She tried to imagine what this Colin Vester might look like, but all she came up with was a vague image of a man wearing a vest who was unworried about the terrible vagaries of existence because his college was better than hers.

JOHN DOE DEAD AT 51

The famed bartender, author, TV host, and world traveler has taken his own life in Belfast

"Whoa," she said.

Katie liked John Doe. Everyone liked John Doe. He was basically a model human. She had never actually watched one of his shows, but she'd seen some stuff about him on Instagram, and this was unquestionably a great loss. And yet . . . Katie felt nothing.

That's not true; she felt something.

She felt the impulse that ruled the lives of writers like her: the impulse to take a moment of great import, strip it down, and sell it fast for parts on the internet.

Katie began rooting around the dirt cellar of her own consciousness, picking up any potentially fruitful thoughts, insights, and memories. Outwardly, she remained frozen, though her hands kept stuffing pretzels into her mouth. At a certain point, River was standing beside her, announcing the tragedy and offering condolences to those affected, and saying that, yes, while it's super important to mourn, times like these are also when teams like ours can really shine, can really band together to deliver meaningful fire content to our users. As a result, he said, he's offering $150 to the writer who can produce the most-shared piece about John Doe by noon.

One hundred fifty dollars.

Katie had read stories about people suddenly possessed of superhuman powers. Parents who lifted garbage trucks off children; women who fought off bands of assailants; a twelve-year-old who swam across a rushing river to save some kind of dog. She'd long wondered if there was such a power like that within her, and what it would take to awaken it. At what level of debasement would something else just take the wheel? And now she knew: it was *this* level of debasement. Because sure enough, something did. Something gently but firmly picked Katie up like a cat, set her aside, and just started doing things. It was as if after months of doldrums, a wind kicked up behind her. It was a thunderous onset of cavalry, a flotilla of battleships appearing over the horizon. Only in this case, it was coming from within, like a possession or the beating of a second and better heart.

Whatever it was, the entity made Katie's hands wipe pretzel crumbs off her outer pant layer and position those hands on her keyboard. It made them type letters and words, and those words formed four short sentences: "I knew John Doe. I had lunch with him once. It was at a little place called Lobio. And it happened because I was crying . . ."

Whatever it was, something had finally taken over, and in an instant, the solution to all of her problems was clear.

Katie Horatio had begun to lie.

5.

VLADIMIR "LAD" BENSHVILI

QUEENS, NY

Monday, July 1, 2019, 2:07 p.m.

If you asked Vladimir "Lad" Benshvili, proprietor of the restaurant Lobio, what he liked best about America, he would tell you the nightshirts. He had moved to America in 1989, right as everyone seemed most concerned that an earthquake in California had caused two teams to stop playing baseball. When he got there, he settled in the Jackson Heights neighborhood in Queens, right next to a store specializing in men's sleepwear.

At first, Lad marveled that (a) a store could specialize in such a way and still be in business (though it was run by an Albanian, so he remained dubious of its true financial situation); and (b) that any self-respecting man would need to wear anything other than underwear and a sleep scarf to bed. But one day, after receiving his first paycheck from the video rental store he cleaned, he walked into SlumberJacks on a whim and was born again.

There were some typical pajamas with pants and a button-up shirt, as well as a handful of silly zip pajamas with feet, but in one corner of the store sat an entire section of what were just very long T-shirts. There were flannel Henley nightshirts in plaid patterns and Bengal-striped shirts and printed cotton ones with designs that looked like optical illusions and woven broadcloth shirts and sexy satin nightshirts and hilarious ones featuring Bugs Bunny and the Tasmanian Devil in what appeared to be teenage streetwear. Lad spent most of that first paycheck on a conservative nightshirt, a cotton one with black arms and a gray body. And when he slept in it that night, he realized what he had been missing his entire life.

It wasn't just the erotic freedom of going bottomless as you slept, of feeling that Marilyn Monroe–style breeze travel up the nightshirt on hot nights if you positioned the fan just so at the foot of your bed. It was also the idea that this could be perfectly acceptable. That it, in fact, *was* acceptable. That there might be a store with an entire dedicated section of shirts made for this very purpose. It was the dumbest, most needless thing Lad had ever seen, and he loved it. America was truly the land where dreams come true, thought Lad, because dreams are kind of fucked up and usually do not make sense when you try to explain them to people after the fact.

AS THE YEARS PASSED and Lad grew from a man working at a video rental store into a man working at a Greek restaurant (also run by Albanians) and then into a man who purchased said Greek restaurant from the Albanian family when they retired and moved to Armonk, New York, his tastes in nightshirts grew more exotic.

He found an Austrian-Swedish man named Helmet who was married to an American woman named Sheila whose family owned a farm in the San Joaquin Valley in California. The San Joaquin Valley was where 93 percent of Supima cotton was grown. Helmet made custom clothing using Sheila's family's Supima cotton, its extra-long-staple fibers ensuring it maintained its shape and retained its color and three hundred thread count. Supima was so much better than Egyptian cotton, which was a false marketing name that specified only country of origin and had nothing to do with the length of the fibers, but most people didn't know that. Lad, however, was not most people.

He contacted Helmet and commissioned him to make a custom nightshirt using Supima cotton. The shirt cost $600. Lad mostly wore it to bed on holidays like Saint Andrew the First-Called Day and Valentine's.

On the day Lad's life irrevocably changed, he wasn't wearing one of his Supima cotton shirts. Or Egyptian cotton shirts. Or even terry cloth. No, on this day, which was a Monday, Lad came downstairs from the apartment he kept above his restaurant wearing a navy-blue short-fiber cotton-polyester-blend nightshirt with the phrase "Schwing" on the front in white block letters.

LOBIO MEANS "BEAN" in Georgian. Lad loved beans, and when he opened Lobio, he wanted to showcase how bean-forward Georgian cuisine could be, so he decided to eschew some of the more popular Georgian dishes like khinkali and khachapuri and focus his menu around beans. Originally, he'd wanted to use the actual Georgian script and call it ლობიო, but the Albanian sign maker he went to wasn't familiar with Kartvelian languages, so he settled on English lettering.

When Lobio first opened, Lad's wife Mariam ran the front of the house, and Lad cooked. It was not what he wanted. Lad was not a chef, and he had no interest in being a chef. But they could not afford to hire anyone, and so Lad learned how to cook lobio professionally, which was different from cooking lobio at home, mostly because of the size of the pot. In those days, the restaurant was not busy, but it did okay. Mariam came from a big Georgian family with lots of relatives in New York, and many of them came to eat at the restaurant in support. Oftentimes, Lad would come out of the kitchen on a Saturday night and look around and realize that 75 percent of the people in the restaurant shared Mariam's lineage.

Though he wasn't made to cook, she was absolutely made to host. Mariam would put fresh flowers on every table and sometimes play the piano the Albanians had left in the corner, singing old folk songs or, if she'd had a brandy, new American music. Her voice was beautiful, high, and almost haunting—Georgian, in other words, a world away from the shrill, hollow deceitfulness of Albanian music, Lad thought—and she would sing and Lad would watch her be absorbed into the music, as if into a portal to another world.

After they had their son, Jann, they put his crib in the office and worked lunch and dinner six days a week. The restaurant made them little money, but, as Mariam put it, "a lot of happiness." But then one summer when Jann was five, Mariam went out to buy more flowers for the tables and never came back. Lad called everyone he knew, including the police, but she was gone. And then her aunt came by the apartment. Lad never liked this aunt. Once a well-known singer in Georgia, she carried herself as if everyone else owed her a debt they both couldn't repay and weren't aware they owed.

"Lad," she said, a satisfied look on her face. "Mariam is gone."

"I know," he said. "This is why I'm worried."

"No," the aunt said. "She is gone to pursue her dream."

"And what is that exactly?"

"Music," the aunt said. "Mariam was born to perform. She is in Europe now. Do not try to find her. She said she will send for you and your boy when her dream is realized."

"You are a hag with a screeching voice," Lad told her. "Mariam thought this."

Mariam's family kept coming to the restaurant, but Lad let them know they were no longer welcome. He didn't want them to eat his food out of pity. He couldn't stand to see their faces judging him. He also needed someone else to work. And so he found Victor, a Georgian who actually liked cooking, and hired him to make the beans. And Lad began working the front of the house. But, of course, it wasn't the same. He didn't have the patience, friendliness, or the singing ability of someone like Mariam. He did not put fresh flowers on the tables, or send out extra pieces of bread, or put down another glass of wine with a wink, even when it wasn't asked for. If someone asked him a question he found bothersome, he would tell them. If they complained, he told them not to come back. That, combined with the lack of Mariam's extended family's support, ensured Lobio would, at best, tread water for the rest of its life.

Occasionally, a postcard would come to the restaurant for him and Jann. The front would feature gorgeous beaches with turquoise water and bright white-and-blue buildings. On the back, there were never personal notes but instead, poems or original lyrics to songs. And always, in the end, they were signed, "Missing you in Mykonos."

Sometimes, in bed by himself in his nightshirts, Lad would reread the lyrics to the songs and try to imagine how they might sound aloud.

THE FIRST ONE arrived at two p.m., alone.

She was in her twenties and wore jean shorts and a T-shirt emblazoned with French words. She stood across the street for some time, occasionally staring at her phone, pacing back and forth. After five minutes, she went into a bodega and emerged holding a single flower and a bottle of sparkling water with natural lemon flavoring. She drank half the water and dumped out the rest. A few minutes later, she gathered the courage to cross the street and placed a card and the empty bottle holding the single flower against the front facade of the restaurant. And then she left.

Three minutes after she put down the card, a strong gust of wind blew it down the street until it wedged under a parked car's tire. But that mattered not. She had made her mark.

By three p.m., it was happening every few minutes. A solitary figure would skulk over and drop something on the ground, stand there for a minute, then walk away. A single flower. A bouquet of flowers. A handwritten note. A teddy bear. A book. A DVD. Women's underwear. A cocktail shaker. An old MP3 player. A basket of fruit. A shot glass. A giant cross. After dropping off their wares, every single one took a picture with their cell phone. The younger ones turned the cameras around, putting themselves in the pictures. The older ones did not.

At first, Lad assumed that a white American had been murdered in front of his restaurant. But once outside, he realized many of these perverse manifestations of grief had something to do with Lobio. Along the sidewalk, nearly a thousand items now formed a massive memorial. Lad looked at the pile of goods and wondered who would clean it up.

There was more, though. Past the memorial, the people had not gone away. In fact, they seemed to have formed a loose line. He walked down the line a bit and saw it go all the way to the end of the block, then veer left. He counted 116 people before the line disappeared around a building.

A boy wearing small eyeglasses and a shirt like the sad blanket child Linus in the Charlie Brown comics approached Lad. "Excuse me?"

Lad looked at the boy. The cotton in his shirt was low quality.

"What are you doing here?" Lad asked.

The boy seemed confused by the question.

"What?"

"Why are you here?"

"For Doe."

"Dough?"

Lad was puzzled. They had bread, but they bought it from an El Salvadoran bakery. A young woman in a T-shirt that read "YURT LYFE" seemed to sense his confusion and stepped forward.

"John Doe, sir. He loved Lobio. Here, see?" The woman held up her phone. Lad assumed it was to show him a picture of the dead American, but it was just tiny words under a bright purple banner that read "SWVLL." The woman put the phone down.

"We want to eat his favorite meal at your restaurant as a tribute to him. It's what he'd want."

She spoke with the unwavering confidence of someone who had never been asked to clean a video rental store bathroom. Lad's mother back in Kutaisi had a phrase for this type of person: "They speak as if god was constantly ruffling their hair."

As he started to walk back, the Linus lookalike asked him a question.

"Sir! What time do you open?"

Lad peered down the line, then turned to the boy. He started walking back to the restaurant. Over his shoulder, he spoke.

"When the beans are ready."

6.

CHEF PATRICK WHELAN

HENDERSON, NV

Monday, July 1, 2019, 11:48 a.m.

"'Hey Julia, this is Chef Patrick Whelan from The Pu—'"

"Julie."

"What?"

"Her name is Julie. Not Julia."

"Christ. All right, all right. I'll go again. . . . 'Hey Julie, this is Chef Patrick Whelan from The Pub wishing you the happiest sixtieth birthday. Your daughter Caitlin tells me—'"

"Kaylee. The daughter's name is Kaylee."

"Kaylee? Are you fucking serious?"

"That's what it says."

"Is this for a den mother at a Texas cheerleading academy? Who the fuck names their kid Kaylee?"

"It's actually Irish."

"Oh, fuck you, Declan."

"We need to finish these today, otherwise the request expires and you don't get paid."

"All right, ALL RIGHT. Give me a finger of Bushmills and I'll finish it."

"After."

"Give me the whiskey or I'll deport you back to Galway—"

"Belfast."

"Whatever, it's all Ireland." Patrick cleared his throat. "Okay, all right. You ready? 'Hey Julie, this is Chef Patrick Whelan from The Pub wishing you the happiest sixtieth birthday. Your daughter Kaylee, which is a beautiful name by the way, tells me you were a huge fan of the show and you've still got my 2001 Sexiest Man Alive *People* magazine. Wow. I'm hugely flattered. Anyway, I wish I could spend your birthday with you, but I've got mouths to feed at my restaurant. As you know, you can always find my mother's grub at The Pub. Take care!' . . . Is that good enough for you?"

"They want the voice."

"What?"

"It specifically asks for you to do the catchphrase in yer daft fuckin' Oirish accent."

"Are you fu— I just . . . ugh. Why the fuck do we do these stupid things?"

"Because each one pays $199 and they take two minutes if you read the request and the wee script notes beforehand?"

"All right, this is the last fucking time. And if you talk to me in that tone again, I'm going to meticulously outfit you like the thieving leprechaun you are and stuff you back in the Lucky Charms box where I found you."

Declan feinted as if he might throw a punch and Patrick instinctively flinched, nearly toppling backward.

"While you're being so open to feedback, may I just say one more thing? You doing these out here by the pool in front of the statue and the water feature makes the audio shite."

"Would you prefer I do them in the kitchen? Is that on the nose enough for you?"

"You don't even use your kitch—"

"I KNOW I DON'T USE THE— Look, now the gardeners are here. We can't even do this shit outside anyway."

In a huff, Patrick walked through the French doors into the kitchen and took a seat.

"All right. I'm going to sit here at the chef's counter and be as on the fucking nose as I can. Declan, are you taping this? Because I've just about run through all the Lee Strasberg acting tips I can remember, and I need this to be over."

"Go."

"'Hey Julie, this is Chef Patrick Whelan from The Pub wishing you the very happiest of sixtieth birthdays. Your daughter Kaylee, which is a beautiful, incredible name by the way, tells me you were a very big fan of the show and you've still got my 2001 Sexiest Man Alive *People* magazine. Wow. I'm just blown away by that. Anyway, I wish I could spend your birthday with you, but I've got mouths to feed at my restaurant. As you know,'" Patrick slipped into an affected Irish lilt, "'you can always find the best of me ma's grub at The Pub. Happy birthday, again! Take care.'"

"Felt more like Stella Adler to me, but— Ah Christ, Patrick, your phone is ringing. It's T. Kendall Sun-Ramirez from *Urgent Fare*."

"Send that needy fucker to voicemail."

Declan now glanced at his own phone, which was lit up with messages. "Pick up, Patrick."

"Why?"

"Because yer man John Doe is dead."

CHEF PATRICK WHELAN didn't pick up the call. He needed a minute. He'd known Doe since the late nineties, when he hired Doe as head bartender at Áise, the thirty-five-seat restaurant Whelan opened in Boston's South End neighborhood when he was twenty-eight.

Irish for "Asia," Áise was a testing kitchen for Patrick's experiments utilizing the flavors of his Irish-Catholic, suburban Boston upbringing in Weymouth, Massachusetts, and merging them with his real interest: Asian cuisine. His gyoza-style shepherd's pie, with a wasabi mashed potato crust and a scallion-and-ginger-flecked ground pork filling, horrified his Irish mother but set the culinary world ablaze. Boston, which was long considered New York's provincial culinary stepsibling, suddenly found itself celebrated by the national food media.

Though a few critics voiced concern that a young white chef seemed to be cherry-picking random Asian ingredients according to his whims, this was the nineties and those voices were drowned out amid the hype tsunami, especially once Patrick won three consecutive James Beard Awards, first for Emerging Chef of the Year, and then twice in a row for Outstanding Chef.

Reservations for Áise became nearly impossible to get less than six months in advance, though Patrick kept a small portion of the restaurant and bar area open for walk-ins. The blocks around the restaurant, historically Black and working class, gentrified quickly as wine and cocktail bars sprang up to try to entice the crowds waiting for Áise (an urban studies professor at Harvard even coined the term "the Whelan effect" to describe his specific contribution to changing the neighborhood), and Black families and businesses, for the most part, retreated southwest on Washington Street past Ramsay Park.

Patrick was young, personable, and handsome, with just enough of a Boston accent and working-class background to give his story the type of pick-yourself-up-by-the-bootstraps American Dream flavor advertisers got hot and bothered about, and he was soon starring in national commercials for American Express, Hertz, and GMC. He had deals with Wüsthof to use their knives and a clothing manufacturer to wear their chef's coats and L.L.Bean to design a specific style of rubber-soled slipper to wear in the kitchen (once they found out via a *Boston* magazine interview that he peculiarly wore their slippers when he cooked).

He was profiled in *GQ* and *The New Yorker* and was famously featured naked on the cover of *Gourmet* holding a sack of potatoes. He went from dating a bartender who worked at the Waterclub Marina Bay, to being romantically linked to Tiffani Amber Thiessen and Neve Campbell. He got a booking agent, a literary agent, a stylist, and a personal assistant. The latter came in the form of his Northern Irish cousin Declan Toomey—brother and son to Catholic Republicans best known for smuggling plastic explosives out of New York in the door panels of cars on the *Queen Elizabeth 2*. Declan had run into some unspecified trouble in Belfast, which made him quite motivated to experience the sights across the pond in America. Patrick took him in, figuring his cousin could handle mundane tasks Patrick felt were beneath him. But Declan quickly proved a greater usefulness. When Patrick was being harassed by a stalker at the restaurant, Declan, who had been ironing Patrick's underwear when he got the call, promised to take a wee peek. Within twelve hours, the stalker had abandoned his apartment and most of his belongings, and, at least according to Facebook, moved back in with his mother just outside of Moline, Illinois. Patrick never asked how Declan did this. He was appreciative, but even now, years later, he still found the episode alarming.

Meanwhile, Patrick kept stepping on the gas. He signed a deal with Paragon Casino in Las Vegas to do a 350-seat version of Áise in their new resort with an unprecedented licensing deal that paid him $2 million up front, $100,000 a year for the use of his name, menu, and recipes, and a small percentage of net profits and sales. It also included entertaining perks like unlimited use of the Paragon suites (when available) and a $40,000-a-year tab at the casino. With his windfall, he purchased a 7,200-square-foot second home in Henderson that allegedly was once owned by Frank Sinatra, clad in yellow stucco that perfectly matched the color of the dress Ava Gardner was wearing when she left him in 1957.

But then, one fateful day, he took a meeting with network studio executives. Patrick had always planned to open an Irish bar back in Boston with his mother and call it The Pub, and in the midst of making awkward small talk, he told these executives about his plans.

They said, "What if we filmed behind the scenes as you opened The Pub?"

And he said, "I couldn't. This is a personal project with my mother."

And they said, "Well, what if we covered all the costs of opening the restaurant, added another $500,000 for you, and a cash bonus for your mom?"

And he said, "The world should really meet her."

This was early in the reality TV game, Patrick was naive, and the deal seemed great outside of the fact that they insisted he open The Pub in New York. And so, at the peak of his fame, Patrick left Boston to come to New York City to open what was essentially a standard

Irish pub. It was an unmitigated disaster, but in the kind of car-accident manner where you can't take your eyes off the screen. Patrick looked every part the egomaniacal, narcissistic celebrity chef, and his mother, who was never happy about opening in New York, seemed sad even for an Irishwoman. The entire show made his favorability ratings plummet in a way America hadn't seen since Gary Hart. But it did something else. It introduced the world to John Doe.

Only appearing in three episodes, Doe was a very small part of the show, but there was something about him that caught the eye of one of the young producers. There was a slow burn to him, a hard-edged worldliness. But he was also thoughtful and witty and well-liked—the guy the other staffers went to when they wanted to talk through problems. He spent much of his time reading or writing things down in a little notebook and talking books with a small clique of other literary-minded industry folks. This was strangely irritating to Patrick. One of the last nights The Pub was open, after advising Justin Timberlake on the best spot to open a barbecue restaurant ("Fuck Nolita, you gotta be in Hell's Kitchen"), Patrick noticed Doe talking to a woman at the end of the bar. He listened in on their wide-ranging conversation about the best time of day to write, how to get an agent, and whether they should both shell out money for some writer's conference in Vermont.

Unable to help himself, Patrick interrupted.

"Fuck you going to write a book about?"

"Bars," Doe replied.

"Well," Patrick said, getting up to leave. "That sounds like a stupid fucking idea."

The show ran for just one season and The Pub stayed open for only six more months after that. The producer took Doe's name and filed it away. When Patrick finally, mercifully shut The Pub down, Doe stayed in New York. Patrick returned to Boston. Everyone assumed he would lick his wounds back in the kitchen of Áise. But this did not happen.

With no real warning to staff or investors, Patrick closed the original Áise in Boston, packed his stuff, sold his place in Weymouth, and permanently made the move to his Vegas house (which an intrepid local reporter uncovered was not ever owned by Frank Sinatra but, in fact, built by actor Corey Feldman in 1991 with money made from voicing Donatello on the original live-action *Teenage Mutant Ninja Turtles* film). And then something even more remarkable happened. Chef Patrick Whelan just . . . stopped cooking.

At first, this sort of thing was explained away. He was doing a cookbook. And judging a cooking show. Plus, he had his Vegas restaurant! Surely he cooked there. And for years there was a rumor, started by Patrick's team, that he was going to do a totally new concept "unseen in North America" and once again blow the roof off the cooking world. That bought him some time. So he did an Atkins version of his Áise cookbook. And one based around the South Beach diet. And keto. And paleo. And, somehow, the Master Cleanse.

He had lines of cookware and ready-to-eat frozen dinners and a four-leaf-clover health powder he got sued over when it was discovered it wasn't actually made from four-leaf clovers but just spinach. He had a couple of cooking shows, one in which he, ironically, judged Irish pubs in America. But as the original Áise became a distant memory and the Paragon restaurant slipped from top-tier status to a place most routinely frequented by deal-seeking tourists with calf tattoos from California's Inland Empire, Patrick started to fall out with the food world. One notable essay called his alleged new concept "the restaurant world's *Heaven's Gate*."

Meanwhile, that young producer from the reality show had become an older producer with more clout. And when Doe's book about bars became a bestseller, that producer tapped him to star in a travel show titled *Last Call*. Over the next decade, he became the sun that the rest of the food world rotated around. And Patrick, who had once known what it was like to be a perfect sphere of fame's hot plasma, heated to incandescence by brownnosers and promotional ad campaigns, felt himself shift out of orbit, moving farther away in fame's planetary hierarchy until he was basically Pluto, no longer even classified as something to pay attention to.

PATRICK WHELAN HATED that all of this had happened.

And, in truth, he hated T. Kendall Sun-Ramirez too, with his stupid name full of obnoxious hyphens and excess periods. But Patrick also knew T. Kendall was a powerful cog in the food-world hype machine, so he wasn't in a position not to return a call.

"Hey, Chef, how are you?"

Declan stood just to the side of Patrick, listening in. He'd tried to get Patrick to write down some thoughts on Doe's passing so he'd have something coherent to say when asked, but Patrick had waved him away. ("I shoot from the hip," he'd said, by way of explanation.)

"Hey, T. . . . Kendall."

Patrick never knew whether to say both of his names.

"Chef, I was just calling because of course I wanted to offer my condolences on John Doe's passing—"

"Absolutely tragic," Patrick said, cutting in. "And devastating to me, personally. Doe was one of my closest friends in the industry. My brother in service. I am gutted to the core."

Patrick hadn't spoken to Doe in seven years.

"Yes, yes, I'm sure. Well, as someone who gave Doe his start in the industry, I wanted to get your thoughts on the whole thing. I'm working on a piece about the mental health struggles people in the restaurant industry face, and so any insight you could offer on either Doe's frame of mind when you worked with him, or even just mental health struggles in general, would be helpful."

Patrick looked at Declan. Declan shook his head and mouthed the word *simple*. Patrick smiled and stood up and started to pace. He thought better on his feet.

"Of course, of course. When I hired Doe, he was just some kid who'd been kinda moping his way around the Boston bartending scene. I picked him because he was cheap and reliable and because, frankly, I wasn't too worried about him leaving for another gig. Not too aspirational. But I came in and started showing him proper bartending techniques. I would have him taste through the menus to see what ingredients might work and told him to start thinking about incorporating those flavors into the mix. And he grew into the role."

T. Kendall started to ask something else, but Patrick wasn't finished.

"I remember coming in one day and seeing him writing in his little notebook. He always had these notebooks. And I remember him trying to hide it from me and I was like, 'No, man. No. You write your truths. Never hide who you are. Not from me, not from anyone.' And he was so grateful I did that. He said it motivated him to write his book."

Patrick looked at Declan and winked. Declan put his fingers into the shape of a gun and stuck them in his mouth.

"So I tell you what, T-Ken. Because you've caught me in this emotional place, I want all your readers to know that we're honoring Doe by offering 5 percent off any cocktails or even appetizers at the bar at Áise Vegas, just by mentioning the Doe discount. And 5 percent off all of my books through my website if you put the promotional code, um . . ." Patrick hadn't thought of a promotional code. "DoeDeath—just type it in at checkout. And that includes the special edition hardcover holiday keto cookbook and *Pale'O: 100 Irish Recipes Fit for Any Hunter-Gatherer Diet.*"

Declan went to the bar, poured himself a shot of Jameson, and downed it.

T. Kendall was quiet for a second.

"Okay, Chef. Thank you. I'll let you know if I have any follow-up questions."

"Do you need my PR people to link you to the discount?"

"No, no. All good. Have a good day."

The phone went silent. Patrick turned to Declan, who was pouring himself a second shot of whiskey.

"And that, my friend, is what you call the money quote."

A FEW HOURS LATER, Lavi came over.

Lavi was Patrick's Krav Maga instructor. Lavi was always dropping hints that he had been part of Sayeret Matkal, Israel's Navy SEALs equivalent, but Patrick could never verify that and it seemed unlikely, given Lavi worked as a doorman at the fourth most popular nightclub on the Strip.

Patrick had a casual attitude toward martial arts in that it was hard for him to stay committed to just one, and, thus, he never really mastered any. He'd been one of the millions of young teenagers who'd started doing karate after seeing *Karate Kid,* and over the last forty years, Patrick had dabbled in jujitsu, aikido, judo, hapkido, kung fu, tae kwon do, tai chi, and, for a brief time after seeing the 1993 film *Only the Strong,* Brazilian capoeira. He'd done Muay Thai in the late eighties (the movie *Kickboxer* was influential in this decision) and Tae

Bo in the late nineties. He did laamb, a form of Senegalese wrestling, for three months after a line cook from Dakar told him about it, and bataireacht, or Irish stick fighting, for a weekend after finding some YouTube videos. The only things holding Patrick back from martial arts success were skill, commitment, athletic ability, and discipline.

Patrick was not good at Krav Maga either. He was not great at the strikes or the throws or the takedowns or the groundwork or the escapes or the weapons defenses, but he kept taking it for one very important reason: he was scared shitless of Declan. Watching Declan in violent situations was truly astonishing to Patrick. He would slow down, get calm, and, most unnervingly, smile. When he did move, it was decisive and utterly effective. Once, Patrick asked him what sort of training he'd had. Declan snorted.

"It's called growing up gay in the Falls."

When Patrick was famous early on, he could be as mean to Declan as he wanted, even though Declan was a hard man. That was the natural order: famous men could be mean to hard men. The problem was, Patrick kept getting less famous and Declan stayed tough as ever. And yet Patrick kept shitting on him because he knew that as soon as he stopped, Declan would know he knew it was all over—that Patrick had become, definitively, the beta. So Patrick took Krav Maga in the hopes that when that day finally came and payback arrived, he might at least avoid total embarrassment.

But during that uninspired hour going over the best techniques for defending against upward and downward stabbing knives, Patrick had a different sort of realization. An epiphany that had nothing to do with Declan's lethality.

He thought about it as he walked through his great room, and his arcade room, and his screening room, and his awards room, and his pub room, and out to the shower in his backyard by the side of his pool, which looked like the T-shaped Tetris tetromino. He thought about it while he lathered himself vigorously under his antique-bronze Langford thermostatic cross-handle rain shower, staring at the statue above said pool, which he'd originally thought was a Celtic water goddess until Lavi informed him it was actually the Slavic water demon Rusalka.

He was so caught up in this epiphany, so overcome by the way it had centered his thinking, that he didn't even bother putting on clothes after his shower. Still naked and standing outside by his pool, Patrick called his agent Gloria. A spindly hippie in the sixties turned cutthroat agent in the eighties, Gloria Laughlin had represented Patrick since the early days, but, as his options had dried up, their talks had grown less frequent.

"Patrick! To what do I owe this pleasure?"

"Gloria, I've got a fucking great idea. A killer."

As he talked, Patrick looked at himself in the slightly mirrored reflection of his sliding patio door and involuntarily sucked in his stomach.

"Oh?"

"Yes. You sitting down?"

Patrick flexed his tricep in the window. At one point in his life, it had looked like a horseshoe. Now it looked more like an indent in his skin, the type of mark you might accidentally get leaning too long against the side of a desk.

"No."

"You should sit down. Are you ready? Are you ready for this? I need you to be ready for this."

"I'm on pins and needles, Patrick."

"You sure? Because this is big. This is like Áise-level big. Maybe bigger than that. This is my way back."

"Enlighten me."

"Okay, so you know that John Doe died?"

"I heard, Patrick, and I'm so sorry. I know you guys hadn't talked in—"

"Never mind that. Gloria."

"Yes?"

"Gloria."

"Patrick, why do you keep saying my name?"

Patrick paused and watched as the water shot menacingly out of Rusalka's mouth into his pool. He took a breath.

"I," Patrick started, "am going to be the next John Doe."

Patrick swore he could hear church bells ringing. Fireworks exploding. Jewish wedding glasses breaking. He got the chills. Well . . . he didn't really get the chills, but he made a silent note to himself to say he got the chills at this exact moment when he was being interviewed for the inevitable *New Yorker* profile. He wondered who would write it. He hoped Adam Gopnik. Adam was a friend.

There was complete silence on the other end of the line.

"Hello? . . . Gloria? Did I lose you?"

PART II

THE MACHINE

7.

KATIE HORATIO

NEW YORK, NY

Monday, July 8, 2019, 7:22 a.m.

"Katie?"

". . ."

"Oh . . . I'll just let you finish chewing."

"Ank ooo."

Katie Horatio was eating her sixth KIND bar in the green room of *Top of the Morning*, the top-rated morning show on a local network TV affiliate, when the cohost Mark Fowler entered. She froze for a moment, like a squirrel surprised while eating an acorn, and then resumed her feed while he watched, grinning. Katie simply could not believe how good these KIND bars were. Her body had gone so long without proper nourishment that after one bite it sang like a harp. Katie had eaten granola bars before, of course, but they were always the Quaker kind: narrow and without joy, squared at the edges and shellacked with that corn-syrup glaze that made your throat burn a little. But these KIND bars: They tasted like food and they looked like food. In fact, they looked beautiful. They were even arranged beautifully, in a wicker basket on the coffee table in their little windowed packages, a mosaic of colors and textures. She imagined such a display serving as the centerpiece on that very first Thanksgiving. It was hope. It was freedom. It was life.

Katie had been led to this windowless chamber by a harried production assistant in a flannel shirt and jeans who spoke to her with great admiration for what she had written about John Doe. She seemed sincere, but Katie had gone so long without being complimented to her face that she simply didn't know how to respond to the praise. She just sat watchful and absolutely still.

"I just think it was really brave," the young woman said.

"Are those free?" Katie said to the KIND bars.

The space was intended to resemble a living room. There were floor lamps and a couch and a table and a television, which was currently showing some woman doing something with a bowl and another much older woman being interested in it. The room was comfortable, but also a lie, its aesthetic undercut by the stark overhead lighting, lack of windows, and rough-textured hotel-room couch. But while some might have found the space's artificiality off-putting, Katie did not. There was food here and it cost nothing, and the air was dry and the carpet was dry and the floor wasn't strewn with bodies and roaches. She was safe here in this false living room, ensconced inside this labyrinthine studio. There were so many layers of building and so many tons of human flesh and sinew between her and the outside world. Combined, it could absorb almost any blow. If Katie could have bricked off the door at that very moment and lived out her days inside, she would have done so happily.

But then Mark Fowler came in.

"Hey, I don't blame you," he said to Katie, grinning, as she chewed and swallowed the last of her bar to keep him from taking it from her. "Those KIND bars are gold. My cupboards at home are full of them. And I've even been known to sneak a few out of the studio from time to time. Perk of the job."

Katie stared at him. Her hand instinctively moved toward her phone.

"Listen," he said. "I just wanted to come in quickly and say that I thought your story was just extraordinary. It was brave and beautifully told. I knew John Doe a little, and he was a great soul. It's a terrible loss. But if one bright spot has come out of it, it's your piece. I just wanted to say that. I think you're uncommonly talented, Katie. I hope you don't mind my saying, we're really glad you're here."

"Thank you, Mark."

"So," he said, closing the door. "First time on TV, right? Are you nervous?"

"A little," Katie said, suddenly finding herself standing as well.

In truth, she was petrified—by the prospect of being on television, but also by this figure standing before her with bleached white teeth who seemed to pulse with something: moderate fame, probably a decent salary, magnetism. He was certainly very handsome. He looked like a former high school football player from a place that was poor enough to care about football but not so poor that it made everyone look stressed-out and unattractive. His success was the product of careful calibration. He landed dead in the middle in terms of temperament and sensibility. He was unthreatening without seeming weak or undisciplined; he was funny but not caustic; he was fit but he didn't look like he'd be gross in the gym; he was confident but not cocky. He'd pull you out of a burning bus without hesitation, but he wouldn't mug about it afterward; he'd fix your car and tell you that the terrorists have hit the capitol with equal aplomb. He was transfixing. She looked down. He also had the hands of a man. A man who gets manicures. But man-hands nonetheless.

"You're going to be great," he said. "Just follow us. We'll make it really easy."

"Okay."

"Can I confess something, Katie?" he said. "I still get a little nervous too. There's nothing wrong with being nervous." He pointed to his skull. "It keeps you sharp. It makes you good."

And he was good, there was no question about that, Katie thought—this masterwork of a secret middlebrow laboratory hidden somewhere under a mountain in Idaho. He was reassuring. He made people feel safe. He made her feel safe as he moved closer. He made middle-aged women wish for better fathers, and better husbands, and better sons. It made them hope. It made them yearn to return for a simpler past that never really existed in the first place. To his adoring fans, he was simply *good*. And the fact of his being good meant that people could be good too, like they were in the olden days.

Fowler smiled that smile, like they were the only two people in the world. And she smiled back.

And he said, "I want to eat your pussy like a hamburger."

"What?" she asked, her face a picture of total incomprehension.

He slid his hands into the front pockets of her jeans.

"I just want to . . . wait, how many pants do you have on?"

The answer was three pairs of pants.

"No matter," he said, checking the screen and unzipping his fly. "I can be quick."

Katie was rigid.

"C'mon. Seriously? This is *Mark Fucking Fowler.*"

Katie was unmoved. Fowler stopped and huffed.

"Okay, how's this sound, then? We'd go out there, and I'd throw you some curveballs, and you'd feel those hot lights on your face, and you'd feel all those sad, fat assholes who came here on a bus staring at you, and you'd start to sweat. And I ask you another question, and you lose your train of thought, and you'd look like a fucking idiot and a laughingstock and your TV career ends today."

"Right."

"Now take these fucking pants off. We only have a few minutes."

WHEN KATIE HORATIO had written her elegy for John Doe, it was as if she'd been taken over. Something came and started doing something, and that something was good. That something got her $150, and a raise, and health insurance in a highly gratifying impromptu meeting with River once the magnitude of the story's success became clear. That something gained her more renown and attention and praise in an hour than she'd gotten in her whole life. Internet praise, but still. Now she was about to go on TV. She had a lunch meeting with an online editor from *The New Yorker* later. Whatever had happened had set her sagging life to rights and given her a future greater than just a few more nervous years before ultimately being crushed under a crane that fell off a skyscraper.

But since she had left work on that fateful day, that thing, that force, had gone AWOL. Katie had returned to the Tomb-for-Youth loaded with fresh confidence and ready to finally confront her roommate Jarvis about his habit of leaving raw chicken on the counter. But when she did, she not only lost the argument, she somehow ended up encouraging him to leave *more* raw chicken on the counter. Then she pulled a back muscle getting up off the toilet, stubbed her toe on a doorjamb, and hid in bed until dreamless sleep arrived. She had hoped that this was temporary, that her new power just needed to recharge. But then she would wake up again with fear in her heart and roaches on the floor and scenes of imminent disaster swirling through her head. She checked her phone. A sanitation worker in Staten Island had had his arm sheared off. A woman crossing Eighth Avenue in Manhattan was crushed by a truck carrying bananas. *Bananas!* Katie got up and put on three pairs of pants and a few sweatshirts, even though it was hot and the network would be chauffeuring her to the studio.

And she got here and this happened.

But then, as Fowler leered at her: a tiny flame. A faint knock. Katie could feel something requesting permission to board. She happily granted it and smiled as she handed the wheel back to her controller. Fowler took the smile as encouragement—at first, anyway. He kept trying to figure out the tangle of pants she had on. But then Katie kept smiling, and it gave him pause.

"What?" he said.

Katie's eyes were directed downward toward her hand. In it was her phone. On the phone was an icon indicating that the recorder was running—and had been running! For three minutes! Katie had no recollection of turning the recorder on, but something had. And now she knew what it was.

"You were here all along," she whispered.

She hit the "stop" button. She tapped "play." She turned it up. Katie looked on from deep inside herself with wonder. In tinny but nonetheless clear and incriminating tones, there was talk of sandwiches and cunnilingus.

Fowler reacted as though shot. "Will you turn that fucking thing off?" he shout-whispered. He tried to grab the phone, but Katie snatched it away from him and stowed it deep within her layers of pants where no one could ever hope to retrieve it.

"I want to be put on contract with your show," Katie heard herself say. "One appearance a week to discuss food or matters of my choosing. Get it done or I post the tape."

There was a knock at the door.

"Five minutes!" a PA called.

Katie brightened. "Coming!" she said.

TWENTY-FIVE MINUTES LATER, Katie Horatio emerged from the studio a star. In her time on air, she did not sweat, she did not falter. She somehow remembered all the shit she'd made up for that story: how Doe confessed to struggling with depression; how his lust for life was inspired by his fear that it was meaningless, or worse, that it was some kind of curse; how the beans at Lobio—a place she'd never actually been to—were "life-changing" and how she's "totally obsessed with them."

But death is a tough sell on morning TV, so Katie was also quick, funny, charming. At the behest of her controller, Katie skillfully steered the conversation toward herself. When she did, she was equal parts self-deprecating and authoritative. She said things about food and life that vibrated the human lumps in the audience. She made Mazie the cohost laugh out loud. She teased Mark about his "hamburger habit," adding that "everyone knows about it, am I right, folks?" and the lumps issued knowing laughter—*We do!* they seemed to say—and he sat there and took it with a glint of terror in his eyes that was so delicious they could have made KIND bars out of it.

Katie did so well, in fact, that they kept her on longer. A guest was bumped: a notch for her ax handle. When it was all over and the applause yielded to the din of commercial break, Katie strode offstage, passing a man in khaki shorts holding a pangolin. Some zookeeper, she figured. "You're only going on because I'm letting you go on," she said, taking off her lapel mic and dropping it on the floor before adding, "Pangolins suck." That was a little weird, as she didn't even know what a pangolin was, but fuck it, she was riding the tiger.

Katie returned to the green room and picked up the basket of KIND bars. She threw a half dozen water bottles on top of it, and then added other foods: muffins, cookies, apples. She put so much in that the basket split and everything fell to the floor. As Katie got down on her knees to pick it all up, the PA came back and told her she was great and they couldn't wait to have her back. The compliment disappeared into the ether. Katie's mind was set to heist.

"Can you get me a garbage bag?" she asked. The PA conjured one from a drawer—this was not, apparently, a novel request—and as the pair stuffed Katie's spoils into it, Mark Fowler appeared in the doorway. Seeing this, the PA disappeared, knowing full well by then what these appearances usually meant. Katie saw that Fowler was smiling. He seemed to be back to his old self. The door stayed open this time.

"Kiddo," he said, "you are a star. You're a natural. I've never seen a rookie do so well on her first time out." She said nothing. "Listen, I talked to the producers, and they'd love to have you back. And we'd love to make it worth your time." He waited for gratitude but none came. "This is a big deal, Katie. Play your cards right and you could be hosting this show someday."

Katie cinched her garbage bag and stood to face him. She threw her sack of plunder over her shoulder and moved to go.

"See you real soon, Mark," she said.

. . .

AND THAT WAS IT. Katie was flying. Out into the glaring sun she went, but she faced it, unafraid of melanoma. Across the street she strode, unafraid of careening taxis or runaway Central Park horses. Her head was held high, exposing her tender throat to potential assassins, but she didn't care. It would all be taken care of by this blessed thing that had taken residence within her. This avenger. Katie remembered riding a horse as a teenager on vacation. When the animal walked, it was fine. When it trotted, it was a rough ride, and she worried it was going to throw her. But when the beast hit its stride, something locked in, and the ride became perfectly smooth and exhilarating. Such was the ride she was currently experiencing, in this, her twenty-seventh year.

The hours passed and the horse did not tire, did not stumble, did not even hesitate. The lunch meeting with the online editor from *The New Yorker* was a rout. Like a concert cellist, Katie's controller took her into her hands and coaxed all the sounds it wanted out of her. And Katie, in turn, did the same with the editor: a small, tense young man with thick-rimmed eyeglasses and the hands of a spider monkey. At the lunch, which went on for three hours, Katie was brazen in all the right ways—ordering lobster and martinis, mentioning her TV deal. She deployed subtle disinterest, but she also was careful not to come across as unobtainable. She added touches of deference, even outright fandom. She began pulling random lines from Nick Paumgarten and Masha Gessen pieces. She quoted yards of John McPhee, Dorothy Parker, E. B. White, and James Thurber, though she had no recollection of reading any of them. She took the editor on a quick trip through John Doe's hidden recesses, quoting Thurber as she did: "People are not funny. They are vicious and horrible—*and so is life.*"

After she stuck that landing, she gave her head a little shake and took a long draw from a fresh, cold martini without spilling it all over herself like she had in the past. She actually abhorred martinis. The editor nodded his appreciation. He thoughtfully lifted up his water glass with two hands, and a thin little smile stretched across his thin little face. *A deep cut*, he seemed to say. *We like deep cuts at* The New Yorker. And she saw this, and she winked back: *I'll bet you do, you little prick.*

For a moment, Katie wondered about this thing that had taken her over. She wondered what gender it was. And why it was sometimes making her talk like a male advertising executive from the 1950s. And what it was really after. But you can't argue with results, she reasoned.

Once the bill was settled, Katie, born again as a creature of agency and impulse, took the trembling editor into the ladies' room and ordered him to service her orally. Upon obtaining satisfaction, she walked out onto the street with an offer to write a series of chef profiles, leaving the boy there on the floor of the stall feeling around for his glasses. Profiles were probably a lot of work, but she figured she could just place her body in front of a computer and space out for a while as the thing took care of business.

There was no question that her circumstances had improved enormously in the last twenty-four hours, and the way Katie saw it, she had absolutely nothing to do with it. She was a vessel for a superior being: *New Katie*. New Katie was confident and smart and cunning. She took no shit and got what she wanted. It was New Katie, for instance, who texted her roommates to tell them she wouldn't be coming back to the Tomb-for-Youth, that she'd be living somewhere "with class" from now on, and that "some dumb son of a bitch from Fiverr is going to come around and collect my effects." It was New Katie who booked a suite at a nice hotel for the interim, with the spa package. And it was

New Katie who summoned an Uber without worrying about the cost, and then, after Old Katie threw up a quart of martini in the car, dabbed at her lip with a cloth napkin she had stolen from the restaurant and responded nonchalantly to the driver's panicked screams.

"Put it on my tab," she said.

8.

CHEF PAOLO CABRINI

NEW YORK, NY

Tuesday, July 9, 2019, 10:53 p.m.

In the West Village, on a block not far from the one tour buses ventured down to ogle the fake residence of a fake relationship columnist on a real cable show, sat Chef Paolo Cabrini's French Restaurant with the French Name.

The French Restaurant with the French Name had been awarded three stars by the Michelin Guide, four stars by *The New York Times* ("an almost excruciatingly perfect meal"), Best of the Best twice by The World's 50 Best Restaurants (a dumb award but infuriatingly influential nonetheless, Paolo thought), the Grand Award by *Wine Spectator*, and a baker's dozen James Beard Awards.

Reservations were set up with a lottery system and booked and paid in full (the restaurant was gratuity-free) nine months in advance. Everything about the experience for each of the forty-eight guests during the twice nightly seatings was meticulously preplanned. Guest bios were scoured for personal details, including which hand they favored, their city of birth, and their astrological sign. Rumor had it that the staff would study guests' online reservation histories at other restaurants alongside any food-based social media posts to determine tastes and palate. Each week, Paolo and his staff would pore over the 384 potential guests that might come through the restaurant during the four days they were open and talk menus. Anyone on the staff, not just back of the house, could pitch or propose a menu item. Much to the chagrin of every single person who ever worked there, every single table had a slightly different menu every night. One actor who had worked as a server at the French Restaurant with the French Name compared the restaurant to *Saturday Night Live*: each week everyone started over from scratch, and very quickly you either loved it or it drove you insane.

Servers, all salaried and making over six figures, claimed it took at least a year to learn how to pour the water correctly. Sommeliers said mastering the wine list's intricacy and depth was by far more challenging than any master exam they'd ever taken. Dishwashers, almost all of whom came from a specific town in El Salvador, did not readily make themselves available for anecdotes.

Chefs who worked in the French Restaurant with the French Name all claimed it was simultaneously the hardest and best job they'd ever had. Paolo was exceedingly tough and demanding but also generous, friendly, and kind. He was not known for holding grudges or lording mistakes over people. He did not throw pots or swear or sexually harass or snort coke in the bathroom or make comments about gender pronouns or tear people down publicly or dress up as Santa Claus and make anyone sit on his lap and tell them what they wanted for Christmas at the holiday party. But he also didn't tolerate multiple mistakes.

"Are you familiar with strikeouts in baseball?" Paolo would ask his staff. "Well, I believe everyone should make one mistake, a few people will make two mistakes, but three mistakes are intentional. And it means you're out." Another difference between Paolo and other chefs was that, except in extreme circumstances, he would always find another job for those he kicked out of his kitchen, and he worked tirelessly to find the right fit. If chefs fell into the role of either teaching professor or research professor, Paolo was absolutely a teaching professor. Perhaps the best there ever was.

The family tree of successful restaurants stemming from his alums would have to be *Sequoiadendron giganteum* because it was so massive. There were thirty James Beard Awards among those who had worked for him. Twenty-nine Michelin stars. Twenty-eight former staff members had married each other, and only two had divorced. The French Restaurant with the French Name was basically the restaurant industry's Ivy League finishing school, and working there ensured others who'd also gone through the FRWTFN process that you were reliable and skilled and unflappable and a dozen other positive descriptors. People who worked there would talk about it for the rest of their lives.

AFTER DINNER, guests were shown out of the dining room and into the Bibliothèque. Upon entrance to the Bibliothèque, a bottle of Pink Lady apple brandy made especially for the French Restaurant with the French Name by a French apple farmer in Big Indian, New York, was placed upon the table alongside petits fours and crystal brandy snifters. Tiny Goyard bags made exclusively for the French Restaurant with the French Name were discreetly placed at the guests' feet, with a gibassier and honey butter for the morning, as well as personally signed and inscribed copies of Paolo's first cookbook, which always included a bonus recipe handwritten by the chef on a random page (when this was first discovered, someone devoted an entire blog just to document all of the extras). Once, when actor Samuel L. Jackson dined at the restaurant, Paolo delightedly wrote out his recipe for the perfect "Royale with cheese" inside his cookbook, even though he was sure Jackson would never actually read the recipe. Paolo didn't care about that. He cared about what he could control. The rest was, as his mom put it, "a vontade de Deus."

In the middle of every table in the Bibliothèque sat three cyan-blue robin's eggs in a delicate nest. But those in the know knew that, while two of the eggs were real, one would have the words "Joyeuses Pâques" stenciled ever so lightly on the shell, and you could bite into the top of that egg and a fortune cookie–esque scroll of paper would come out with a phrase on it.

Though the phrases themselves would vary, they would inevitably be in Italian, and if you uttered said phrase to your server, they would excuse you from the table and usher you through the back of the Bibliothèque into what looked like a private washroom. Once inside, a giant painting of the Tunisian-born Italian actress Claudia Cardinale would slide to the side and guests would be able to enter one of the most exclusive drinking clubs in New York, in a space that suggested a typical Italian bar centrale. Upon sitting at their new table, each guest would be handed a tasting-size version of the Cardinale cocktail, with Italian gin, Campari, vermouth, and a lemon twist, plus a tiny plate of stuzzichini that ranged from simmered veal shank mondeghili, to crostini topped with baccalà mantecato, to oven-roasted olives, hand-cut and fried potato chips, and various nuts simmered with saffron oil.

But within the secret speakeasy, there was yet another secret chamber that almost no one knew was there, a private drinking room hidden behind a painting of an iconic soccer photo, with just one table, made to look like a tiny Brazilian boteco. A chest in the corner was stocked with ice-cold Brazilian beer, and bolinhos de abóbora com carne seca were always available upon request.

The secret bar, and the secret-secret bar within the secret bar, were created in collaboration with John Doe a few years back, after the restaurant had made enough money to purchase the spaces behind and next to it. As a bartender, Doe had always bugged Paolo to have a bar in his restaurant, and the Italian and Brazilian themes were an inside joke, as Doe said Paolo covered up his Italian side but actually buried the Brazilian one.

That much was true. Paolo's father was Italian, an engineer from Modena, in the wealthy north. An entrepreneur, he'd tired of the defeated complacency of post–World War II Italy and, despite pressure from his family to stay in Modena, had moved to Santa Catarina, Brazil, in the fifties, seeing it as a place where he could create. There he met and married an Italian Brazilian woman whose family had emigrated from the Aosta Valley in the Alps of northwestern Italy the generation before. Though Paolo's mother was born in the Canasvieiras neighborhood north of Florianópolis, she spoke Portuguese, Italian, French, and a sort of Franco-Provençal dialect called Valdôtain fluently, and she would regularly mix the four when speaking to him.

As an only child, Paolo was burdened and blessed with his parents' full attention, and like many only children, he essentially thought of himself as an adult well before the age of sixteen. At that age, he left Florianópolis to begin his apprenticeship in France, staging for free at the best restaurants he could find, sleeping in dangerous apple-picking hostels and on floors as he worked his way up Escoffier's brigade de cuisine ladder through Michelin-starred restaurants. With dark hair, dark-blue eyes, and fluent though strangely accented French, Paolo never once let on that he was actually Brazilian, and it wasn't until years later, after he'd come to the States and opened a boring, traditional French restaurant on the Upper East Side with the backing of his French wife's wealthy family, that the truth of his background actually slipped out to the public.

"Everyone knows you'll never be French," his ex-wife had told him as he stood in the kitchen reading the mediocre *Times* review that would seal the restaurant's fate. She knew what she was doing when she said it, and the worst part for him was she knew that he knew she was right. The entire experience had shamed him, branding him in a way he'd likely never shake. The money he'd gotten from his French father-in-law, the way the father guilted him with menu and decor decisions, it made him hate himself. Which was impressive, because as an Italian Brazilian Catholic, he was basically born into a volcanic eruption of perpetual and intense self-shame.

Reeling, he'd moved from New York to Boston and started working as the executive chef for a dumb French hotel restaurant, drinking every night after work at the bar of a strange Irish-Asian fusion restaurant in the South End called Áise. The food, he thought, didn't make any fucking sense, but at the same time, he couldn't stop eating it. Judging by how crowded it was, neither could anyone else. One night, as he sipped Scotch and finished another shepherd's pie, he noticed the bartender, in the midst of all the chaos of a crowded bar, reading a book by George V. Higgins.

"How can you read in this place?" he asked.

"Well," the bartender replied, casually pouring Paolo another Scotch "the Milky Way is around 105 billion light-years in diameter, and our sun is just one of hundreds of billions of stars in our galaxy, and there are fifty galaxies within the Milky Way. So it is entirely possible and even plausible that our universe is one of hundreds of universes out there, and therefore the actions of one man at one time of day on one planet among the billions and billions of planets out there is meaningless. So if I decide to stop for a minute before pouring someone else a Sam Adams to read Higgins, I don't think it's going to cause a main sequence star to puff into a red giant, violently shed its outer layers, and turn into a white dwarf."

"I'm Paolo," Paolo said.

"John," the bartender said.

From there, Paolo and Doe became friends. It was Paolo who had encouraged Doe's writing, introducing him to an editor at the underground paper the *Weekly Dig*, which started publishing his Behind the Stick column. It was the popularity of that column that got him the book deal that came along after Doe moved to New York to continue working for this strange Irish American chef as the chef filmed a show based on a new restaurant he was opening.

And it was Doe who prodded Paolo to move back to New York and encouraged him to start working on the idea for the French Restaurant with the French Name, and a few years later—after Doe became wildly and unexpectedly famous—it was Doe who introduced Paolo to the types of people who might invest in an extremely expensive, high-end concept restaurant without attempting to repeatedly stab him in his back and front and sides like his ex-father-in-law. But it wasn't until his own father passed away and left him a sizable inheritance that he decided to push it forward, and so he bet every single penny he had on the French Restaurant with the French Name, and in that bet, he won, and he won big, and life seemed to have rewarded the meticulous and studied way Paolo had lived it.

. . .

IT HAD BEEN one week since Doe had died, and Paolo was finally able to function through the sadness. It had taken all his composure, focus, and attention to detail to lie to the constables, but they had seemed satisfied with his story and didn't press him much. In this very specific and particular case, Paolo's Catholic upbringing actually seemed to help him, because it gave him a mechanism with which to compartmentalize and suppress his grief and dedicate himself fully to his job. It also helped that, almost universally, everyone seemed to rally to his side, knowing he'd been Doe's best friend, and suddenly he'd found himself in a new tier of recognizable celebrity, with access and interest from decision makers all over the world.

And it was in that vein that he found himself in his little private boteco within his semiprivate bar centrale talking to Greg Oldenburg, an executive from Doe's network. And it was during that conversation with the TV man that Paolo was tentatively offered the chance to replace Doe.

"We were thinking we want to do a documentary to honor him," the executive said. "Something rad but tasteful. And I was thinking—if this was something you might be interested in—we could . . . announce you as the new host on the doc? I know it's super soon, but again, this whole thing is a ways away. And anyway, you're the only one we think makes sense. You're his best friend. You were already on the show all the time. The audience would be stoked. Everyone would see it as the honorable choice. The inevitable choice. Plus, it's what he'd want."

And with that last sentence, whatever compelling case the executive might've actually had was lost. Paolo knew this wasn't what Doe would've wanted for him. Doe knew the restaurant was Paolo's child. And he'd never leave his kid. But just as he was about to explain that to the executive, there was a quiet knock on the door. One of his floor managers peeked her head in.

"I'm so sorry to interrupt, Chef."

"No problem, Alice. What is it?"

"There's someone here to see you."

"Well, did you tell him I was . . ." Paolo gestured to the executive.

"I did, Chef, yes. But he said it was an emergency. He. . . ." She paused and glanced ever so quickly at the other man. When she spoke again, she did it in a nearly silent whisper directly into Paolo's ear. "He said he's here from Belfast."

WHEN PAOLO WALKED OUT to the front of the restaurant, he saw him. For a brief moment, he contemplated rubbing his eyes, as he'd seen people in movies do when they saw mirages in the desert, and maybe that would make him go away. But the man was not a mirage. It was indeed the black-haired bellhop from the hotel in Belfast. No longer in his uniform, the man wore a black duster and yellow T-shirt. As Paolo approached, he thought he might be doing a card trick for a couple of servers on his staff. But as he got closer, he realized with a sort of sinking terror that it wasn't a card trick at all.

He was showing them a picture on his phone.

Paolo walked closer, faster, and tried to say something, but his vocal cords short-circuited and what came out sounded like a gargled yelp, as if he was trying to sing while using Listerine. It did, however, have the effect of making the bellhop and the servers turn in his direction. The bellhop's dark green eyes glimmered, his smile growing longer and wider, unfurling like a banner.

"Chef Cabrini! Sorry to drop in like this, I was just showing the lads here an image I thought they'd like."

His stomach somewhere behind him on the floor, Paolo glanced down at the phone and saw on the slightly cracked screen what appeared to be a woman's naked behind, with the word *Arse-nal* painted across her cheeks. "Yer man said he was a Gunners fan, so I figured this would bring a laugh." He popped his phone back in his jacket, and Paolo found himself exhaling for the first time since he'd walked into the dining room.

"Why don't we . . ." He motioned with his head and walked the bellhop over to a table in the corner and sat down.

Charlie sat in the leather upholstered chair and ran his fingers along its arms. "Jaysus, is this real? This chair is absolute heaven. Class all the way. No shocker there, Chef."

"What brings you to New York?" Paolo said in a voice he hoped sounded even and pleasant. The back of his mouth felt sticky, as if he were stress-sweating directly from his sinuses. He still couldn't recall the bellhop's name.

"I was at the hotel working the other day and recalled your words about how if I was ever in New York, to look you up, and I thought, 'Smilin' Charlie, you've earned a holiday, haven't you? And now you know this nice man in New York City who's made such a generous offer.' And so I found a cheap flight and here I am, looking you up."

For the first time in his life, Paolo was actually relieved a person spoke in third person. But now he needed to take control of the situation. First, he needed to get Charlie the bellhop out of his restaurant. Ideally to a confined place with a locking door. Sure, going somewhere private would hypothetically make him more vulnerable to attack. But he didn't think that's what Charlie had in mind. If Paolo was going to be blackmailed, he preferred it happen somewhere private.

"Well, I'm thrilled you've made your way out here. I'm afraid I can't offer you a meal tonight," Paolo said. "Service is done. But—" He searched around for the best, quickest idea, but his mind was gummy and only one thought shook out. "Why don't you come by my apartment? For a beer. I live just upstairs."

Charlie smiled yet again. Or maybe he never stopped smiling from before.

"Grand."

Paolo gathered up his stuff and quickly motioned to his manager, Fred. Fred had been with him since the beginning. Fred would understand, and if Fred didn't understand, it wouldn't impact the way that Fred handled the situation. Fred was a pro. "I've got to see to this gentleman. Can you please inform Mr. Oldenburg that I've been called away for an emergency and maybe offer him a drop of—"

"I know what he likes."

"And can you—"

"Of course, Chef. I'll see you tomorrow, and call if there's anything else."

Fred glanced ever so quickly at Charlie.

"Are you okay, Chef?"

Paolo ignored the inquiry.

"Thank you, Fred."

Though there was an internal staircase that led directly from the restaurant up to his apartment, Paolo and his brain agreed in tandem that they didn't want to show it to Charlie, and so they walked outside for a minute. It was a lovely summer night, a soft breeze in the air.

Charlie looked down the street one way, then the other.

"Stop the lights. Isn't this where they filmed that show where posh city women ate fancy breakfasts and fucked about?"

"That's down a bit that way."

"Fuckin' brilliant. One of those ladies stayed in bandit once. I won't say which. Bad tipper. Had a problem with the taste of the ice cubes. And clogged multiple toilets. Wasn't any craic. Not like yer man." Charlie crossed himself. "I've been reading about him on the internet," Charlie said. He did the sign of the cross again, in case the first one hadn't taken. "God rest his sweet soul."

Paolo opened his front door and waited for Charlie to come through before showing him upstairs. Upon entering the apartment, Paolo instantly realized he'd made a mistake.

Paolo Cabrini's apartment was three bedrooms with two full bathrooms, and featured, after several renovations, an open layout that was rare in old West Village buildings. The kitchen was exactly as he'd wanted it, with a Lacanche range and a Smeg refrigerator featuring a hand-painted mural of his mother's family's Valle d'Aosta mountainside home taken from an old photograph she had at her house. His German-made Nesmuk chef's knives were made from 640 layers of Damascus steel and worth nearly $100,000 in all.

As he looked around, he suddenly saw the price tags of nearly everything in his apartment, and he knew Charlie, as a bellhop at a fancy hotel, likely did too. But if Charlie was appraising the place, he didn't show it. He just whistled softly, removed his coat, and took a seat on Paolo's burgundy-red leather couch.

"What can I get you to drink?"

"I'm not picky," Charlie said. "As long as it's brown, liquor, and not made by Protestants."

Finding a bottle of Jameson's Rarest Vintage Reserve, Paolo took down two whiskey tumblers and poured a couple of ounces into each. He slid a glass across the coffee table to Charlie.

"Sláinte," Charlie said, raising the glass. He took a sip and set it back down, then removed his phone from his pocket and set it next to the tumbler. Paolo didn't look at it; in fact, Paolo made it his singular mission in life not to look at Charlie's phone.

"So . . . what are your plans while you're here?" Paolo asked, keeping his eyes on Charlie's head as Charlie examined the room.

"Oh, you know. A little of this, a little of that. Bout ye?"

"Excuse me?"

"Apologies." Charlie spoke slowly in an overenunciated American accent. "What. About. You?"

"Well," Paolo said. "I'm just working at the restaurant and—"

Charlie cut him off and proceeded to tell a fifteen-minute story about his previous weekend in Belfast, listing off all the bars he'd visited, what they'd had to drink, and so on. Paolo looked for an opening where he might cut in, waiting for Charlie to at least run out of breath, but he never once paused to breathe. Briefly, Paolo wondered if he maybe had a blowhole, like a whale. Finally, after Charlie started singing a song about a woman named Kitty, whom he'd assured Paolo he'd had sexual relations with many times, "though all for her pleasure alone," he stopped to take a sip of his drink.

Paolo smiled broadly and put on his best hospitality face. A look that was both sympathetic and, he hoped, firm.

"I love these stories, Charlie. I truly do," he said. "And I could listen to them all night, but I'm so sorry, I'm incredibly exhausted and have to get up early to be at the farmer's market. If there isn't anything specific I can do for you, do you mind terribly if we call it a night? I'd be happy to call you a car to take you to your hotel, and you can pack up the rest of the bottle if you want to continue your night back there."

Charlie's face became quizzical for a moment and then his eyes narrowed. Paolo recalled a time from his youth in Brazil when he was playing out in the woods by his house and saw a maned wolf. Seeing a maned wolf was rare, and when he'd told his classmates the next day, no one believed him. But Paolo had seen the maned wolf in the woods. It was gnawing at something, something he couldn't see, and as he got closer to try to get a better look, it stared at him, narrowed its eyes, bared its teeth, and unleashed its famous roar-bark, and he ran all the way home. He had nightmares for weeks.

Charlie's eyes remained narrow for a beat longer. Then he blinked, picked up his phone, and looked at it for what Paolo determined was the exact amount of time it took him to whisk eggs for an omelet. When he finally looked back at Paolo, his smile had returned.

"So which bedroom, then?" he asked.

Paolo looked confused. "I'm sorry?"

Charlie took the last sip of his whiskey.

"Which bedroom is mine?"

9.

CHEF PATRICK WHELAN

HENDERSON, NV

Sunday, July 14, 2019, 3:32 p.m.

It is said that it took the entire twenty-year reign of the pharaoh Khufu to build the Great Pyramid. Patrick Whelan figured he could become the next John Doe in three weeks. First, he watched all 152 episodes of *Last Call*, often while pacing around his home theater in just boxers and a threadbare Aerosmith *Permanent Vacation* T-shirt, murmuring to himself and writing on a whiteboard. From the outside, it might've appeared that Patrick was mourning Doe in a very specific way, honoring the man in his passing by watching all his creative work. But anyone who remembered Patrick in his actual heyday might recognize something else: Patrick was cooking.

When he used to make menus, Patrick would go to sleep and vividly see finished dishes in his dreams. He was the only chef he knew of who worked backward, who started with a vision of a completed dish and figured out how to make it in reverse. Doe and his success were a finished dish to him, and Patrick figured all he needed to do was break the dish up into its ingredients. Over that week, he thought of nothing else. He slept in one of the theater chairs and made sure to keep playing episodes of Doe's show even as he slumbered, hoping something would come to him. And on the seventh day, the day even fucking god took some me time, it did.

On that day, he emerged from the home theater with a crazed look in his eye. "I've got his sauce, Declan," he told his startled, deeply sunburned Irish assistant, who, freed from any real tasks for those days, had taken to falling asleep out by the pool.

"Is that a semen reference?" Declan asked, but Patrick ignored him. He was focused. And now he needed to implement step two: understand social media.

IN PATRICK'S CASE, access to the young minds of America who spoke fluent social media was not difficult, because he was (kind of) dating one of them. Jackie Fletcher was twenty-two years old and a sommelier at a beautiful Austrian restaurant in a casino considerably newer and cooler than the one housing Áise Vegas. The sole daughter of two late-eighties NYC house music club kids who loved parenting in theory but never got around to the practicing part, Jackie had grown up in Alphabet City during the credibility-optimizing sweet spot between actually unsafe and utterly gentrified. Never very engaged throughout her time in the NYC public school system, Jackie had worked in restaurants since she was eleven, though early onset puberty allegedly brought on ("Purposefully!" claimed her mother, blaming her father's love of sushi) by excess soy consumption had made her look sixteen.

By the actual age of nineteen, she had decided to forgo college but passed both the certified and advanced sommelier coursework for the

Court of Master Sommeliers. She plied her trade for a year, sourcing and pouring exclusively natural wines at an extremely hip vegan restaurant run by two extremely chill lesbian chefs in an extremely expensive part of Nolita.

One sweaty day in August when Jackie was twenty-one, a famous Austrian chef came into the vegan restaurant and asked her recommendations on four bottles. So impressed was he by her knowledge and poise that by the time his strawberry rose cake was plated for dessert, he told her he wanted her to move to Vegas by Columbus Day to take the head sommelier job at his restaurant.

"You mean Indigenous Peoples' Day," she replied, saying she wouldn't consider it unless he also wanted to become the chief investor in her line of natural wines.

"Will you do a Grüner Veltliner?" he said, biting delicately into the pink frosted cake.

"Fuck no."

"Then we have a deal."

PATRICK MET HER a month into her time in Vegas, at Homies Cinnamon Rolls. Patrick was not going to Homies Cinnamon Rolls, and had never heard of Homies Cinnamon Rolls, but he happened to be walking out of a Thai massage parlor in the same strip mall. She was standing outside on Tropicana, taking a photo of her pastry.

"What are you doing?" Patrick asked her.

She looked at him. And back at her roll, which she tilted slightly higher.

"I like the light."

"Are you a photographer?"

"Aren't we all?"

Patrick introduced himself and laughed, even though he didn't quite get it. And then he asked for her number, and he didn't quite get that either.

But a month later, as he sat at the nearly empty bar in Áise drinking a whiskey, she came in.

"Who does your wine list?" she asked.

"Our sommelier, Diedrich."

"Does Diedrich know it is a steaming sack of grape shit?"

"You can ask him," Patrick said, pointing to the improbably thin man with the jagged beak polishing glasses within earshot. "He's right here."

After that, they started to (kind of) date. But it was in the old parlance of the word, which is to say, they saw each other nonexclusively. Patrick—who had spent his twenties hooking up with bartenders and servers from the inner suburbs of Boston; his thirties hooking up with B-list celebrities from the inner suburbs of Fame; and his forties hooking up with bartenders and servers from the inner suburbs of Vegas—didn't have a set romantic agenda for his fifties.

He liked Jackie because, seeing how she was born during his rise and was a toddler during his fall, she didn't come with any of the judgment baggage some of the older women he'd gone out with did. In fact, she didn't come with any baggage at all. Attempting to derive meaning from the types of people she dated was as fruitless as trying to explain chaos theory to a bird. Whether she was out with a valet from the Hard Rock, or an NHL defenseman on the Vegas Golden Knights, or a department head at Kaiser Permanente, she genuinely only seemed to care about whether she was having a good time in the moment. There was no status anxiety on her part. Perhaps it was generational, thought Patrick. He'd never felt such jealousy, both about the other men she dated and the lack of self-consciousness with which she dated them.

And so, for the last few months, Patrick and Jackie were (kind of) a thing. They would occasionally go on dates. Patrick would bring her to Vegas industry events, though more often than not she was invited anyway. Some nights, she would stay over and they would fuck and it would be glorious and athletically impressive and he would try to remember a time in his twenties when sex was freeing and fun but then realize his twenties were mostly spent with repressed Irish Catholic women, pulling out on pullout couches in the common rooms of shared triple-decker South Boston walkups, both of them still wearing their shirts and coats and sometimes even hats. Other nights, Jackie would kiss him on the mouth after a movie and commandeer some off-hours pink limo to take her to her house in the Arts District (a true New Yorker, she refused to get her license), and he wouldn't see her again for eight to ten days.

Patrick, who was never clear about relationship boundaries, had originally bragged about their open relationship to Declan ("I can fuck anyone else I want!"), but Patrick's dating reality was not the Ted Danson in *Three Men and a Baby* (but before the baby gets there) fantasy he'd hoped to convey. Especially considering most people he knew were too young for that reference.

A few days after he emerged from bingeing on *Last Call*, and following a particularly aggressive fuck involving light scarf-based bondage and 30 percent more ass play than he was realistically comfortable with, Patrick asked the question.

"What are we?"

Jackie contemplated for a minute as she folded the scarves.

"We're both busy," she'd said, and though it wasn't entirely clear who the "we" in the scenario was, given how Patrick spent most days, he'd left it at that. That was now ten days ago, though Patrick hadn't been paying attention the way he usually did because Doe had skipped to the front of the queue in his brain.

On that tenth day, Patrick texted Jackie and got the proper endorphin injection of an immediate response. She wanted him to meet her and her friends at the Velveteen Rabbit, a female-owned cocktail bar in the Arts District. "It's #WhitneyWednesday," she'd explained. "And Tabby is reading."

Though he didn't know what #WhitneyWednesday was, and he disliked both Tabby and readings, he wanted to see Jackie, and so, thinking about it like a focus group, Patrick packed a notebook and a pen and fifteen minutes later found himself in a booth with three twentysomething women drinking natural wines Jackie had selected for the night as a fourth performed the poetry of Isabella Whitney, the music of Whitney Houston, and the comedy of Whitney Cummings.

In between readings, Patrick quizzed Jackie's social media influencer and strategist friend Beth about what he needed to learn, dutifully taking notes as she peppered him with phrases like *long-tail keywords*, *UTM parameters*, and *HAS Been* (her own shorthand for *High Authority Source*).

Patrick had tried to understand social media before. His personal Twitter and Instagram accounts each had over a hundred thousand followers thanks to a combination of his past fame, Belarusian bots, and the aggressive social media team he'd hired for Áise a few years prior. But with his former staff scattered to the winds, he mostly just tweeted out specials at the restaurants, discounts on his books, and links to appearances on morning shows for cooking demos related to said books. Jackie, on the other hand, managed to post to Instagram several times a day while also somehow seeming over it.

When Patrick was with Jackie and her friends, he tried hard to tell himself generational differences were just made up by academics and marketers and not really a thing. But as he sat listening to them say they were "obsessed" with old *Muppet Babies* cartoons while, in the background, Tabby started a dramatic reading from Whitney Port's MTV reality show *The City*, he couldn't help himself.

"But you're not actually obsessed with them, are you?" he said, finishing off his wine. "It's not like you are tracking down old VHS cassette tapes of *Muppet Babies* episodes from 1989 at estate sales and writing letters to the families of the creators of the show to see if you can purchase Baby Rowlf memorabilia, right?"

The three women at the table all stared at him. Well, two did. Beth was on her phone.

"A girl I dated in my twenties," Patrick began as Jackie rolled her eyes. "She was incredibly into the whole riot grrrl scene, right? Bikini Kill, Heavens to Betsy, Bratmobile, all of that. And she would actually call up these indie record labels, Kill Rock Stars, Slampt, and others, and ask if she could send money orders—"

"What are money orders?"

"—for cassettes, and I remember she looked up Tobi Vail in Olympia, Washington, in the white pages—"

"White pages?"

"—because she'd created this zine, *Jigsaw*, and they became pen pals, and she'd get all sorts of zines sent to her and she subscribed to the *Action Girl* newsletter, and she just . . . I dunno . . . she just earned it. Like she really had to be fucking into it, she couldn't just spend a couple of hours on YouTube listening to songs from *Pussy Whipped* and suddenly become . . . obsessed."

Jackie looked at him quizzically, the way a retired person stares at a particularly challenging sudoku, then turned to her friends. "Sorry, he occasionally has to do one of his old-guy rants so he can try to rationalize the inconvenience of pre-internet culture. I'm going to get us another bottle of this funky white I found at La Dive Bouteille last year and attempt to shake off the fact that I'm hanging out with Andy Rooney."

"See!" said Patrick, pointing triumphantly. "Another unearned cultural reference!"

LATER THAT NIGHT, after they had sex on his kitchen counter because Jackie said they might as well "use it for something considering you never fucking cook on it," they went outside, laid down naked in chaise longues by the pool, and smoked a joint. Declan was gone for a couple of days on some trip to Boston, so they both remained al fresco. The heat that day had been scorching, but the night was comfortable. Patrick stared at the half-peeled-banana float still making its way around his pool.

"You remember my friend John Doe?"

Jackie took a hit and turned on her side in the chair to face him, blowing the smoke in his direction.

"I know who John Doe is, of course. Was. Is?" She cleared her throat. "I didn't realize you guys were friends."

"We were, yeah. We were good friends," Patrick said quickly. "Anyway, the network wants to offer me his job. I just have to go to New York to figure out the details."

This was not true. Gloria had secured a meeting with EEN at the end of the month, and it was in New York, but no job had been offered. Patrick, however, figured that was a foregone conclusion, and calculated that saying it aloud would make it a self-fulfilling prophecy. And hopefully impress Jackie. And she did in fact seem impressed!

"Holy shit! Patrick! That's incredible. I'm so thrilled for you!"

"I'm thrilled for me too. Pass that dutchie."

"The what?" She took another hit and handed him the joint. "Are they having a memorial service?"

Patrick made a mental note to call Gloria to find out, and make sure he was invited.

"Yeah, I'll probably make just one big trip out of it," Patrick said. He'd planned to stop there, but he was on a roll so he kept going. "They asked me to speak but I probably won't. Just rather keep those memories between me and Doe, you know?"

Patrick took a small hit, exhaled, and looked up at the cloudless sky, listening to the sounds of water rush through Rusalka's demon mouth. He felt confident and daring. And so he said the phrase that was beating against the back of his mind.

"You should come."

"I did, babe."

"No, no. I mean to New York."

Jackie turned over all the way onto her stomach and put her hand under her chin.

"Huh?"

"Come with me to New York."

Jackie didn't respond right away. The sound of water streaming out of that Slavic water monster felt like it was roaring in Patrick's ears. Finally, Jackie spoke.

"Yeah, sure. I haven't seen my friends in forever. And Lucas just got back from Brazil. That'd be so fun."

Patrick didn't know who Lucas was, but he didn't care. He was getting the girl. He was getting the job. He was going to go to New York.

He took another deeper, more triumphant hit.

"I've got his fucking sauce," Patrick said. Then he coughed for thirty seconds straight.

10.

NIA GREENE

NEW YORK, NY

Tuesday, July 16, 2019, 10:33 a.m.

For the first time in two weeks, Nia had time to think. So she thought about her friend.

After John Doe's first book hit, back in 2000, all of Hollywood came for him. They sent him gift baskets. They threw him parties. They told him he could make whatever he wanted. "If you sign with me," one agent told him from a convertible darting through traffic on the 405, "I will make you bigger than Justin Timberlake." Doe told the man he would sign, but only if he delivered Timberlake's head on a silver plate. "And the hair has to be *intact*," Doe said. "It has to be perfect. I want it specifically for the hair." The head never arrived, and Doe never signed.

As Nia saw it, the mistake agents and producers made with Doe was that they all assumed he was some dirtbag bartender who would be easily dazzled by attention and money. He'd come in for a meeting at an agency and there would be people applauding him. Maybe an agency head would even stop by. This might work for most people—almost all of them, really—but you don't spend decades working in bars and restaurants with drug addicts and ex-cons without learning how to tell the difference between a real smile, a desperate smile, and a malicious smile. And as Doe scanned all those gleaming white teeth in gleaming white rooms in gleaming white offices, he saw nothing but greed, treachery, and simian terror. His heart pumped hate, and he turned, and he left.

This was inconceivable to Hollywood, and it only made them want him more. As vicious as they could be to one another and to those who wanted in to their business, they were hopelessly enraptured by those who didn't give a shit about the very thing for which they were willing to saw off their grandmothers' legs. Disinterest disordered their minds and made them mad with lust and existential confusion. A redoubling of their efforts only resulted in a multiplication of their failures.

That was the state of the world when Doe arrived for a meeting at AAE on that shining summer morning. The sleek elevator chimed and the doors slid noiselessly open. He stepped out into AAE's offices wearing a battered leather jacket, jeans, motorcycle boots, and hangover hair, and he was greeted by every single employee of AAE. They applauded. Then one hooted, and then three more hooted, because they did not want to be penalized later for not hooting. Doe stopped amid this wall of sound, stuffed his hands into the pockets of his jeans, and rocked back on his heels. A grin spread across his long, prematurely lined face.

"Who will you make me bigger than?" he demanded to know.

They went silent. They looked at one another. No one quite knew what to do with this prompt. At least no one wanted to be the first to answer it. Then someone yelled, "Tom Cruise!" And you could tell people instantly regretted that they hadn't yelled Tom Cruise first. So then another one yelled, "Will Smith!" And another, "George Clooney!" Pretty soon everyone was just yelling out the names of random stars. "Eminem!" "*The Sopranos!*" "*Monday Night Football!*" "Santana featuring Rob Thomas!"

Doe stood there taking this all in. He seemed pleased, and his pleasure heartened them. And then he got back on the elevator and left.

Certainly, Nia figured, John Doe would enjoy money. Like many people occupying the more bohemian rungs of the social ladder, he surely had better taste than he had resources to satisfy it. And he seemed as if he'd enjoy fame, at least based on his appearances on Patrick Whelan's horribly misbegotten reality show. But Nia also saw something in Doe that the others had missed—a more complicated motivation. She saw a man who was, first and foremost, interested in cultures. She saw a fellow anthropologist. So, while her colleagues milled in the reception area of AAE, quietly devising ways to blame one another for the agency's failure to sign Doe, a twenty-six-year-old Nia Greene slipped into the stairwell, raced the elevator down three stories, and burst through a door leading to the lobby. Doe already had his sunglasses on, and he was smacking a pack of cigarettes against his palm. She appeared next to him, panting. He looked down at her and raised an eyebrow.

"Hollywood," she said, struggling to catch her breath, "is the NBA. For white people."

Doe laughed as he continued walking across the lobby. She walked alongside.

"You one of them?" he said, nodding at the ceiling.

"I am," she said.

"Not really my ilk," he said.

"Not mine either," she said.

"That's what they all say."

"Let me take you to lunch and I'll tell you some stories."

"Nah," he said, pulling ahead. "Nice meeting you."

Nia stopped, and she watched for a moment as Doe approached the glass front doors. His form began to turn black against the LA sunlight. It would be years before Nia could put words to what she felt in that instant. In the moment, it felt like a compulsion to succeed, or to show her colleagues that she could do what they failed to do, or to make some money. But it was more than that, she came to realize in later years. It was a sense of pending loss. Not just as an agent, but as a person. For some reason she felt like she was losing an alternate future, a life that she might really enjoy.

"Hey, John," she said.

He turned, halfway through the doors.

"My boss weighs his own shit."

"Say again?"

"He weighs his own shit. He has a special toilet in his office with a scale built into it. I just saw it."

Doe's face brightened. He studied her for a moment. He withdrew a cigarette from the pack, practically tossed it into the corner of his mouth, lit it, took a drag, nodded, and pushed out the smoke in a thin, hard jet that made everyone in the no-smoking lobby nervous.

"I know a pretty good Thai place on Sunset," he said.

IN THE END, there was fame and money and adventure, but it all began in a little storefront in a strip mall in Little Armenia, ironically. Doe made her eat something called the Chef's Spicy Dynamite Challenge—with lamb, because anyone who gets chicken with it is vulgar. Nia had to show the owner her ID to prove she was over eighteen before he'd bring the dish out. When he did, she could practically feel her hair recoiling. It was horrible beyond reckoning, but she ate the food because she'd learned that when doing fieldwork, you always eat the food. If you hate it, that's fine, you can say you hate it—they'll probably think it's hilarious if you make a big show of how gross it is—but you always eat the food. And while she ate it, and sweated and drooled and tried to ignore her body's emergency warning system, they talked.

"So," he said. "You're a Black agent."

"John, you noticed."

"That must be a pain in the ass."

It is, she told him. But there is an upside. It led people to underestimate her, which was useful. She told him about how everyone assumed she was an affirmative-action hire—they'd even tell her that—even though she went to Princeton on a merit scholarship. It didn't mean her colleagues were mean to her, she said, just that most of them swung between being dismissive and "nice," and the nice ones were the worst because they seemed to think she owed them something for tolerating her, like tolerance is such a great moral achievement.

"Right," Doe said. "I shall *tolerate* you, like I tolerate lactose."

"Right. They get to decide to tolerate me. I don't have that luxury with them."

They ate more food—mercifully no more Spicy Dynamite Challenge—and he told her all about the dishes. He did this with a surprising command of the subject matter for a bartender, but also with a sensitivity that she found captivating. He told her stories of motorcycle trips he had taken in Thailand, and other places—Java, Vietnam, Morocco—how these journeys had changed him, and how travel has always changed him, and food has always changed him, and how, when you think about it, food and drink are a form of travel, of communion.

"It's borderline impossible," he said, by way of example, "to love Indian food and not love Indians. Not totally impossible. But pretty fucking difficult."

As he talked, the wised-up New York cynic pose yielded to something else, something more human, more vulnerable, more curious. He came to life. He became boyish. And there she saw her opportunity. The next twenty years of her life laid themselves out before her.

"These people who are after you," she said, "they're probably talking about, like, movies and barhopping shows and gigs on *Good Morning America* showing people in Oklahoma how to make an eggnog martini for Christmas, right?"

"A man in a convertible said I could be the new Justin Timberlake."

"You're not pretty enough for that job."

"Fuck you I'm not."

"Here's the thing, John. These things people are promising: none of that is for you."

"No?"

"No. Look, you sold a lot of books. You've got some money in your pocket. The next book will probably get you more money up front. As long as you're not a total idiot, you should be able to live off that for a few years. And when that runs out, you can always go back to work, which you love anyway."

"Overstatement, but go on."

"So don't do anything you're going to feel gross about. Don't whore. Don't do a John Doe line of cocktail jiggers for QVC. Don't do a branded bourbon that's actually just two years old. But on the other hand, don't be a caricature, because that's whoring too."

"Okay, so what should I do?"

"You should do Hollywood on your own terms, or don't do it at all," she said. "Here's my pitch: You sign with me for six months. Literally, a six-month contract. And we pitch a show together. And it's not a barhopping show. It's a travel show, where you go around the world, to all these exotic places, with a little crew—a little pirate band of your very own—and you drink, and you eat, and you learn, and you talk to people, and you struggle to understand, and you convey that to us, to the viewers. Just like you're doing here."

"Interesting."

"And when you do this, John, you will show them how to live. What's the line—beer is evidence that god loves us and wants us to be happy? You can embody that. By your example, you can show them the potential for life in this world. And *that's* something. Anyway, I'm not interested in anything else. And I won't try to pitch you on anything else. Just this. And if it doesn't work, no hard feelings. I go back to being yelled at by a man who weighs his own shit, and you can go host the Teen Choice Awards or whatever it is they're pitching you."

"The new Justin Timberlake."

"You shouldn't be the new anything. You should be John Doe, writ larger. That's what I want for you."

He leaned back and scrutinized her with a hint of a smirk but a light in his eyes. And then he smiled and took a pull of his beer.

"I won't do anything that's not fun, Nia," he said.

"It'll be fun."

"Promise me, Nia."

"I promise."

And it was fun. The two decades that followed were the best of her life. She saw John become a global star. She saw him go from a cynical wiseass to a genuine humanist. He made a lot of money, and at first she made 15 percent of a lot of money, which was still a lot of money.

When his literary agent dropped a couple of balls, Nia studied the book business and took over there. When his publicist stopped doing anything more than sending out email blasts to the media, Nia picked that up too. She left AAE and started her own one-woman shop. He became her full-time job, and she was so good at it that other stars, huge ones who shall remain nameless due to bales of nondisclosure agreements, begged her to take them on. But she wouldn't, and it made them crazy.

She never had a husband. She never had a kid. Instead, she had John Doe, and she figured she won on that deal. They traveled the world together. They ate, they drank, they got into weird scrapes with foreign customs officials, spent more than one night in the woods with armed rebels, and once got a Saudi princeling's new Rolls stuck in a sand dune in Dubai and just left it there. They could barely even walk away, they were laughing so hard. When shooting for the show was over, they still talked almost every night, as business partners but also as friends. And now they'd never talk again.

IT HAD BEEN a brutal couple of weeks, but Nia had done her job well. The BBC story led the coverage, full of money quotes from culinary celebrities. Other reports followed, also rich, evocative, and full of star power. She'd coached Doe's friends in advance—be shocked, but not skeptical; tell your favorite stories about him, even if they're off-color; don't make him a saint, just tell the truth—and they had more than delivered. She figured if she could load enough great testimonials into the news cycle, that would keep even the lowliest blogger well fed for seventy-two hours and keep conspiracy theories at a minimum.

The first wave of stories in legacy media outlets led to a second wave of columns, essays, and personal remembrances. That second wave broke into a million posts and tweets, and the overall message was that this was a great man, a magnificent and riotous soul, and his loss was a lesson to the rest of us about the hidden depths and struggles of even the most seemingly self-assured person. Most of the stories ran with a tag at the end telling those who felt suicidal to call a hotline, and for everyone to take care of one another. Nia heard from the CEO of a leading suicide-prevention nonprofit that donations were up 50 percent in the week after the news broke. She got a call from *Good Day*. They wanted to dedicate a full hour on an upcoming Sunday show to John. And not some shitty hour. The good one. The third one. She agreed to it and offered to help wrangle people. It was unpaid, but it was a huge audience, and he deserved such a send-off. He deserved a sultan's farewell.

As the story developed, Nia received an onslaught of emails, letters, DMs, and texts from all creatures great and small within the Hollywood ecosystem that purported to offer sympathy and support, but in reality were just attempts to secure her representation or hire her. "If you ever need to talk, I'm here for you," wrote some actress Nia had never heard of. "We can be the family you've lost," said a leading agency head, a large, damp, bristly, sinister boil of a man who would soon thereafter be indicted for assaulting starlets.

Nia dismissed these out of hand. But she still replied to every single message with a vow to "seriously consider this amazingly generous offer," followed by an effusion of gratitude so patently insincere and excessive that in any other industry it would be viewed as an insult. But Hollywood had a curious relationship with the word *no*. Most rejection didn't look like rejection. People loathed saying no outright, opting instead to utter things like "Let's keep talking about this," which actually meant "Let's stop talking about this." *I will not tell you no,* it said, *in the hopes that you'll eventually go away on your own, and if by chance our paths should cross again, and we find ourselves in public together, I will sing your praises and call you a genius.*

Nia had studied a phenomenon called cultures of honor —how in some cultures, life was so unstable and people were so afraid of one another that everyone went to absurd lengths to be nice in order to avoid being killed. Hollywood was one such culture. "Smile until your eyeballs water," a mentor had told her. "Never tell anyone no. Always hide the bodies."

Whatever. It was nice to be thought of, she figured. Her main priority remained her press barrage, and two weeks in, it appeared to have gone off just the way she'd hoped.

There was just one thing that concerned her. There was a story on some website—*Swizzle*, or *Swivel*, or *Tizzy*, or *Navel*. It wasn't a negative story. In fact, it was quite beautiful and played right into the narrative Nia was pushing. She'd been monitoring it, but unlike the hundred other stories by no-name grief-parasites claiming they'd had a revelatory beer with Doe at an airport or locked eyes with him in a way that somehow granted them unmatched insight into the dark multitudes at the man's core, this one hadn't disappeared in a day. In fact, it was still growing.

Why did it matter if it was a good story? It mattered because Nia had never heard of the author, and she'd made a point of knowing everyone John knew. It mattered because she'd never heard of the restaurant the author had supposedly visited with John. And it mattered because the story was becoming *the* story: the takeaway from the tragedy. Nia had started getting calls from reporters who referenced it. It had become the substance of the suicide narrative. It wasn't what the kid was saying that worried her. It was that the kid might be seizing control of the story and using it to advance her own interests, which were a mystery to Nia.

The kid was good too. A natural. Nia had watched her on TV a week prior. She was composed, articulate, engaging. She presented well. She had that thing that made you like her right away. The only indication that she didn't do this for a living was a chyron that said she worked for a website, and the strange padded-looking outfit she had on. "I was literally crying when I met John Doe," the girl had said. "It was this past winter. I was standing on the corner in the snow crying—which is such a New York cliché, I know." The audience chuckled knowingly, sympathetically. "And he walked up, and he asked me, 'Are you okay?' "

At the time, this setup had sent a frisson of mild panic through Nia. *Ex-girlfriend? Sexual harassment allegation?* But the kid assured the hosts that nothing untoward happened. He was just being kind. She said she and Doe talked a bit, he about being a writer and TV host, she about being a journalist. "We just felt this instant connection," she said. Doe told her he was headed to one of his secret favorite restaurants—"a little place called Lobio"—for lunch, and he asked if she wanted to join him. She said yes, and they went and had lunch together.

This struck Nia as perhaps a bit unexpected but not wholly out of character for John. He liked to talk to strangers, and he actually was the kind of guy who would ask someone weeping in the street if they were okay. The kid said the beans were "life changing," and that Doe revered this little hole in the wall for elevating such a humble item to such a lofty height, "which is what food, and life, are all about." It didn't sound like Doe, but the general idea wasn't totally out of character for him either.

Nia hadn't been terribly concerned at the time. But as the story showed real staying power, she revisited the segment online and something began to nag at her, something that really did not sound like Doe—which also happened to be the very thing that made the story such a hit. It was that, according to Katie Horatio, Doe confessed to her, seemingly unbidden, that he had suffered from serious depression for as long as he could remember, and that every day was a struggle to resist the relief that only death can bring to a troubled soul. "He told me the belt sometimes called to him at night," the kid had told the hosts. "Sometimes he'd be holding it and not remember even getting it out of the drawer." Mazie made her empathy face at this. Mark tried to, but he looked a little under the weather.

"Did he tell you how he pulled out of it, in those moments?" Mazie asked.

"He made a cocktail," she said. "A single gimlet."

"Amazing," said Mark.

"So amazing," she agreed. "He told me, 'Katie, good drink doesn't just sustain life, it creates life, and it makes it worth living.'"

Nia started poking around. She searched for "Katie Horatio" online and found the original story. She clicked Horatio's byline to see what else she had done, but she found only the usual internet dreck. Nothing to suggest this woman was a gifted writer.

Next, she searched for "Lobio NYC." It had no website, but it had accumulated dozens of Google reviews. Most of these were five-star ratings, paeans to John Doe and beans, but they were from the last couple of weeks. Only three reviews predated John's death.

Doe loved odd places, but even by Doe's standards this place was pretty obscure. She wondered if he had gone there a lot. Usually she knew about all his secret haunts. He kept a Google document of every restaurant he'd ever gone to, which Nia and Paolo contributed to as well. She checked it. No Lobio. She logged in to the corporate credit card account and searched the statements for Lobio. Nothing over the last year. She dug into previous years—nothing. She did find records of a slew of purchases from Bulgaria the previous December. Boxes of Bulgarian pottery, traditional embroidered garments, spooky religious icons, vintage pornography that featured more hair than a dumpster behind a barbershop, a dozen weird T-shirts featuring mangled English phrases that didn't mean anything, and a metal sign in Cyrillic reading, simply, "PLACE FOR TRASH."

Nia had missed that trip because of the holidays, and Doe had sent her all of this: a mountain of Bulgariana for Christmas. The postage cost $700. "Dear Nia," read the card. "Elvis had a jungle room. Now you can have a Bulgaria room, like you've always dreamed of. Please have it ready upon my return next month. We miss you. Sofia sends its love. Nazdrave! John."

Anyway, maybe he paid cash at Lobio. But he usually wrote off everything he could—even her Bulgarian Christmas bonanza—so if he did pay cash, the receipts should be in their taxes. She pulled those up. No Lobio in the last seven years. She searched his calendar. No Lobio. There was the possibility that he didn't want anyone to know he had gone there, though she didn't know why. It could have been drugs, maybe. Or a woman, though he'd never been shy about that in the past. A friend's wife? But then why would he bring some random kid down there?

She texted Paolo: "Did u ever go to Lobio?"

A few seconds later he replied, "No."

Finally, Nia Googled "Lobio" with "Katie Horatio." She scrolled through the detritus of commentary on the Doe piece and came at last to a capsule review Horatio had written more than a year before, for a package regrettably titled "Ain't Too Proud to Beg(umes)."

It read: "Eastern European foodies come here at all times of day to nosh their signature: *lobio*, a bean dish swaddled in rich, salty, yum-inducing cheese. Just don't sleep on the *tkemali*, a traditional condiment made with plums. And pro tip: if they ask you if you want *mchadi*, the traditional Georgian cornbread, the answer is a resounding 'Da!'"

Anyone who worked in and around the food world had the misfortune of having read hundreds of these sorts of things, which were generally produced very quickly, and researched via Google and not from actually having eaten in the places themselves. But even by those standards, this was bad. What's more, it was dated months before John Doe had supposedly plucked this Katie off a snowy sidewalk and whisked her to his secret bean sanctuary that his closest friends had never heard him speak of, to confess that not only did he suffer from bouts of acute depression, but when he did, he consumed a cocktail that Nia had never once seen him drink.

Nia Googled "SWVLL" and found a main number. A young woman answered.

"Could you connect me to Katie Horatio, please."

"I'm sorry, I can't. We have a landline-free culture."

"But I called you."

Silence.

"Right. Well, could you just grab her for me? This is Nia Greene. I represented John Doe. She'll want to talk to me."

"I can't *grab* her."

"It's an expression."

Silence.

"Is there an email I can use?"

"Sure, it's info@swvll.com."

"That sounds like a slush-pile email."

Silence.

"Okay, let's try this. Can you just connect me to the editor in chief?"

"We don't have an editor in chief."

"Then can you connect me to whoever Katie's boss is?"

"We don't have bosses here."

"Then who does Katie report to?"

"No one reports to anyone here. SWVLL has a horizontal culture. We're all autonomous."

"Oh my god," Nia said. "Is there someone who gives speeches sometimes? Who stands up in the middle of what I'm presuming is an open-plan office with exposed wood beams wearing fucking $500 high-tops and gives speeches about value and meaning?"

"Yes, that's River."

"Is he the editor in chief? Or the CEO?"

"He's the Firestarter."

"Can you connect me to the Firestarter then, please?"

"Sorry, we have a landline-free . . ."

"Dear god. *Can you just fucking tell me how to get in touch with Katie Horatio*?"

Silence.

"Maybe try DMing her on Insta?"

So Nia did. She hung up. She found Katie on Instagram. She explained who she was. She congratulated Katie on her marvelous story. And—this was risky, but she needed to get a net over this kid—she invited her to John Doe's memorial party that evening.

THE MEMORIAL WAS HELD in a large function room in a facility on the Hudson River in Manhattan's Chelsea neighborhood. It was a sad occasion, but the party was shaping up to be a riotous good time: loss, fused with the sense of collective effervescence and camaraderie that can only occur when you gather a couple hundred brilliant and profane people who have dedicated themselves to creating beauty with edge weapons and combustible liquids, and give them a night off and access to bottomless drink. The loss of John Doe had impelled everyone involved to reach for higher levels of decadence; to celebrate him, and, in doing so, celebrate themselves and the fact of being alive. *This may be the last time,* the old gospel song goes. And the attendees, arms thrown around one another, singing and yelling and staggering in rugby scrums from table to table, behaved as if it were.

Often while drinking gimlets, curiously.

Nia was happily absorbed by this mass. By virtue of her proximity to Doe, these had become her people, much more so than Hollywood. While chefs, bartenders, and brewers pushed through the mob to offer condolences, they always sheathed their kindness in the language of insult, which she liked, because it showed actual solidarity and didn't assume you were fragile or broken.

"You're fucked now, sister," shouted Ally Toback, the Harlem-based vegan soul food visionary, before hugging her.

"If you're looking for more coattails to ride, I've got a spare pair," said Jeffrey Simó, head bartender at Flamingoes & Fauna, a proto-tiki speakeasy in Stamford, Connecticut, that paid winking homage to the fern bar movement of the 1970s. He was pushed aside by Cliven Thompson, chief distiller of Bayou Bourbon, a premium spirit aged in barrels fashioned from Acadian shrimp boats that was owned by a hedge fund also based in Stamford.

"Oh, Nia," Thompson drawled, enveloping her in a bear hug as he choked up. "If you need work I can always speak to someone at the barrel factory."

"Great."

"You're gonna be dazzled by East Baton Rouge. Don't worry," he said, patting her arm, "you'll get used to the humidity."

There were real offers too. Most people in the room would happily pay Nia a fortune to manage their brands, and many of them pitched her. But what she loved about this crowd was that she could just reject them. The beauty of restaurant people was that they had no time for passive aggression. They lived life on deadline, they had to perform at all times at a very high level, and there was nowhere to hide. So they not only asked for candor, they were also psychologically equipped with the ability to deal with it. Nia could even be mean, which was phenomenally gratifying. When the British chef Robby Wareham insisted, rather rudely she thought, that he be the next Doe, Nia calmly explained a core principle of American entertainment. "Robby, in England, an actor can be fat and still take serious parts. But in America, if an actor is fat, fatness has to be his brand. That means he has to be jolly or ridiculous. If we put a fat man on TV and he is earnest and intelligent it would just confuse the shit out of everybody and the whole culture would collapse."

While Wareham licked his wounds, Nia scanned the room. She was hoping to see Paolo. Instead, she saw Patrick Whelan pressing copies of his cookbook into people's hands. Knowing him, it was probably a hustle, like those kids selling rap CDs to tourists in Times Square: walk up, stick it in their hand, and then harass them until they pay you. Before his agent had reached out about attending the memorial, she hadn't thought of Whelan in years. Now she regretted inviting him. He'd always struck her as a cautionary tale: everything Doe wasn't. He'd still be a great chef, if only he hadn't self-commoditized with such desperate abandon that it killed his art. She ducked away before he could notice her, only to be accosted by another scrum of scarred and vulgar geniuses.

What finally settled the mob—or at least brought it as close to stillness as it was capable of getting—was the tribute to John Doe. There was a reel of greatest hits from the show, introduced by the chair of the Tales of the Cocktail Foundation. Paolo gave the eulogy, striding onto the stage tailed by a smallish black-haired man she'd never seen before who was grinning like a maniac and waving to the crowd for some reason.

After Paolo came Katie Horatio, who seemed to have gotten a modern haircut and some fashion sense since her television appearance. Nia had to admit Katie looked fantastic: jeans, Chuck Taylors, and a blazer over a lavender silk top. Her speech was a masterpiece of control—sadness, humor, hope, self-deprecation, boldness, and a touch of saltiness to show the crowd that though she may be a stranger, she was one of them. And she destroyed the place. When she was done, she slipped the mic into its holder like a gun into a holster, descended from the dais as the gathering resumed its bacchanalia, and was swarmed.

"Nia?"

It was Paolo.

"Oh god, Paolo." She hugged him. "How are you?"

"I'm okay. How are you?"

"I'm okay. Are you going to do this *Good Day* thing? This Sunday morning thing?"

"Do you want me to?"

"Yeah, could you?"

"It'd be my pleasure. Uh, can we talk for a second?

"Sure."

He led Nia across the room and out a set of doors leading to a deck overlooking the Hudson. He found a quiet spot and instructed his assistant to keep people away. Nia was slightly amused at the cloak-and-dagger business. But Paolo was serious.

"There is a man living in my apartment," he said.

"Lucky you."

"It's not like that. It's . . . I'm going to tell you something. And you're going to be very upset."

Paolo was flustered. Nia had never seen him flustered—save for the day Doe died, and at least that time she didn't have to actually see it. It was unsettling. It was like seeing your father cry.

"Just tell me, Paolo. You can tell me."

"Remember that day, when you asked me if anyone else knew."

"Yes."

"Someone else knew."

Nia rocked back. She wanted to scream at him. But she channeled it into a harsh whisper. "Are you kidding me, Paolo?"

"No."

"Who is it?"

Paolo said nothing. Nia studied his face.

"Oh fuck," she said. "It's the man in your apartment."

"Yes."

"Goddamn it, Paolo."

Nia watched as Paolo scanned the deck for anyone who might be listening. It was empty. He turned toward the large windows of the function room. There stood the strange man who had accompanied him onstage when he gave his eulogy. He smiled and made a drinking gesture at Paolo. Paolo shook his head, and the man made the sign of the horns with his hand and exited, presumably heading for the bar.

Barely holding himself together, Paolo told her everything. The lemon, the ten-pound note, the sudden appearance of Charlie in his life, and this sense he had that he wasn't being blackmailed so much as . . . occupied? Inhabited? He'd come home the night before, he said, and found Charlie wearing his shoes and cooking at the stove, only the stove wasn't on and there was nothing in the cast-iron pan. Later, Paolo noticed that Charlie had scratched his name into the center of the pan.

"What does he have?"

Paolo took a deep breath.

"There's a photo," he said.

"What do you mean, a photo? A photo of John?"

"Yeah, with me in it. Covering . . . covering *it* up."

"He took the photo?"

"Yes."

"He hasn't asked for money?" Nia asked.

"No. He hasn't even mentioned the photo. But he doesn't seem to be leaving either."

"Right."

"Maybe if I could get my hands on his phone . . ."

Nia shook her head. "Wouldn't do any good," she said. "It'll be in the cloud."

"Of course."

"Let me think about it."

"Please do."

"I'm going to need to meet him."

"I don't know, Nia."

"I'll be discreet. We can bump into each other or something. I can come by the apartment."

"Come by the restaurant tomorrow, around ten a.m."

"Okay," she said, and drained a glass of champagne. "What a fucking world."

They peered out over the Hudson at New Jersey.

"Paolo?"

"Yes."

"You ever lie to me again and I'll fucking kill you."

NIA WALKED BACK INSIDE. She needed to talk to Katie Horatio. She was fairly certain the kid was lying, but she needed to see if this was something she had to worry about. But whenever she got close, Katie moved farther away, swept toward the bar by her new fans. Nia tried to catch up but was intercepted by a third-place contestant from some cooking competition show insisting that *he* be the new John Doe, and offering Nia the opportunity to represent him.

She didn't know him, and thus reverted to her customary Hollywood blow-off.

"Thank you so much!" she replied. "I will seriously consider this amazingly generous offer."

That was the story of the rest of the night. Katie was so hard to get to that Nia began to suspect she was fleeing. If that were the case, good. It meant Katie was afraid. Nia was more than comfortable working with fear. It was only later, at one of the three after-parties, that Nia was able to get Katie alone for a moment. She followed her into the ladies' room, pantomimed doing her business in one of the stalls, and ended up next to her at the sinks.

"I loved your speech," Nia said.

"Oh, thanks," said Katie, studying her face. "That's so sweet."

Nia thought she looked cagey. Her smile was wide, but her eyes were cold. "And I thought you were great on TV the other day," she said.

"Thank you. Beginner's luck, I guess."

"Where are my manners? I'm Nia Greene. I was John Doe's agent, and publicist, and everything else for twenty years."

". . ."

"I invited you tonight?"

"Oh, amazing! Hi!"

"I just wanted to say, you really captured him in that essay. It was extraordinary. You're really very talented. In fact, I can't believe we've never met before."

"I know, right?" said Katie. "I'm so glad we finally did. John told me so many amazing things about you."

"Oh, I'm sure. Listen, I know you're busy, but I wanted to say, we should talk sometime."

"I'd love that," Katie said. "I'm doing this weekly thing on TV now—it's no big deal, but I'd love to see what else is out there: books, national TV, I'm really open to anything."

"Definitely that, yeah. But some other stuff too."

"For sure. Like what?"

Nia glanced around at the busy ladies' room and smiled. She leaned over and whispered in Katie's ear: "John Doe's never been to Lobio."

Katie's face hardened.

"You cocksucker," she said.

11.

CHEF PAOLO CABRINI

NEW YORK, NY

Wednesday, July 17, 2019, 8:23 a.m.

For fifty-two years, four months, and three days of his life, Paolo Cabrini's bowels had performed with the punctuality, predictability, and efficiency of a Swiss train. Every day, he would have his espresso, eat a bowl of Familia muesli with hot oat milk and seasonal berries, and between twenty-six and forty-two minutes later, nature would make its gentle call. He would head to his bathroom, take care of business quickly (no reading material!), and be on the way to a productive day.

But in his fifty-second year, during the fourth month, on the fourth day, Charlie had walked into his bathroom and interrupted his routine.

"Where do youse keep yer biscuits?" he'd asked as he went to the sink and started flossing his teeth. By that point, Charlie had been at the apartment for two days.

Paolo was incredulous. "Excuse me, I'm in here!"

Charlie looked at him full in the face and then down at the toilet. "So you are. Apologies." He switched to a whisper. "Just pretend I'm not here, I'll be quiet as a field mouse." Then he'd continued to floss.

Shocked by the disturbance to his routine, Paolo's body had protested. Both his rectum and his anus had closed up shop. His intestines had taken off on a French-style grandes vacances. And now, for the first time in his life, it had been over a week since Paolo Cabrini had taken a shit.

THE PLAN WAS FOR NIA GREENE to stop by the restaurant without seeming like she was stopping by. It had to feel like a drop-in. Paolo worried that if it seemed like they were having an actual *meeting*-meeting, Charlie might feel trapped, in which case he might panic and do something rash. Or worse, he might feel emboldened. If Paolo tipped his hand and revealed that he needed not only outside help with the matter of Charlie McCree, but outside help from a heavy like Nia Greene, then Charlie might see that as additional leverage to help him enact his grand plan, whatever that was. Paolo wanted to get out of this mess, but he wanted to do so without paying one cent more than he had to.

Paolo shifted in his seat. His insides felt like they had been filled with concrete. He hadn't slept well in several days. He'd seen some hairs on his comb that morning. He'd found a pimple on his inner thigh. He and Charlie were sitting in the restaurant, having what was supposed to be breakfast. Paolo was eating a bowl of Familia muesli with hot oat milk and seasonal berries. Charlie was eating hamburgers from Wendy's in Paolo's dining room. Paolo had offered him food from the restaurant, but Charlie passed. He only wanted Wendy's, he said, because he liked the redhead on the bag. "We went to school together," he said. "She's a dirty bird."

There was a tapping at the window. Paolo looked up and there was Nia. She was pretending to be on the phone. Paolo waved her in, and then got up and unlocked the front door. A passerby actually craned his neck to look inside the restaurant. Such was Paolo's reputation. Such was his mystique.

"Nia! What a pleasant surprise!" Paolo managed.

"I was just stopping over at Makala's," she said, effortlessly referencing something that was not real in a way that put Paolo at ease. "How are you feeling?"

Paolo recognized that she was referring to the party last night. He composed himself.

"I'm mourning the late loss of my sobriety," he said. "Please, have coffee with us."

"No, I should be going."

"I insist," Paolo said. "Besides, I'd like you to meet a—"

Paolo turned and Charlie was already standing right behind him.

"You was at the wake last night," Charlie said.

"That's right. I'm Nia," she said.

"I'm Charlie," said Charlie, standing very close and looking her in the eye.

"Um, how about that coffee, Paolo?" Nia said.

"Of course," Paolo said.

"Of course," Charlie echoed.

"Whole milk is fine," said Nia.

"Whole milk is fine, Chef," called Charlie to Paolo, without breaking eye contact with Nia. He was still smiling.

OVER FOUR CUPS OF COFFEE and about two hundred questions, Nia had failed to extract anything meaningful from Charlie whatsoever.

He mostly just praised Paolo and America for making his dreams come true. She asked him how long he figured he'd stay for, and he told her that "dreams have no timeline." She asked him if he was a fan of John Doe and Charlie just nodded absently. "Oh, sure, sure," he said. "Yer man was quite a man." But he didn't seem to know who Doe was. Or, if he did, he was concealing it, which was a weird thing for an aspiring blackmailer to do.

Growing desperate, Nia asked if there was anything she could do for him while he was in town, and he said he'd like to meet "the girl on the hamburger bag," whom he'd named Kitty, even though her name was clearly Wendy. Trying to remain conversational, Nia asked about his past. He told her he grew up in Divis Flats, a notorious Catholic housing project that was a hotbed of paramilitary activity during the Troubles. She asked him what it was like to live there. "Good craic," he said. He told her his uncle Seamus smuggled in the mortars they used to blow up 10 Downing Street. And his uncle Sean helped blow up the Europa Hotel five times before being lured out to Armagh and "head-jobbed by some fuckin' SAS cowboy." Charlie was grinning conspiratorially by this point.

"Some people," he said, "believe the McCrees to be bloodthirsty." He winked.

"Are they?" Nia asked. "Bloodthirsty, I mean?"

"Oh, some are, for certain," said Charlie. "Proper hard men."

"Are you, Charlie?"

"Smilin' Charlie? Bloodthirsty? You're mad."

"Are you thirsty for other things?" she asked.

"Yes," said Charlie. "I am, as a matter of fact."

"Okay, good. What are you thirsty for?"

Charlie grinned. He leaned back in his chair and crossed his arms. He cocked his head and pursed his lips. And then he gave his answer.

"Fame," he said. "Proper. Fucking. Fame."

"Fame for what?" Nia asked.

Charlie lit up. He turned to Paolo. "Have I told you about my band, Chef Cabrini?"

"Your band?"

"Yeah, my band. We're called the Bad Friday Disagreement. Because—"

"No, I think I understand. What sort of music?"

"You know Tommy Makem? The Clancy Brothers?" he said, turning back to Nia.

"No," said Nia. "I'm sorry."

"Well, it's that, the Irish rebel stuff, but in a ska sort of way. Like if the Clancy Brothers met the Mighty Mighty Bosstones." Charlie's face scrunched up as he seemed pained by that comparison. "Nah, not the Bosstones. Maybe Less Than Jake, actually."

Paolo, who mostly listened to classical Spanish guitar while riding his stationary bike, didn't know who any of these bands were. Nor did Nia. Charlie could sense that and tried again.

"The Wolfe Tones had a musical baby with Fishbone? The Chieftains fucked the Pietasters? Did you catch any of that, Nina?"

Nia just smiled.

"Anyway, that's my band," said Charlie. "We're class. And I feel like with all the love for Ireland over here, we could find an audience in America. I read 40 percent of America thinks they're Irish, right? That's a big audience. Bigger than anything we could do in Belfast. We just need to meet the right people. Martin Scorsese. Couple of the lads from *Star Wars*. Anyone. It's about who you know, right? That's half the battle?"

Nia smiled. She leaned forward and said in her gentlest voice,

"Charlie, would you like us to get you a gig for your band? Would that . . . satisfy you?"

"You serious, Nina?"

"It's Nia. And we'd love to," Nia said. "Wouldn't we, Paolo?"

"Yes," said Paolo. "We would love to."

"Then it's settled!" said Nia. "The Bad Friday Disagreement is coming to America!"

Charlie exploded. "Fuckin' gorgeous!" he exclaimed as a small gray morsel of chewed hamburger flew out of his mouth, sailed across the table, and landed in Paolo's hair.

DESPITE THE PETRIFICATION of his digestive track, Paolo had an exceedingly productive couple of weeks, all in an effort to secure a music venue and an audience for Charlie and his band. Charlie spent much of their mornings together in his skivvies, addressing a long litany of knocks against the band, which he insisted were baseless, such as the claims that the Bad Friday Disagreement "wasn't a proper ginger wrecking crew" or that "Seamus had burned all those cars." Meanwhile, Paolo set about mounting his first concert, which was challenging. First, he had no connections in the music world. Nor, historically, had he wanted any. Frankly, the people involved in playing music and promoting it always struck him as erratic and slovenly. Second, even in his ignorance, Paolo knew that music venues in New York were booked weeks or even months ahead of time. Booking something quickly would be challenging. He could book a function hall, or try to find an open mic night, but he knew that would not take care of the Charlie problem. Charlie required a real gig, at a creditable venue in which people of influence gathered. And third, Paolo never asked for favors. Never. He was not that person. The prospect of putting himself in a situation where people could call him and make him do things for them at a time of their choosing further upset his digestion and made his skin tighten.

And yet here he was, asking for favors. This was the course of action he had chosen, and he had to execute it at a high level. He'd cornered one of his servers, a talented musician who knew people in the business, and asked for connections and introductions. He had texted friends of friends, asking them if they would like to come to a concert in exchange for a dinner on him at the French Restaurant with the French Name. He begged an ex-girlfriend who worked in event planning for introductions to club managers, offering a dozen of them dinner if they agreed to bump an act they'd booked to free up a slot. He even combed through music listings and reached out to the bands themselves, offering them dinners with wine if they agreed to step aside.

Because it was novel and because he owned the most prestigious restaurant in New York, people responded to Paolo. After a few phone calls and the promise he would cover the bar and take care of a $15,000 minimum, he was able to secure seven p.m. the following Monday at the Pluto, a well-respected small music venue on the Lower East Side. Paolo, true to form, insisted on controlling most of the particulars of the event, though he did permit Nia to contribute to the publicity effort. In exchange for seventeen comped dinners (for two) at the French Restaurant with the French Name, she was also able to secure a somewhat substantial mix of A&R scouts, older music bloggers, younger music podcasters, and a few relatively famous people who knew musicians. About 40 percent of the chefs Paolo had asked had agreed to come based solely on the promise of an open bar. And he got most of the staff of the restaurant to commit to going to the show on their night off and bringing two guests. When all was said and done, Paolo and Nia had personally gotten commitments from 169 people, with the promise that they might lug along another thirty or forty. If they all came, it would be a pretty packed house.

When Paolo told Charlie what he had planned for him—including round-trip airfare for what turned out to be an alarmingly large band—Charlie beamed and said, "That's massive of you." Then he took a big pull from Paolo's cold-pressed beet, spinach, and apple juices that he had mixed with Mountain Dew ("Looks like a proper Code Red now"). Red streaks of liquid dripped down each side of his mouth and onto his "I Fought the Ska and the Ska Won" T-shirt. "I've got to text the lads," he cried. "We're playing the bloody Pluto!"

PAOLO DIDN'T LIKE LIVE MUSIC. He didn't like the unpredictability, the way songs sounded different when you heard them live. He was a man who prided himself on consistency, on delivering the same level of service to anyone, anywhere, no matter who you were and when you came to his restaurant. The whole thing was tightly choreographed. There were no freestylers in a Paolo Cabrini kitchen. So on the night of the show, Paolo tried to do what Paolo did: exert control.

He got to the venue two hours early to talk to the bartenders about drinks and sub out some of the terrible low-end American and Australian wines they had with French and Chilean ones from his own inventory. He changed kegs himself and cleaned tap lines. Pluto didn't have food, but Paolo made sure to bring along a large quantity of the French Restaurant's own specialty toasted nuts, and he set bowls at intervals along the bar and on the high tables in the back. He lit candles to see if he could blunt the smell of angry sweat and mildew.

By the time the doors opened and people started filing in, Paolo had briefly forgotten about why he was doing the things he was doing, losing himself in the details of the buildup. He was roaming around, offering to help anyone and everyone with even the smallest of tasks: taking out garbage, breaking down boxes, wiping down surfaces, sweeping floors.

And as he stood at the bar mindlessly cutting up lemons for the well, Charlie and the band members came through. Every single one of them, save Charlie, had almost offensively bright orange hair, like Class 2 neon safety vests.

As Charlie walked past Paolo, he snatched a lemon off the cutting board with unnerving quickness, popped it in his mouth, and started to chew the rind. Paolo shivered.

BY SEVEN P.M., the Pluto was full. The crowd was truly impressive—Paolo had been introduced to some label folks, as well as two different roving packs of music journalists. The younger ones, who worked for online outlets and podcasts, all wore glasses and were appealingly clean looking, but otherwise embodied no unified aesthetic. Since the internet, time had ceased to be linear—it was now one thing reacting to the previous thing and influencing the next thing, an endless swirl into which barrels of cultural signifiers were dumped. Some of these people looked like they came from the seventies, with bell-bottoms and tie-dye. Some looked like they'd come from the eighties, with neon sweatshirts and poorly fitting jeans. Some from the nineties, with flannel shirts and poorly fitting jeans. One looked like a cowboy, one looked like Betty Boop, one looked like Betty Boop run through some Japanese fetish translator.

The older music journalists, the ones who worked for legacy media, were more consistent, however. To a man, and they were all men, they looked like hell. Clad in black jeans and Western-style shirts, they resembled Dickensian ghosts, gray and wasted. Most were stubbornly holding on to the dated hairstyles of their youth in what Paolo could only assume was an unfortunate bid to trap a vestige of their better days in amber. But their faces! As he watched them unselfconsciously consume vast quantities of nuts and drink, Paolo simply could not get over how bad they looked. It was as if they had all just concluded two terms as wartime presidents. *What did they do to look like this?* he wondered. *Don't they just listen to music and write?* But they were here, and he was happy about it, even if their presentation troubled him.

Then there were the chefs. Paolo saw two large groups of the mostly male, mostly white chef cliques that dominated the New York food scene walk into the Pluto and head straight to the bar to get shots of brown liquor. All facial hair, testosterone, and overinflated egos, they carried themselves like varsity volleyball players walking into a high school lunchroom, Paolo thought: brashly confident that they were great though wildly insecure because it was at something so inconsequential.

He watched his staff come through as well, quietly led by Fred, who was still wearing a blazer. Each one greeted him with a hug or a handshake and then made their way over to a corner to watch this strange scene together.

Just before the club abruptly turned off the house music to signal the beginning of the show, he watched Nia come in by herself. For a brief period before the show actually started, as he glanced around at a good crowd buzzing with excitement and wonder and the first rush of alcohol into their bloodstream, Paolo allowed himself to believe that Charlie's band might actually be good. Who knew? Paolo understood the transitive properties of greatness—the way the right view can inspire a poem, the way a better room can make someone a better cook. Maybe some of his own precision and elevated taste had rubbed off on Charlie.

Around seven thirty, Charlie and the rest of his band made their way onto the stage. They all wore matching black suits, and Paolo had to admit, the contrast between all that fire-orange hair and the black actually looked pretty good. And Charlie, with his black hair combed and his suit on, appeared composed. Handsome even. As Charlie made his way to the microphone, Paolo found himself taken. Even his greeting—"This one's from fuckin' Belfast!"—wasn't altogether unsexy.

But as Charlie's band started playing a song called "Skankin' Bobby Sands," even Paolo, who knew virtually nothing about popular music, was still able to realize something: Charlie's band was terrible. For one thing, they all started off on a different beat and stubbornly stayed that way, giving the song a sort of Doppler effect. For another, there was an electric violin. It made the worst sound Paolo had ever heard, at a volume that drowned out all the other instruments, even the horns. It made him feel like his skin was shrinking, and it caused a quarter of the crowd to start filtering out the exits.

"Yeah, you better run, ye fuckin' twats," Charlie sneered as they went. "Soldiers of ska have no need for fuckin' twats in their ranks."

By the end of the second song, "Dinner with the INLAs," in which each member of the band again started on a different beat, most of the chef crew had dispersed through the double doors to the venue's bigger bar and demanded the bartender turn off the live feed of the stage and put on the rebroadcast of a New York Red Bulls friendly against FC Tulsa. By the fourth song, a reggae number called "Belfast, Freedom Slow," in which Charlie attempted a Jamaican accent, most A&R and other music folks had also floated to the larger bar, or at least to the back of the room. The older journalists backed away too, but not so far that the free drinks would be out of reach. Everyone gave Paolo the same look. He'd never gotten such a look before. Not that he could remember. It took him a moment to recognize that it was a look of disappointment.

Seeing that he was losing the crowd, Charlie upped his game. He issued a long and profane diatribe against U2 drummer Larry Mullen, who Charlie hinted had taken something from him. "If ye hate the cunt Larry fucking Mullen, scream!" he shouted. A couple of people took him up on it. "I said, I wanna hear you scream!" he cried. No one screamed that time, but Charlie was undeterred. He told the crowd the band wouldn't play another song until the crowd screamed loud enough that he could hear it. They declined. He demanded again. It was a stalemate and it went on for some time. Eventually he gave up and the band set to mangling a song called "Skankin' on the Shankill," which featured a forty-eight-bar electric violin solo.

That sound did what was previously believed impossible: it separated the older rock journalists from the free drinks and nuts. They actually left. Many of the bloggers and podcasters, with their natural inclination to find a contrarian angle against the opinions of the mainstream gatekeepers, stayed on. They puzzled over a few more songs, perhaps trying to figure out ways to convince themselves it might actually be good, or funny, or some kind of art prank they didn't want to *not* get. It could be that, they thought. Why else would this singer keep inviting the crowd to sing along with choruses they had never heard before? But even they gave up and absconded when Charlie began accusing them of carrying water for the Protestants and also "not having the balls to fuck like Smilin' Charlie fucks."

"Cool band, Paolo," said one journalist, walking past.

"Can't be great at everything, I guess," said another fifty-year-old man with an earring who Paolo had observed picking his nose just minutes before.

During this punishing ordeal, Nia sidled up next to him. "It reminds me of that *Onion* headline," she said. "'Ska Band Outnumbers Crowd.'"

"Maybe they're good and I just don't understand?" Paolo said.

"No," Nia said, draining her beer as Charlie ripped his suit jacket doing a somersault and tried unsuccessfully to start another "Fuck Larry Mullen" chant onstage. "They're the worst fucking band I've ever seen, and I saw Kevin Federline live."

By then, Charlie apparently decided he actually didn't want his ripped suit coat anyway. He shouted, "These suits represent the rapaciousness of capitalism!" He and the rest of the band stripped off their suits, doused them in a bottle of brown liquor, and tried in vain to light them on fire, chanting, "Up yer arse, capitalism!"

"I sure hope this does it," Nia said.

Paolo just stared.

And Charlie, even as he played a song called "Sunday (Bloody) Funday" and skanked around the stage wearing only what Paolo suddenly realized were a pair of his boxers, stared directly back at him. Charlie reminded him of something he'd seen when Doe had insisted, two days before his death, that they take a black-cab tour of the working-class Protestant Shankill neighborhood in Belfast. Along the side of one of the council estate buildings, there was a mural featuring several flags of Protestant paramilitary groups. In the middle, a man wearing fatigues and a black balaclava aimed an assault rifle straight ahead. The tour guide had pointed out that it was an optical illusion.

"No matter where you're standing," he'd said, cheerfully, "the gun is pointing at you."

12.

VLADIMIR "LAD" BENSHVILI

QUEENS, NY

Wednesday, July 24, 2019, 4:11 p.m.

For weeks on end, these small American teenagers with soft, wet hands had come to Lobio to talk to Lad about the dead man.

They would begin by introducing the publication they were from, but these were not newspapers or magazines or even persuasive pamphlets. If the *New York Post* had come to see Lad, he would've been happy. Or the *Daily News.* Or even the socialist *Times.* But these had dumb names like *Chewy* or *Swallow,* or pornography names like *UrbanDaddy.* They existed only on computers, and Lad didn't own a computer, so what, really, was the point?

His mother had a saying, which she used to repeat to his father frequently: "Tell it to the bog wolves." In his youth, Lad interpreted this to mean that ultimately all big decisions must be run by the wolves who inhabited the local bogs, but as he grew older, he realized what she was really saying was that she didn't believe him. That his story lacked value.

And that was how he felt about these elfin children asking him questions and holding their phones to his face. They never made eye contact. When he was a child, his father had stressed to him that you had to make eye contact for at least twelve seconds when you shook hands with or talked to an adult. His father told him only liars and Albanians had shifty eyes (and they were essentially one and the same). He used to count in his head as he interacted with elders, and as he got older, he realized that this eye contact, while not only being polite, also gave him power. In any social interaction, Lad would never be the first to look away. But these miniature toy humans with their damp dish-towel hands couldn't even start a handshake by meeting his eyes.

As such, all of their stories lacked value for him. But still, he tried his best to answer their questions. When they asked him about why he only served bean dishes, he told them that it was because beans were very cheap. When they asked what made his dishes so unique, he said that they were not unique, and that his own restaurant recipe came from a very popular Georgian cookbook. When they asked what was the best part about owning a restaurant, he stared at them for a count of twelve and said, "Pass." All of these answers seemed to delight these fairy-size, water-handed scribes. The more curt he was, the more they seemed to relish the interaction. And yet they refused to look him in his eyes.

To accommodate the crowds and his restaurant's newfound popularity, Lad did . . . nothing. He didn't hire more servers. Or cooks. He didn't put more seating in the dining room even though, for three years, two of his booths in the back lacked tables. He didn't even order more beans. This meant that by the time half the crowd got to the front, the restaurant would already be out of food. Lad wouldn't tell anyone beforehand. He would just wait until the beans ran out, then shut the door, lock it, and put up the დახურულია sign.

He'd expected these inconveniences would mean the crowds would thin out. He thought that after the oversize toddlers wrote their phone stories, things would return to normal. But judging by the line already forming when Lad walked into the restaurant weeks after the first of them had come, that was not the case.

When he got to the office in the back of the restaurant, his son, Jann, was sitting at his desk. Jann was twenty-seven, a first-generation Georgian American, born in Queens, the only child Lad had had with his wife before she'd left when Jann was five. Jann was an average soccer player, an average student, and made acceptably long eye contact with adults, which made Lad proud. When dropping his son off at Rutgers for college, Lad had briefly cried in a lockable public restroom on campus.

But at Rutgers, Jann had fallen in with a crowd of other first-generation Americans. No Albanians, thank god, but Greeks and Russians and Turks and some others from smaller Baltic affiliates. Soon he was spending weekends out in the city until five a.m., when he would come back to their apartment with five other intoxicated, overgroomed young men. Lad was perplexed by the way they all lifted weights for no specific purpose and used hot wax not for candlemaking but to strip their chests of body hair.

Jann, who before leaving home had the beginnings of an impressive thatch of thick Georgian wool on his chest, had been plucked and tweezed and waxed and lasered into something Lad thought resembled a human greyhound. He'd gotten tattoos that made little sense and shared no common themes, and branded himself on the sternum with a cigar as part of some inexplicable bonding act, which had the effect of making it look like he had a third nipple. Within a year, Jann had failed out of school and had started working as a club promoter in New Jersey. Eight years later, he still mainly worked as a club promoter in Jersey, though if someone asked him, he always said he was an entrepreneur.

Until very recently, Jann had shown no interest in the family business, mainly content as far as Lad could tell just to take pictures of his calf muscles. But after the man had died and the people started showing up, Jann had begun to come with him to the restaurant.

At first, Jann had been upset with Lad, thinking he had hidden this man from him.

"Dad, this story is everywhere," he'd said. "Why didn't you tell me a famous dude came through our restaurant?"

It wasn't that Lad was above celebrity culture. In fact, in his office, he had various pictures of himself with celebrities who'd been to Lobio. Yankees infielder Luis Sojo's brother Tito. New York State comptroller Thomas DiNapoli. Actor Karlo Sakandelidze, whose portrayal of Aristo Kvashavadze in *The Stepmother of Samanaishvili* was well above average. But this man, he did not know. He had said as much to Jann, staring into his eyes for a count of fourteen. Jann had eventually looked away. He believed him. And he wanted to help.

Jann's first order of business had been to print up a hundred T-shirts (half red, half white) with "Lobio" and Georgia's five-cross national flag printed on the front, and a stenciled picture of the dead man on the back, along with a quote from the most popular phone story: "Doe had the power to change restaurants, and he didn't want Lobio to change. It was already perfect."

The first day Jann had peddled them (twenty dollars each, cash) for the crowd in front, he'd sold out in less than an hour. The next week, he'd come back with three hundred and sold out in two days.

Lad could see how proud Jann was of the T-shirts and so, when Jann had said he was quitting his club promotion job to work strictly at Lobio, Lad had pretended to take it in stride but was secretly elated. It was what he'd wanted all along. And when Jann had said he wanted to "make the decor fresh," Lad did not stand in his way. Perhaps this explained why his office was now a storeroom for eight different-size mirrors, each of which seemed to be framed with cast-iron spikes. And why there was now a mural that stretched along one of the interior walls of the restaurant.

The mural featured a beach scene from Georgia's Black Sea coast with the Caucasus Mountains in the background. It looked sort of like the coastal resort town of Batumi, except in the waters sat a life-size khachapuri bread boat filled with famous Georgians like Tamar the Great, George V the Brilliant, and NBA basketball player Zaza Pachulia. Tamar held a giant bowl of beans and both George V and Pachulia were dipping spoons into it. When Lad had seen the mural artist sketching it out, he was angry. Why, he'd asked Jann, would you commission such an absurd picture, especially considering that Lobio did not sell khachapuri and a vessel that size made of bread would disintegrate quickly in the waves, drowning these notable figures? But Jann had waved him off.

"People will go crazy for it, Dad. They will all want to take pictures and post it."

"But it doesn't make sense."

"Exactly."

Jann was right. Every single customer of Lobio who was not old and Eastern European took a photo next to the mural with their phones. Jann told him that the Instagram account he'd started for the restaurant only two weeks earlier now had seventy-eight thousand followers.

"Followers?" Lad had asked. "Like a cult?"

"Exactly."

After the shirts and the mural, Lad wondered if his son, the same son who'd once taken a grown woman on a first date in a yellow truck limousine to a business that rented hot tubs by the hour; who'd once eaten a glow stick on a dare when he was nineteen; who'd once gotten second-degree burns on his anus while trying to light his flatulence on fire with a butane torch, was actually a genius in a way he couldn't comprehend. *Was this what Dimitri Arakishvili's parents felt like when he first wrote music?* he wondered.

"You fuck with the mirrors, Dad?" Jann asked.

Lad stared at the mirrors and felt nothing.

"Do you like 'em, I mean?"

Jann got up and picked one off the ground, its heavy iron base digging into several gold-plated Cuban link bracelets on his wrist. "Feel how heavy they are. Going to make the place seem huge."

Lobio sat nineteen people (when the booths were fixed) and so this seemed like an exaggeration to Lad, but he let it go and walked back out into the dining room with Jann following behind.

"Why are you here so early today?"

Jann had taken to calling himself the restaurant's "chief operating officer," and had even made up business cards for himself featuring the golden lion from the Georgian coat of arms wearing a red headband with "Lobio" on it and shooting a machine gun that somehow had tattoos on it. "But look closely, the bullets are actually beans," Jann had told him proudly when he'd first showed him the cards. Lad had nodded appreciatively even though he couldn't tell.

"We've got that meeting with the producers for the morning show."

"The show?"

"The one about Doe."

Lad stared.

"About the dead man, Dad."

Lad sighed. Outside, a teen child with earrings that made his earlobes look like novelty bicycle tires stared in, snapping photos with his phone through the glass. Instinctively, Lad picked up a broom and banged it against the window. Everything seemed to be about this dead man.

Lad headed back into the kitchen to check on the beans. Victor, his cook, stirred away, nodded at him, and held his palm up. They would be ready in five minutes. He walked back to his office, took off his nightshirt, pulled up a pair of black dress pants, buttoned his overly starched white dress shirt, and walked back out to open the door. He was still the restaurant's only front-of-house staff. Jann sometimes wandered around handing out business cards and taking photos, mostly for women, but did not handle food or drink, explaining that the "business side should be separate from the service side."

"The producers are coming around six."

Lad looked out at the line. It stretched to the end of his block and then bent down the cross street. There were at least two hundred people. On a Wednesday. He looked back at Jann, who was balling and unballing his fist, trying to make the vein in his bicep jump.

"There will be no beans by then."

13.

CHARLIE McCREE

NEW YORK, NY

Wednesday, July 31, 2019, 3:22 a.m.

If Charlie could have swum out into the humid Manhattan air the night of the gig, he would have. He would have floated off the stage after the triumphant stateside debut of the Bad Friday Disagreement, and drifted above the delirious crowd. Men and women alike would strain for just a passing touch of his face and hair and bollocks. A single trainer would be torn from his foot by a supermodel carrying on like those girls he'd seen in the old news footage of the Beatles, tears streaming down their faces and soaking their white T-shirts. But Charlie wouldn't need trainers anymore. Never again would his feet touch the lowly earth. Never again would he work in a hotel. Never again would he be who he was—some smiling papist pack mule, a bit of local color to be sampled by rich foreigners and forgotten. The beefy, black-shirted bouncers, their faces aglow with wonder, would throw open the doors of the club, and Charlie would swim out into a city of light and flesh and money, propelled by the irresistible alchemy of ska and Irish rebel music.

But that wasn't the end of it. Charlie would then rise—past the tops of buses, and then trees, and then small buildings and then larger buildings and then all of the buildings. Having attained the appropriate altitude, Charlie would orient himself to the north and begin to travel, and while he did, he would expand, growing larger and larger until he finally eclipsed the sky itself, replacing a firmament of stars with just one star—himself—and one moon with another: his great big, fucking Belfast arse. He'd travel north until he arrived at the lights of Broadway, the Great White Way, which from this height resembled a gleaming, beckoning electric fanny. Charlie, who by then would have grown to half the size of Manhattan, would look upon himself and see that he was naked. His clothing must have torn off as he assumed his new dimensions, his proper dimensions. He was also massively erect.

Having sighted his quarry, Charlie would then descend to the noisy welter of Times Square, and, once down, begin making passionate love to the crossroads of Broadway and Forty-Second. The vigor with which he went about this act would impress the citizens of the City of New York, who would then accept him as one of their own, even if he did inadvertently level a great many buildings in the bargain. Charlie would then finish his business with a tremendous eruption of sound and fluid. He'd roll over and snap off the top of the Empire State Building and smoke it like a fag as Broadway gasped with satisfaction and coursed with his seed. There would be no doubt then that Charles Ulysses King Kong McCree had arrived. He was the King of New York, and now they'd never be rid of him.

When Charlie opened his eyes, he was sitting in a grimy cell in a Midtown police precinct facing several charges of public lewdness. He was wearing strange drawstring pants that weren't his and had writing all over his torso. It read: "IF FOUND, PLEASE CALL CHEF PAOLO CABRINI," along with Paolo's personal cell phone number. He'd been arrested in Times Square. A family of tourists who had seen him coming up the center of Seventh Avenue initially took him to be the famous Naked Cowboy and unsheathed their phones in anticipation. But then they noticed he didn't have a guitar, or a hat, or boots, and was in fact completely naked and also Irish, and they put the phones away. When he began having sex with a crosswalk while singing the horn part of "New York, New York," the family quickly fled and the police became involved.

Charlie got to his feet—bare, he noticed—and appraised the situation. There were five other men in the cell, quiet and watchful. He turned and smiled at one who had blood in his hair. He seemed like a good lad.

"Grand town, am I right?" The man didn't reply.

But it *was* a grand town. A short while ago, Charlie, like so many immigrants of old, had arrived at the port of New York (aka Newark Liberty International Airport) with nothing in his pockets but a dream, a couple of quid, the personal cell number of a rich and famous man he barely knew, and a bit of rotting lemon. And what had happened? The man had welcomed Charlie into his beautiful home without hesitation, and allowed him to eat from his plate, sup from his bar, wreak havoc against his toilet, and even sometimes sleep in his room because Charlie liked the mattress better in there. And all this for what? What possible cause could the man have for extending such gracious hospitality? It was a miracle. It was America.

And that wasn't even the whole of it. Charlie had shyly confessed to the great man that he dreamed of being a rock and roll star. And what did the man do? Did he scoff? Did he say, "Charlie, you're thirty-seven years old: go get a job"? No, he stuck his bloody neck out is what he did. He made inquiries to top people. He got him a top gig, flew all his mates to New York to perform, bought them the best gear available, and uttered not a word of complaint when Charlie made copies of his apartment keys and gave them out to all the lads. And was that even all? *No!* When the day arrived, the man brought his rich and famous friends along to watch. He put his own reputation on the line to help this humble immigrant. Of course, this wasn't mere altruism. There was a clear upside for the man. Charlie wasn't naive. Paolo's association with the Bad Friday Disagreement would in time be very fruitful for the man's business and public profile. It would be studied in business schools as an example of perfect synergy, like ska and Irish rebel music.

Charlie did not begrudge the man his selfish motives. He appreciated the show of faith and vowed to repay it a hundredfold once the Disagreement got its record deal.

"Charles McCree?"

Charlie snapped out of it. There was a policeman before him now.

"Present," Charlie said.

"Time to go," the cop said.

"See ya, lads," he said to his fellow prisoners.

The cop led Charlie down a grimy hallway and through a pair of heavy doors into the main receiving area of the station. And there stood a fraught-looking Paolo. One of the cops had recognized the name scrawled across Charlie's chest as that of a famous chef and called the number for shits and giggles. He was so surprised when Paolo Cabrini answered that he forgot to hang up. Instead, he told the chef about the man they had in their custody, and the chef said he'd be right down. Now, with the promise of a free dinner with wine for twelve at the French Restaurant with the French Name, the police agreed to drop the charges and produced a topless Charlie McCree.

"Jah, but aren't you a sight for sore eyes," Charlie said, warmly.

Paolo just stared at him.

"He can retrieve his personal effects over there," said the desk sergeant, indicating a window off to the side.

"That's where his clothes are?" Paolo said.

"There weren't any clothes," grinned the sergeant.

Paolo sighed. He proceeded to the window. He gave Charlie's name to the exceptionally slow-moving woman behind the glass.

"What happened, Charlie?" Paolo asked.

"Ah, just a spot of craic," Charlie said. "No harm. You hungry? I'll call the lads and tell them to meet us at the restaurant."

The woman reappeared. "Nothing for Charles McCree."

"What?" said Paolo.

"No personal effects."

"Bugger," Charlie said.

Paolo looked up at the ceiling and exhaled for about ten seconds. Then a thought entered his head, and he looked back down. "Charlie," he said. "What did you have on you when you went out?"

"Fuck," Charlie said. "I don't know, Chef. Everything. Me passport. Me wallet. Me phone. Me fuckin' pants even."

"Your phone? You lost your phone?"

"Fuck, I think so, Chef."

A strange expression clouded Chef's face. Charlie had never seen it before. He hoped he'd never see it again. It wasn't anger, nor sorrow, nor fear. It was sort of all three at once. Charlie thought he'd gone mad. He watched as Paolo strolled elegantly over to a trash can and puked his guts into it.

"Found it!"

Charlie and Paolo both turned. The woman behind the glass had reappeared and was holding something up, a little plastic bag. She stuck it into a metal tray and slid the tray through a hole in the glass.

"Sorry," the woman said, "they put it in the wrong locker."

Paolo picked up the bag. In it was a phone and nothing else.

"You lost your passport," Paolo said.

"Looks that way," said Charlie.

"You lost all of your clothes."

"Right."

"Even your shoes and your underwear."

"That would seem to be the case, yes, Chef."

"But you still have your phone."

"I have. I guess someone upstairs is looking out for me."

Paolo, numbly and at half his usual speed, handed him the phone.

"You all right, Chef?" Charlie asked.

"I just need a minute."

"You look like death. C'mon. Let's go get a few drinks in you. Sort you right out."

"Charlie, it's four o'clock in the morning."

"Perfect! Loads of hours yet before that demon sun arises. I'll just round up the lads."

14.

CHEF PAOLO CABRINI

NEW YORK, NY

Wednesday, July 31, 2019, 4:12 a.m.

Paolo had begun to worry that Charlie was the devil.

During the moment at the police station when Charlie had thought he'd lost his phone, Paolo's mind had skipped right past the possibility that the threat had vanished with it and had landed at a near certainty that disaster was now truly, finally upon him. Did someone else have it now? Someone worse than Charlie? Someone more dangerous? Was Charlie now outsourcing the dirty part of this job? Paolo had heard a Bulgarian dishwasher once refer to killing someone as "wet work." *Was this the wet work part? Am I going to be wet work?* For the first time, Paolo was legitimately terrified. Then the phone reappeared and now he was merely more tired than he had ever been in his entire life.

Paolo's phone rang. It was a number he didn't recognize. He'd received dozens of such calls over the last two days. As it turned out, someone had tweeted a photo of Charlie asleep on a bar with Paolo's personal cell number scrawled across his chest, and someone else called the number and posted, "Holy shit! It's really his number!" Since then the calls had not ceased. Paolo couldn't turn the phone off in the event they needed him at the restaurant. He just had to deal with it.

Even more disturbing, however, was the fact that Charlie didn't seem to realize that his bender had gone on for more than a week. He'd spoken as though it was just the day after the gig. When Paolo had pointed out that, no, a full nine days had actually elapsed, Charlie had said, "Of course it has. I just figured I'd give you a little break. Get out of your hair for a bit." But Charlie had not gotten out of Paolo's hair. He had, in fact, come home to Paolo's apartment every single night, blackout drunk. Worse, he had done strange things. Paolo would be trying to fall asleep and he'd hear the front door open. Then there would be sounds of exertion. One night, he'd found Charlie shadowboxing in the corner of the living room. Another night, he'd been jumping rope without a jump rope. Still another time he'd been standing in the bathroom, muttering. When one night he'd appeared in Paolo's bedroom, Paolo had thrown a shoe at him. It had hit Charlie square in the chest. Charlie had just turned without a word and left the apartment.

The lads were already at Paolo's place by the time Paolo and Charlie returned from the police station, and they seemed to have multiplied. There were now fourteen of them. The new ones looked and sounded so much like the old ones that he couldn't tell which ones were new. Every single one of them had screaming orange hair, save for Charlie, whose hair seemed to have actually gotten blacker. Paolo had heard them from down the hall when he and Charlie got off the elevator. When they walked in, there was a great roar for Charlie, who had been to jail and returned without a scratch. There was talk of his being a political prisoner, which Charlie encouraged. There were speeches and songs. There was Reel Big Fish's breakthrough album *Turn the Radio Off,* played at a volume reserved for Gabriel's horn, a sound that heralded apocalypse.

Charlie's friends couldn't have been at the apartment for more than ten minutes, but they were well underway. The fridge was wide-open and someone had pried open the liquor cabinet with a $2,700 Nesmuk chef's knife and removed a bottle of Imperial Collection vodka that John Doe had given Paolo after a trip to Russia for the show. It came in a Fabergé egg and cost $4,000, and now a redheaded man was emptying it into a crystal pitcher along with half a dozen cans of Red Bull while singing a song about the hills of Ulster.

Paolo felt something, and that something was fear. He walked through the scrum, careful not to touch or be touched. He stopped at the damaged liquor cabinet and removed a lone bottle of Bushmills that had gone untouched on account of being made by Protestants. The Nesmuk knife was on the floor. He picked it up and carried it as he crossed the room in the opposite direction, sidestepping a small pile of bright orange sick that had been generated in the infinitesimal span of time between his arrival and now. Tucking the knife under his arm, Paolo opened the door to his expansive balcony and stepped outside into the wash of city sound and air. He closed the door behind him with a soft click and took a seat while Charlie's friends destroyed his home.

THE NOISE CEASED around six thirty in the morning. The lads had passed out, or maybe died. Paolo didn't care. He had maintained a lonely watch if only because it was a thing he could control, and he needed to control something. He had not fallen asleep, and he had not once turned around. Instead, he marshaled all his discipline and he sipped and he sat, gripping the Karelian birch burl handle of his knife, and he waited for the first light of day.

The door opened behind him with a soft, expensive click. There was a sound of someone stretching and yawning, and a powerfully sour musk.

"Hell of a night, Chef."

"Hello, Charlie."

"Did you have a good time?"

"I was out here all night, Charlie."

"You was? I hadn't noticed."

Charlie sat down and stretched some more.

"What's the fancy knife for? Thinking of doing some cooking?"

"I was thinking of killing you with it."

Charlie laughed. His breath smelled like gasoline. "Jaysus, that was one for the ages," he said. "What are you drinking?"

Paolo held up the bottle of Bushmills. Charlie took it and smiled.

"Don't tell the pope," he said.

He drank from the bottle and handed it back, gazing out over the scruffy backs of Greenwich Village's town houses as the city stirred itself awake.

"She's a real beauty," Charlie said.

"She is that."

"You're out of ham, by the way," Charlie said.

"Thank you."

The air was cool and still and very wet. It was going to be a hot day. At some point, Paolo would have to take a shower and change. At some point, he would need to go to work. But in order to do that, he would have to turn around and see what the lads had done to his home, which was a prospect he couldn't yet bear. So he had another sip of whiskey and handed the bottle to Charlie, who responded in kind. Paolo breathed deeply through his nose. The Village smelled fantastic at this hour. Sweet and vegetal, like a bar in the morning.

"My whole life, I've wanted to live here," Paolo said.

"Me too," said Charlie. "And now I do."

"Right."

They sat and breathed for a moment.

"I read a bit about yer man, you know," Charlie said.

Paolo nodded. "I bet."

"You knew him well, did you?"

"He was my best friend," said Paolo. "Everything I have: this apartment, this city, my restaurant—none of it happens without John. I owe him everything."

Charlie nodded thoughtfully. "I owe him too, in a way," he said. "If it weren't for him, I'd never have met you, Chef. Your kindness has meant the world to me. And maybe it's not a big thing to you. Maybe you help people like this all the time. But you have changed my life. You have given me the first taste of a better life, a life I've always wanted, better than that shite excuse for an existence back in Belfast. You're making my dreams come true. And I know there's a lot in it for you as well, but I'll never forget it. Never."

"Charlie, I'll give you $10,000 to get the fuck out of here."

"Eh? Why?"

"I don't want to talk about it. That's my offer. Ten grand cash, today, and then you're gone, and our business is concluded."

Charlie was beside himself. "Chef, I can't take your money—I couldn't possibly. You've done too much already."

"Then what the fuck do you want, Charlie? Seriously."

"Seriously?"

Charlie took another swig of the whiskey and stood up. He stretched. He tipped his head back and bathed his face in the sun. "Like I said to Nina—"

"Nia."

"Yeah, like I said to Nina: I want to be fucking famous. Like you."

Paolo chuckled bitterly.

"Do you know how many shitholes I lived in over the last twenty years, Charlie? *Sixteen*. Sixteen shitholes. And I struggled for years. I failed more than a few times before I finally got it right."

"What was the secret?"

"It was what John Doe told me: Fuck fame. Be great. Make the thing you wish was in the world. Let the chips fall where they may."

"Yer man was absolutely right," Charlie said. "Fame is the fuckin' best."

"Is that it, Charlie? That's what you want? You want to be famous? That's what you're saying will end this?"

"End what?"

"End this! Whatever this thing is you're doing to me. The thing with the photo."

"What photo?"

"God, Charlie. The photo from Belfast."

"What photo from Belfast?"

"The photo of John. You took it that day. *I saw you take it.*"

Charlie thought for a moment. Then it hit him. "Oh, that," he said. "Nah. That was two phones ago. I dropped that phone in the River Lagan. That photo is long gone."

"You didn't back it up in the cloud?"

"The cloud? Are you daft, Chef? That's run by the government."

Paolo, in spite of himself, suddenly saw a shaft of golden light. Angels aflutter. He heard a heavenly chorus sounding through the early morning sky above the Village.

"Then what are you doing here, Charlie?" he wondered.

"You said to come visit."

"My god. You never had the photo? This whole time you never had it?"

"I swear upon me nan, Chef."

"But I . . . I thought you . . ." Paolo slumped in his chair. "Well, let's have a drink, Charlie," he said. "Let's have a toast."

"Grand idea, Chef."

"To new friends."

"New friends indeed."

"May all your dreams come true, Charlie McCree, you fucking . . . stronzo . . . idiot."

"And the same to you, Chef."

"Thank you."

Charlie took a big sip of his drink. "Once we make me a famous rock and roll star, and I get my own place, I'm going to throw the wildest fucking housewarming party anyone's ever seen, and you'll be the fuckin' guest of honor. Maybe you can even cater it."

For the first time since Charlie had entered his life, Paolo laughed.

"I can't make you a rock star, Charlie."

"Of course you can."

"No, you misunderstand me. I won't."

"You will."

"I won't. Charlie, you stupid, stupid man. You don't have any leverage."

Charlie looked wounded. "What do you mean, leverage? What's leverage?"

Paolo shook his head. "Leverage is when you have something to hold over someone else. Something to offer, to make someone do something you want. You lost the phone, Charlie. You don't have the photo."

He felt the need to talk to him like you might a small child.

"You can't possibly believe that I would lift a finger to help you at this point," he said, almost gently. "You don't have any leverage."

Charlie laughed. "You're famous. You're rich. You have connections. I mean, Jesus, look what you did for my gig. And that was in just a few days. Imagine what you could do in a *year*."

"You're crazy," Paolo said.

"Is it crazy to have faith in another man?" Charlie mused. "I don't think so." He slapped his hands on his thighs. "Now, how about some coffee?" Charlie stood and went back inside.

Paolo shook his head in quiet disbelief. He almost laughed. His heart rate slowed. His bowels slackened. For the first time in a month, he felt something akin to peace. Paolo looked out over his blissfully empty patio. His eye was drawn to a jay singing in a tree, to the rough corner of a stately old building, to a single cloud sailing on the summer breeze, and then finally to the seat Charlie had occupied just a moment ago. On it lay a cracked iPhone. And on the phone was an image of John Doe, pants around his ankles, dead in a closet in a Belfast hotel room.

15.

CHEF PATRICK WHELAN

NEW YORK, NY

Wednesday, July 31, 2019, 8:04 a.m.

The day Chef Patrick Whelan was to be reborn in Fame's waters almost started with a hand job.

Since they'd flown together to New York a couple of weeks earlier, he'd seen Jackie a total of four times. She had surprised him when they got into the city by telling him she was staying with friends and not at his suite at the Murser Hotel ("But it has a circular bed!" Patrick had told her, though even as he said it, he wasn't sure what that implied). But the night before his big meeting at EEN, she had indeed slept over, coming in at two a.m., three hours after he'd taken an Ambien to ensure he got a proper night's sleep.

And yet, by the time he woke up at eight the next morning, she was already dressed and showered, saying she was about to meet a producer friend for breakfast downstairs. Patrick, who upon seeing her in his room had gotten some sort of Pavlovian erection, pouted and showcased his rigidity as a silent protest, a horny display of civil disobedience.

Jackie hopped on one foot as she put her shoe on the other, then looked at his cock and frowned. "Oh Patrick, I'm sorry. I wanted to fuck last night but you were comatose. I couldn't even turn you over." She glanced at her watch. "Shit, maybe I can give you a quick hand job?"

Patrick's pride wanted him to pretend he didn't want a hand job. But the rest of Patrick wanted the hand job. "Okay, I guess—well, there's lotion in the—"

Jackie's phone beeped and she cut him off. "Ah, fuck. She's early! She's never early!"

She bent down, kissed him on the cheek, and patted the top of his penis like you might an obedient dachshund. "I promise I'll pay attention to both of you later."

"Are we going to hang tonight?"

"Tonight?"

"After my big meeting?"

"Oh babe, I'm sorry, I'd already made plans." She stopped before she got out the door. "But you know what? You should come! It's at Lucas's loft in Nolita. Across from the Supreme store. I'll text you the details. You can meet my friends! And we can fuck!"

Patrick looked confused even as his erection perked up.

"It's going to be super chill and casual," she said, checking her face one more time in the mirror by the door as she applied ChapStick. "We can celebrate! It'll be so much fun, I promise."

It occurred to Patrick fifteen seconds after the door shut behind Jackie that he'd just been invited to his first orgy.

. . .

"MY DUDES! Isn't this just a heavy dose of nostalgia-laced ketamine."

Without even looking up from the EEN conference room table he and his agent Gloria had been sitting around for the past ten minutes, Patrick knew this was Greg.

Greg had been a junior producer on Patrick's show back in the day, mostly known for getting in trouble trying to expense cocaine with forged cab receipts. But he was also the man who'd "discovered" Doe working at Patrick's restaurant while they filmed and had tapped him for his own show years later. Off that success, Greg had steadily risen up the ladder and now found himself chief decision maker, a designation Patrick found completely absurd.

"I'm totally stoked on this meeting, Pat," Greg said.

Greg talked in a weird combination of surfer patois and marketing acronyms, as if he had been birthed by a combination of Da Boys from the Nintendo game *T&C Surf Designs* and a group of competitive air traffic controllers listing off IATA airport codes. Patrick wanted to blame LA, but Greg had grown up in the Catskills, gone to Syracuse, and never lived outside of New York.

"Gloria, always a pleasure."

Greg gestured to the two women with him, both in their thirties. One tall and Korean, the other a short, dark-haired white woman.

"I've brought Kristin, she's our head of development, and Tia, who helped produce *Last Call* for the last few years and was actually part of the crew in Belfast when Doe so tragically passed. As you know, we are super, super conscious of not wanting to tarnish Doe's legacy in any way, but at the same time, we recognize, as a way of honoring him, there might be value for our viewership if we continue the show.

And I know Gloria mentioned you had ideas on that, so we'd love to hear them. Kristin, anything to add?"

Kristin, the tall Korean, shifted slightly in her chair as Gloria leaned over and, employing her long arm like an arcade machine claw, quickly snatched a cheese Danish from the requisite platter of sweating pastries sitting in the middle of the conference room table.

"We're amped to have you here, we're amped on any ideas you've got," Kristin said, mimicking Greg's speech patterns impressively. "Let's just keep it loose and flowing but also be mindful of the time, because both Greg and myself have a hard stop in thirty. Tia, anything else?"

Tia shook her head. Greg looked at Patrick.

"Okay, Chef. The floor is yours."

Patrick got up. *All right, fucker,* he thought to himself. *Show them the guy who cooked Thanksgiving dinner at the White House for two different presidents. The guy* The New York Times *once called "the single most influential chef in America." The guy who'd gotten an actual hand job from Downtown Julie Brown in an elevator. Show them you've got Doe's sauce, motherfucker.*

He took a breath and began.

"John Doe is iconic. He's a legend. There will never be another person like him, I think we can all agree."

The executives nodded.

"Doe had a unique ability to seem timeless. From the early years to last month, you couldn't tell the difference in Doe or in how he talked to people. The bars and restaurants and people he chose all over the world, it wasn't because they were new or hot—they were just the best people to talk to, to tell a story. And Doe did a legendary job of letting everyone tell their stories, and I should know, because he was a bartender for me for many years, and goddamn would I often wish he'd move people along so we could turn over those seats . . ."

He'd left space there because that was supposed to be his laugh line, and Greg and Kristin obliged. Tia did not. Tia, he surmised, would not be on his side. Tia was the cooler. Immediately he wondered if goddamn fucking Coke Cab Greg included her just to fuck with him. That would be so Greg.

"When I was in the kitchen, you could plan all you wanted, but in the middle of service, inevitably things fucked up, and you had to pivot, shift, and adapt. And that's what I want to do with the foundation Doe laid. I want to adapt it for these modern times."

Here he looked down at the notes from his conversation with Beth at Velveteen Rabbit. He wanted to make sure he didn't fuck up any of the terms, so he read them out. From the corner of his eye, he saw Gloria running her finger along the outside of the Danish sitting in front of her.

"I'm talking everything here. Small, snackable content in between shows on Instagram Stories. Interactions with fans on Facebook Live. A dedicated YouTube channel. AMAs on Reddit. Twitter tweetstorms. A paid, dedicated Substack newsletter for the superfans. An accompanying podcast. Spotify playlists from the shows. Paid partnerships and allied content and merchandise and all these other revenue streams we're missing right now. Some sort of TikTok . . . something."

Gloria started to speak, but Patrick cut her off. He wasn't going to let her kill his momentum. He looked directly at Tia. She stared back into his eyes and right through his skull.

"Now, of course, we know Doe never wanted to go for any of that stuff in the show. I know how much he hated advertising and the idea of him selling to his fans. I get that. So, we keep the show itself pure."

He almost compared it to the early Aerosmith album *Toys in the Attic*, but he caught himself. *Keep it cooking, baby.*

"I think about it like cooking. If someone gives me the perfect piece of protein, I don't need to do anything to it. I can just cook it with a little butter and salt and pepper and let it speak for itself. But that doesn't mean you can't add some flourish to the side dishes. And the appetizers. And the dessert. It doesn't mean that you can't make a show of the wine service. We keep the original product pure, and we monetize the shit out of the rest and keep everyone happy."

The executives seemed engaged. Everyone except Tia was leaning forward a bit. Hanging on his words. Now he just needed to bring it home and sell himself.

"But you're probably asking yourself, if the goal is to modernize the show, why bring me in? I'm even older than Doe. As Greg knows very well, I was on TV back in the mid-aughts, before the internet was even born."

Not true, but whatever.

"I have a direct lineage to Doe. I gave him his start. He worked for me. I counseled him, and trained him, and I knew him way before he became the icon he is today. And I think the American people want someone connected to Doe to keep his torch lit. And I also think the American people love a comeback story. Travolta in *Pulp Fiction*. Matthew McConaughey in *The Lincoln Lawyer*. Robert Downey Jr. as Metal Man."

"Iron Man," Gloria said quickly, though the words were a bit garbled as she'd just bitten deeply into the Danish, pushing cheese filling into the corner of her mouth.

"Yes, him too." Patrick watched out of the corner of his eye as a small glob of filling dropped off the side of Gloria's mouth and landed on the table. Summoning all his willpower, he moved on.

"It is my time to come back. People know me, they know my connection to Doe, and they want to root for me. I'm an Irish Catholic working-class kid from Weymouth, Mass. The son of a plumber and an Irish immigrant mother. People relate to that. The show doesn't need a rebirth. It needs a continuation of Doe's legacy, but with a modern makeover. I can do that. Only I can marry those two worlds together. Give me that chance and I promise you I will make you, this network, and Doe proud."

Patrick sat back down. He was suddenly reminded of a Bible verse from Isaiah Something: Something. "But they who wait for the Lord shall renew their strength; they shall mount up with wings like eagles; they shall run and not be weary; they shall walk and not faint."

He looked at the executives and he knew this was a defining moment in their lives. He was sure, assuming cocaine hadn't addled Greg's dopamine responses, that Greg was aroused. He knew in his heart of hearts that decades from now, Kristin, in her self-published memoirs, would start a chapter with this meeting, as it seemed like she was trying to wipe away tears. Even Tia, who earlier had glared at him as if he'd just stepped on her children's heads en route to boarding a lifeboat, appeared to be moved. It was not just that he'd developed a rapport with them—he'd turned fucking chemistry into theology. This was a Higher Power. He was their sauce-based Lord and Savior.

There was a silence—how could there not be? This moment would forever be recorded in the annals of history and everyone aware of that was likely choosing their words carefully—and then, as Gloria mercifully finished her last bites of Danish, Greg spoke.

"Wow, buddy. Epic. I am so stoked on this."

He looked at Kristin.

"Shoot, should we just offer him the job right here? Get the contract worked up now?"

Kristin laughed.

"Unbelievable job, Patrick. You've given us so much to think about there. And I can really tell you've done your homework," she said. "We're just going to huddle up and talk through some things and dot our *i*'s and cross our *t*'s, but this was so killer. Stoked."

Patrick got up, shook their hands, and walked out with Gloria. He felt like he was floating. It was like the time he heard Alexis Lucente, the second-hottest girl at Weymouth High, say his name after he scored sixteen points in a JV basketball game against Duxbury. Or when he walked into the James Beard after-party with the medal around his neck for the very first time. It was almost like a hunger. But he'd put in the time and sold himself and he was going to be the next goddamn host of *Last Call*. He could feel it in his bones. Gloria seemed to agree.

"It was great seeing you with all that energy in there," she said as she got into a cab. "I'll let you know what they say as soon as I hear."

He stood out on the sidewalk in the middle of Manhattan as people streamed up and down and around him. He felt like a motorcycle could crash into him and he wouldn't feel it. He felt like he could lift a car off a baby. He felt like he could single-handedly cook brunch for a sixty-seat restaurant on a Sunday, let people make substitutions on their omelets, and still get generally positive Yelp reviews.

This was his city again. Fuck Boston. He didn't need that provincial, insular shit town full of young dudes with old eyes and military haircuts, all of whom were both eager and disappointed they were spending their one night off from the Malden Department of Public Works drinking eight-dollar Coronas at José McIntyre's. He had New York. Maybe, thought Patrick, it always was his city.

He called Jackie. She didn't pick up, so he texted her: "Headed to your party. Mtg went fucking great. Job = mine. See you soon."

Patrick hopped in a cab.

"We're headed to Nolita. But we've got to make one stop first."

PATRICK DIDN'T KNOW where to put the cheese.

When the elevator opened into Jackie's friend Lucas's Nolita loft, Patrick stepped off carrying the finest cheese board Murray's Cheese had available. He'd handpicked four of the cheeses himself, hadn't cut corners on the jambon de Bayonne, dried fruits, cornichons, artisan flatbreads, and had even sprung for the Red Bee honeycomb, though he viewed its inclusion as needlessly excessive.

But when he walked into the coolest loft he'd ever seen, an amalgamation of uniquely vibed spaces and exposed brick covered in graffiti murals that seemed like they threaded the needle between hip art and political importance, and saw nine people, all of whom were naked and in their twenties and quite possibly the most aesthetically interesting, beautiful motherfuckers he'd ever seen in real life, Patrick no longer felt like he was putting himself in a position to dominate by coming in carrying a cheese board, no matter how tightly curated.

He spotted Jackie sitting naked with her legs crossed over on a long, black sectional couch and headed over, placing the cheese board down on a glass table in front of the couch, careful not to disturb the lines of cocaine also on the table. Jackie got up and gave him a hug and a kiss, and introduced him to the owner of the loft, Lucas.

"What's up, my man," Lucas said, giving him a big naked bro hug. "It's such an honor for you to be here! Jackie was just telling me all about your new job. Parabéns!"

Lucas, Patrick quietly admitted to himself, was the best-looking human he'd ever seen in real life. With caramel skin, bright green eyes, a shaved head, and an effortlessly lanky body that had indents and creases and hard angles even in the soft fleshy areas, he looked like a multicultural Brazilian David, but somehow more jacked, and with a much bigger cock, which was quite visible despite the fact that he very clearly didn't trim his pubic hair.

Over the course of the next few minutes, Jackie introduced him to all her friends. They looked, to Patrick, like the cast of the movie *Kids* ten years after the fact, if all of them had cleaned up, gotten intense personal trainers, and become subtly rich. As he looked at their well-designed tattoos and piercings, he wondered if this specific nouveau Benetton ad was what advertisers meant when they said "influencers."

An elegant, striking Indian woman with a septum ring and half-inch gauges in her ears walked over to him, shook his hand, and gave him a deep kiss on the mouth with a light dusting of tongue. She tasted like peppermint and kindness. Jackie smiled.

"This is my friend Kiara. We went to high school together. She's a painter."

Patrick smiled at her and pulled Jackie to the side.

"So how does this work?"

Jackie looked around.

"How does what work?"

"The orgy! Or whatever. Do you have to pick partners, or how do people do—"

Jackie laughed. "Babe, chill out. It's not like that. There is no partnering or pressure or anything. Everyone just agrees to feel safe and comfortable and go with any moment as long as it's mutual."

She watched his eyes go to the table. "Maybe some drugs would help you here," she said softly and kissed him on the mouth. "You can do whatever you want. Just . . . wait for the moment."

In order to help recognize and act on those moments, Patrick walked over to the drug table. After identifying what he believed to be cocaine, he snorted two lines and, though he was sure he wouldn't need it, quickly added his own crushed up Viagra as a kicker. Just as he'd noticed Kiara's labia piercing, his phone buzzed.

It was a text from Gloria: "Just heard from Greg. Give me a call back. No rush."

This is it, Patrick thought. *This is fucking it*. His body felt electrified and it wasn't (just) the coke, or the Viagra, or his sudden awareness of Kiara's classy vagina jewelry.

And yet. He suddenly craved the extra rush Gloria's good news would give him. Deciding that it would likely be uncouth to make the call while fucking, he asked Lucas where the bathroom was.

"That mirrored door right there," Lucas said, pointing to the wall across from the black couch and the drug table. Then he did a backflip. From a standing position. Naked.

AFTER CLOSING THE BATHROOM DOOR behind him, Patrick dropped his pants and began peeing. During his relatively satisfactory urination, he noticed the door of the bathroom functioned as a two-way mirror. When he finished, he called Gloria and watched through the mirror as Jackie did a back handspring, much to Lucas's delight.

When Gloria answered, she seemed slightly taken aback.

"Patrick! I'm sure you're out and about! If it's easier, we can talk later?"

"You know me, I need that instant gratification," he said, grinning at himself in the bathroom's other mirror.

"Well," she said as she drew in a breath, "they were so, so complimentary of your presentation. They *loved* hearing from you."

As she talked, he looked back through the door. Everyone seemed naturally hairless except for their pubic hair, most of which, he noted again, seemed fully ungroomed. Briefly, he thought to himself that it was strange how even pubic hair length was cyclical.

"That shitbird Greg certainly did well for himself. Too bad that girl Tia was—"

"Patrick." She paused. "They're going in a different direction."

As she spoke, Patrick watched as a naked woman and two naked men lounged, entangled, on the floor beside the black sectional couch, and passed around a commercially rolled joint. To their left, a toned woman with dyed-gray hair was grinding on a longhaired man's face.

"Amaz— Wait. What did you say?"

Patrick's brain, high on coke-fueled confidence, couldn't actually fathom anything other than Gloria lavishing him with breathless praise. She spoke again.

"They've decided to go in a different direction, Patrick. I'm terribly sorry, they were so impressed—"

"Are you fucking serious? I destroyed that meeting!"

"You were the best I've seen you in ages! But you know how . . ."

Patrick felt like he was having a stroke. His brain sloshed around inside his head trying to make sense of what Gloria was saying, but he couldn't fathom it. They'd loved him. He owned them. So, if he wasn't the problem, it had to be . . . her. His voice grew spiteful.

"If *you* hadn't taken the opportunity to deep-throat a week-old cheese Danish, they would've been able to focus on the fact that *I* am the next generation of *Last Call*!"

Gloria sighed.

"Look, Patrick. They have a target demographic. They just weren't going to go with someone older than Doe."

He wasn't done. He was flailing around inside his mind, trying to find knives to throw.

"You want to talk about being old?! Is your baby boomer brain so fried from brown acid and those years as a second-tier Jefferson Airplane groupie that you can't even sell your most famous client in the role he was put on this earth for?"

For ten seconds, there was a dead silence on the phone. During the pause, Patrick noticed Jackie and Lucas had moved on from feats of gymnastic glory to other things. Namely Jackie sucking Lucas's cock with what he thought was an unnecessary amount of enthusiasm. When Gloria spoke again, her voice sounded like sharpened steel.

"Okay, let's think about you for a second: You *quit* the one thing you were put on this earth for, and for what? To chase the dragon of fame all the way to fucking *Vegas*? You decided that your power move was going to be exploiting your mother to open an Irish pub on television. And when it didn't work out, your lack of fortitude in that one moment of adversity—that you brought on yourself, mind you—was one of the most cowardly acts I've witnessed in my, yes, very long, but very. Fucking. Successful. Career."

Patrick watched as Jackie's hand began to move past Lucas's balls, toward his ass.

Gloria continued, her voice a maelstrom of invective.

"I have to admit, you did manage to dine out on your fame for much longer than most. And while I'm complimenting you, I will also say that your ability to whore yourself out to anyone with a shitty kitchen utensil to sell or a fad diet to promote is so all-encompassing as to be genuinely impressive. I may be fried, but you're a shill in a chef's coat who's way past his expiration date."

Jackie began pumping her head faster, and Patrick saw Lucas's unfairly athletic body become rigid as he began to visibly pant.

"You want me to pat you on the back and say 'good job' because you memorized eight social media terms you learned from the teenagers you surround yourself with? Do you even realize what made Doe special? He didn't want to force himself on the world. He wasn't chasing fame. It was never about *him*. His agenda was that he didn't have a fucking agenda. This is something you'll never understand. You tried to pass out your keto cookbooks at his fucking funeral."

"They were signed," he responded meekly.

"Fuck you, Patrick. I could go on, but I'm going to be late for my dinner at Questlove's. This is over. I'm not fucking representing you anymore. Get some fucking talentless Ari Gold wannabe cocksuck to sell your next fad diet, piece-of-shit cookbook."

She stopped. He could hear her breathing into the phone.

"And I'll have you know—I was the fucking White Rabbit."

Almost simultaneously, Gloria hung up on him and Lucas's entire body convulsed as he ejaculated into Jackie's mouth, his arm shooting out into the Murray's cheese plate on the drug table, crushing forty-two dollars' worth of Brebirousse D'Argental with its famous bright orange rind and sweet buttery intensity, and knocking the Tomme de Savoie onto the floor.

PART III

HELL AND DAMNATION

16.

NIA GREENE

NEW YORK, NY

Thursday, August 1, 2019, 10:00 a.m.

After their encounter in the bathroom at Doe's memorial service, which did not progress much further after Katie called Nia a cocksucker, the two women agreed to meet up to continue their discussion. Nia had become doubly concerned. She was concerned that Katie was not only out peddling a bogus story, but that she also seemed to be building a whole career on it. Katie's was a rise that was happening in real time in the public eye, which meant that a fall would happen in the public eye too. And if people were given a reason to doubt Katie's story, which had by then become embedded into the main narrative, then people would begin to doubt the main narrative.

Wary of being seen with Katie until she had a better handle on the situation, Nia avoided all her usual meeting spots: the bar at the Carlyle for drinks, Balthazar for lunch, or Eisenberg's for breakfast. Instead, she invited Katie to her home, thinking it an olive branch.

Katie rejected her invitation, went dark for a week and a half, then suggested Nia come see her at her suite at the Four Seasons.

"That's an unusual choice for a twenty-seven-year-old," Nia had said.

"Tell the man at the desk to buzz me when you get there," Katie said, "and ask him to send up some towels."

On the day of the meeting, Nia took the subway. She could never think in cabs, and she needed to think. She needed to figure this kid out. If Katie had merely been terrified that she was found out, that would be a normal, expected reaction. That was something Nia could deal with. You didn't become a professional in Hollywood without learning how to make fear into something productive. It was the alchemy the business ran on. But Katie didn't seem terrified at all in the bathroom. She just seemed . . . determined? Steely? Imperious? But not afraid.

Nia wasn't afraid of young people. She actually remembered being young herself, which was a rarer thing than it should have been for her generation. She knew what it was to be hungry. To *want*. As a result, she was empathetic toward young people, but she was also wary of them. To her, the young were like the Americans during the revolution, hiding in trees and picking off redcoats from behind rocks. And the olds were like the Brits, complaining about the upstarts' lack of decorum and respect for the rules of proper engagement. "A gentleman does not shoot at an enemy from behind a rock!" they moan as they lie dying in the mud. No, Nia was not afraid, but Katie's absence of a normal human reaction to peril, and indeed to the rules of engagement, augured ill. It made Katie very dangerous, and Nia had to be careful. She would not be surprised. She would not die surprised. She would not die in the mud.

She exited the subway at Fifty-Ninth Street and Fifth Avenue at the southeast corner of Central Park, took a deep breath, and walked a few blocks over to the Four Seasons. She checked in at the desk in the ornate lobby. The clerk called up and announced Nia. "Thank you," he said. Then he listened some more. "Yes, Ms. Horatio," he said, before hanging up. Then he turned to Nia and said, "One second, please," before disappearing into the back. When he returned, he was holding a pile of towels.

"Ms. Horatio asked that you bring these up."

"Happy to. What room?"

"3211," the man said.

"Thank you," Nia replied, leaving the mountain of towels behind.

Nia rode the elevator to the thirty-second floor. She stepped into the hallway, located the room, and knocked. A full minute later, Katie opened the door. She was wearing a pristine terry-cloth robe and slippers. She looked Nia up and down.

"Where are my towels?"

"They're at the front desk," Nia told her, and pushed by. Katie had somehow rented a terrace suite with a view of the park. It was stunning. Baronial. But the room itself was in disarray. There was a room service cart with half a dozen plates of food on it—steak, shrimp, everything—all untouched. There were numerous empty bottles of champagne. There was a stubbed-out cigar on a bread plate. There were towels everywhere.

"Nice room," Nia said.

"It suits me. I haven't seen a single cockroach."

"I bet."

Katie floated over to the living room and sat down in one of two matching leather armchairs. She gestured to Nia to take the other, across a glass table adorned with a bowl of fruit. Katie looked a little anemic, Nia thought. She noticed Katie staring intently at the fruit.

Drugs? Eating disorder? Or maybe she really was afraid. That would be good. That would be useful. But don't assume.

Katie gave her head a little shake and pulled away from the fruit. She fixed her gaze on Nia and smiled.

"Can I offer you some water?" she said.

"Sure."

"It's in the bathroom," Katie said. "There's a fount. It's sparkling white and looks a lot like a toilet. Help yourself."

"Ah."

They sat there, smiling.

"I've got fifteen minutes, Nia, then I have to go to the studio. What would you like to talk about?"

"I thought we'd talk about John Doe."

"Of course."

"So," Nia leaned forward. She chose her words carefully. "I'm not mad, Katie."

"That's a load off."

"Just hear me out. I'm not mad. I've worked with a lot of writers and a lot of TV people, and I know how hard it can be to break in. And I know sometimes we do things that—while not harmful—are not completely ethical."

Nia watched Katie's face for some hint as to where to go, but it was completely placid.

"So . . . first things first: I'm not going to blow the whistle. I think you're very talented, and I'm happy to see someone so talented do well. And between us, you seemed to be on a whole other level with your insights on John. You must have really studied his work."

"I'd never even seen his show," Katie said, eyeing the fruit again. "Guess I just got lucky."

"Right. I'll cut to the chase. I'm not going to go public, and I'm not expecting you to either. What I am going to do is propose an arrangement. All that it entails is that we talk once a day. I need to know what you're going to say about John. And I mean on TV, in print, on Twitter, even to friends. I don't want any surprises. And that's it, Katie. And this stays between us. That's all I need."

"That's all you need."

"Yes."

"And what if I don't give you what you need?"

"You really want to know?"

"Thrill me."

"I'll take you out, Katie. I have all the documentation. Doe had never been to Lobio. You'll be gone in a day. You'll be finished. You'll be a laughingstock. I've got you dead to rights, Katie. Now let's do the right thing."

Katie nodded. She reached over and plucked the cigar off the bread plate. There was a fancy butane lighter next to it. She lit the cigar, took a few puffs, and watched the smoke plume and curl toward the ceiling.

"This cigar cost more than the pants I was wearing the day Doe died," she said. "All three pairs of them."

Katie turned her head and stared out the window at the city beyond, drumming her fingertips on the armrest of her chair. Nia had hoped offering a get-out-of-jail-free card would elicit some sort of reaction, a hint of relief. Instead, Katie seemed bored. She looked back at Nia. "Is it warm in here?" she asked, and untied the belt on her robe and recrossed her legs, letting the robe fall open around her thighs. She took another puff from her cigar.

"Okay," she said, exhaling a plume of fragrant smoke. "I hear your offer. Here's mine: You give me $10,000. And that's just the down payment on *my* silence."

Nia was flabbergasted. "What makes you think—"

Katie came to life. "What makes me think?" she said. "Well, let's see. I sit here and I look at you, Nia, and I think, 'Why is she here?' Right? 'She's a real big shot, right? Why did she come all the way here to see me?' And you say that you're not going to tell the world that I lied about your client and your best friend, and all I have to do is, what? Call you in the morning?"

"Uh-huh."

"That doesn't add up, Nia. You're giving me way more than I'm giving you. You're giving me a life, and I'm giving you a fucking phone call. So that makes me think that you actually have an interest in protecting this lie. It makes me think that if my lie were exposed, maybe one of yours would come down too, and it would be worse for you than it would be for me. Am I on the right track here?"

Katie took another puff and gestured with the cigar as her robe fell open further, revealing her sternum, navel, and pubic hair. "My question to you is: What are *you* lying about, Nia Greene? And what's your lie worth to *me*?"

Nia was speechless. Actually speechless. Ordinarily she'd just talk here—just insert some mindless filler while her brain figured out what to do. But she was truly at a loss. It certainly didn't help that Katie's legs were now fully splayed, her crotch fully exposed, and Katie was staring her dead in the eyes with just a hint of a smile. Nia finally found some words.

"Are you trying to *Basic Instinct* me right now, Katie?" she said.

"I don't know what that is," Katie cooed. "I'm just a young woman." She stood up and dropped the robe entirely, then walked over to a mirror, stark naked save for the cigar and the slippers, and admired herself, her breath visibly quickening. Without taking her eyes off her own reflection, Katie reached down and grabbed a hamburger from the room service cart and took a huge bite, then immediately spat it out onto the floor and placed the rest of the burger in a desk drawer before slamming it shut.

"I'm going to go," Nia said.

"You're not going anywhere until we make a deal," Katie said. Without replacing her robe, she walked back across the room and sat down in the leather chair, tracing circles in the air with her cigar while eyeing Nia.

"What deal could we possibly make, Katie?"

"I'll tell you." Katie moved to the couch, close to Nia, and leaned in. "Nia, I know all about you. I've asked around. You're brilliant. You're tough. People think John Doe invented John Doe, but that's all bullshit. You did. You made him. Without you, he's just some schmuck from Palookaville."

"That's not true."

"I like that you feel the need to say that, Nia. It impresses me. Shows me that you're loyal." Katie stubbed out her cigar. Nia still could not get over the fact that she was completely naked. "Here's what I'm proposing," Katie said. "You take me on as a client. You make me as big as we both know I can be—books, TV, movies, the whole nine yards. You run everything. Same deal as Doe. I give you the same cut as he did, plus five percent. And I don't tell anyone about my lie, or yours."

"What is my lie exactly, Katie?"

"That John Doe wasn't depressed. That he didn't commit suicide. That something else happened. Drugs? Sex? Some redheaded speed-freak Irish rent boy with big hands and a temper? I don't know, but something real nice. And you're worried that if whatever it is gets out, his legacy gets tainted, and your piece of the business is worth jack shit inside of a year." Katie smiled. "Ooh. I can see from your face that I hit that one on the head."

"You have proof?"

"Proof," Katie said, shrugging. "No proof. What's proof?"

Every alarm in Nia's being was sounding, but she fought the urge to rub her face, or squirm in her seat, or jump off the terrace and swan dive to the street below. She stayed cool and kept her eyes locked.

"That's it? You want me to represent you."

"That, and a $10,000 signing bonus, yeah. I have a certain standard of living I'd like to keep up. Plus, I hear that *Good Day* is going to do a full hour on Doe for the Sunday show. I'm going to need to be on that. Prominently."

"Anything else, Katie?"

"No, that's all for now. What do you say?"

"I will seriously consider this amazingly generous offer."

"Don't consider, sweetheart. Do."

"And if I don't?"

Katie held up a single finger and leaned over to pick up her robe. She dug around in the pocket, produced an iPhone, clicked it on, and tossed it to Nia. Nia caught it. The phone was still the phone of a child, she thought. It had ironic unicorn stickers and a sparkly case. The Twitter app was open. Katie had drafted five tweets but had not posted them. They read:

> 1/ Peeps: I have something I need to say about my John Doe story: I never met John Doe. He never told me he was depressed. I made it all up.
>
> 2/ I was going through some serious mental health challenges at the time that I'm not going to get into and my illness caused me to make a very unfortunate choice.

3/ I'm actually hearing that he wasn't even depressed but the depression/suicide angle was better for business but IDK.

4/ But I'm so sorry I lied. I feel so ashamed but it's important to tell my story if I want to ever be well again. TAKE CARE OF YOUR MENTAL HEALTH. XOXOXO.

5/ If you're having suicidal thoughts, call 1-800-273-TALK (8255) to talk to a skilled, trained counselor at a crisis center in your area at any time.

Nia handed the phone back to Katie. Nia played the sequence out in her mind. Katie's tweets kill Katie for sure—at least as a journalist. She might come back as some kind of confessional mental health memoirist. The tweets don't kill Nia immediately, but they open the door for lurid speculation, for questioning, for digging. Maybe some ambitious Belfast politician or cop reopens the investigation. Maybe Paolo falls apart under questioning. Maybe Katie's disclosure somehow triggers Charlie into making a move. It gives him leverage and adds urgency to the situation. Whatever happens, if the actual truth comes out, that's it. Nia's finished. Paolo's finished. John's legacy is damaged irreparably. But even if only uncertainty is allowed to fester and speculation persists, John is damaged, Nia is damaged, the work is damaged, the business is damaged. It may not result in his shows and books being pulled right away, but the demand will soften and then disappear.

"So whattaya say?" Katie asked. "How about we make some money together?"

"Can you give me a week?"

"I'll give you forty-eight hours."

Nia stood and gathered her bag. She stuck a hand out at Katie, who was still sitting, stark naked, and Katie shook it.

"This is going to be great for both of us," Katie said. "Now get the hell out of here. I gotta take a shit."

17.

KATIE HORATIO

NEW YORK, NY

Friday, August 2, 2019, 6:22 a.m.

Old Katie had become concerned. When New Katie finally released her from her grip, depositing her on the floor of that terrifying hotel room that she could in no way afford, Old Katie lay there for an hour, lost in thought. The meeting with Nia Greene had unsettled her. On one hand, yeah, it was fucking righteous. If Katie had watched someone else pull that sort of thing, she'd be envious. But someone else hadn't pulled it. Katie Horatio had. She was profoundly uncomfortable with her role in it—even if that role was meat puppet. She just couldn't believe she had behaved that way to Nia Greene. *Oh god*, she thought, *why did I take off all my clothes?* It was pretty baller, but still she was consumed with guilt, shame, and genuine fear of the bills New Katie was running up.

And she was hungry. She was so hungry. Old Katie had made the mistake of trying to reassert some control over New Katie a week before. She had gone to the bar at the Four Seasons after the memorial party and ordered a cheeseburger, medium rare. She had been famished. But when the burger had come back well-done, New Katie wanted to vehemently object. New Katie had tried to tear into the bartender for his stupidity and incompetence. New Katie had wanted to smash the burger under her heel and break this beautiful boy down into nothing and then fuck the wreckage upstairs. Old Katie had just wanted the burger. She didn't care if it was overcooked. A month before, she would have eaten a burger she found in the men's room of the Four Seasons. A month ago, she wasn't even sure if the Four Seasons was real.

An internal struggle had ensued—not that the bartender knew about it. From the outside, it merely looked as though Katie Horatio had gone catatonic and peed herself a little. But inside, New Katie and Old Katie were locked in a bitter struggle for control of this vessel. In the end, they fought to a draw. Old Katie succeeded in preventing New Katie from destroying the boy, but New Katie retaliated by denying her sustenance. A very long night followed. Old Katie ordered room service. New Katie made her spit out the food the moment it touched her tongue. Old Katie begged for food. New Katie permitted her only champagne and cigars. Old Katie hated cigars. They made your mouth feel like you had just blown a scarecrow. But she couldn't stop smoking them. She must have smoked half a dozen of them. Her fingers were brown. At one point, Old Katie called her mother. She was in Costa Rica on vacation with Katie's father. She had intended to ask for help, but New Katie took over and upbraided the poor woman for maintaining "that charade of a marriage" and counseled her to "dump that fucking loser pronto and get yourself some of that good Latin beef."

For now, thankfully, New Katie seemed to be resting. Old Katie needed a shower. She tiptoed over to the bathroom. On the way, she removed the half-eaten hamburger from the desk drawer and walked quickly into the bathroom, whereupon she gulped it down sitting on the toilet and prayed to whatever god protects young women from salmonella. As her body seized upon and rapidly distributed the nourishment in an effort to stave off death, Katie rose shakily to her feet and turned on the shower. She initially set it to medium-hot, but when her mind presented her with a vivid image—the temperature suddenly spiking, Katie leaping from the shower, slipping on the marble floor, smashing her skull into the toilet, and dying in a pool of glossy crimson—she opted for room temperature. She stepped in and let the tepid water cascade over her, her pores puckering slightly. She was exhausted and weak and a little scared, but the shower felt good and, to some small degree, restorative. It helped her regain her equilibrium. She could finally think.

First, she noticed she was still wearing slippers in the shower. She took those off and threw them onto the bathroom floor, where they landed with a dull slap. Next, she thought about her situation. It was clear Katie needed to make a tally. The good in one column, the bad in the other.

The good: Katie was suddenly on the verge of becoming successful. And not successful in a shameful and diminished SWVLL sort of way, but in an actual grown-up sort of way. If, say, she became a co-host of a network morning show, that was tens of millions. If she made a TV show and it took off, that was millions. If she sold a book, that could pay for untold hotel rooms and hamburgers. For years, Katie had thought of money in units of her basic needs. A freelance story was half a month's rent. A day's work at a temp job was a visit from the roach man. You earned and you spent and every month you started over again. But now . . . now there was the possibility of real money, and with it, actual nice things, actual luxury.

To be young in New York is to spend much of your days wishing harm upon those who have nice things. The town house, the six-room apartment on a high floor, the $1,000 shoes, a car, a washing machine—my god, a washing machine! Katie, if she stayed on this path, could have those things. She could live in comfort and style. She could be hated. It was thrilling, the idea of being hated. Usually she was regarded with either contempt or dismissal. Success, material acquisition, and the envy of others: those were unquestionably good. And they were in reach, thanks to the moves being made by New Katie.

But was New Katie *good*? That was more complicated. Without a doubt, she was very good at what she did. When she wasn't starving or afraid, Old Katie enjoyed riding along with New Katie, watching her operate. It was satisfying and educational. It was thrilling, really. If it was a show, she would watch this show. New Katie was tough, smart, and sexually unafraid. She knew what she wanted and seemed to understand implicitly how to get it in a way that Old Katie never could. She understood the world, she understood how others think, and she acted in service of Katie. Old Katie had always secretly wanted to be the sort of person who could walk into a hall packed with strangers, start tapping a spoon against her glass, and give a toast that leveled the place. Now she was. Even though when she was doing it, all she could think was *no no no no no no no no no.*

Katie stepped out of the shower and wrapped a towel around herself, then walked into the room. New Katie, it seemed, was still latent. Old Katie tiptoed over to the room service cart and stuffed a fistful of cold, limp, salty French fries into her mouth and tried not to have an orgasm. She pulled a pair of jeans out of a gold-and-white shopping bag and ripped off a tag that informed her that they cost $1,200. She slipped them on and continued trying not to have an orgasm.

At her most benevolent, New Katie was her protector, her advocate, and her hero. But was New Katie her friend? That remained to be seen. New Katie was delivering results and improving Old Katie's material circumstances, but she also seemed to have no qualms about abusing Old Katie. Maybe it was like one of those frightening upper-middle-class parents she started reading about one time in *New York* magazine, imposing strict discipline and impossible expectations to help their child succeed at being a concert violinist or getting into Stanford or whatever it is those people want. But do those people starve their children? Would they potentially kill their child for refusing to practice a sonata? Katie honestly didn't know—she was frozen out by the paywall before finishing the article. But the last twenty-four hours were a worrisome sign.

There was a darker thought too, that it might be a mistake to think of New Katie as a separate entity from Old Katie. The dynamic could be more sinister than one party simply guiding another. New Katie might be trying to replace Old Katie—one fetus resorbing another in the womb. Katie could already feel that, the sensation of being devoured. Her old instincts tended toward passivity and cravenness, and early on she was happy to have some help overcoming them. But now New Katie seemed to be taking aim at her kindness too, her sensitivity, and moving to replace them with ambition, greed, hunger, and sex. Which weren't the worst things in the world, but Old Katie would love it if New Katie at least left her the illusion of agency.

But then she slipped on an outrageously luxurious silk button-down shirt and black blazer that cost three months' rent at the Tomb-for-Youth and had a cheerier thought. Maybe the mistake was in imagining that New Katie was even an outside force at all. Maybe New Katie wasn't New Katie, but *real* Katie? Maybe this was who she was meant to be. It wasn't a takeover. It was a revelation of something that had been buried by Katie's recent past, and an unequal workplace, and the expectations of a patriarchal society. Maybe she was growing up. Everyone knows that when you grow up you have to reconcile your old self with your new self. That's why being a teenager is such a nightmare. It's a painful process, but a necessary one.

Katie looked at herself in the mirror. *That's it*, she decided. She had her answer. This wasn't a parasite/host situation at all! There was no New Katie and Old Katie. This was a young woman coming into her own, finding her power, and writing her own story. A young woman being awakened to what the world really was, and boldly stepping into it to take what's hers without apologizing for being a bitch or for wanting things. Sure, she hoped there wasn't going to be a *lot* more nudity in meetings, but if there was, and it worked, she would not apologize!

The logic was bulletproof. Of course Katie wasn't being taken over by an alien force, and shame on the world for making her feel that way. She was just becoming herself! At last! She felt confident. Clear-headed. Eyes on the future. Damn the torpedoes! Katie opened a random drawer. Was that a buffalo wing? It sure as shit was! Katie ate the buffalo wing, feeling no pain. No pain whatsoever.

18.

CHARLIE McCREE

NEW YORK, NY

Saturday, August 3, 2019, 3:44 a.m.

Charlie had started taking all of his meals at the French Restaurant with the French Name. The reason why was a sad one, truth be told. He had grown a little concerned about Paolo of late. The man who had struck him as so flawless when they'd first met was actually quite lax about his standards of cleanliness around the home. Paolo's apartment, sad to say, was a mess. Charlie still slept there, of course, but that only accounted for sixteen hours of each day. The rest of the time he spent downstairs in the restaurant.

Charlie loved the French Restaurant with the French Name. He loved the quiet of the place when he ate breakfast and lunch there, thanks to the kindness and generosity of Kevin, a sous-chef who Paolo had asked to come in to work early just to cook for Charlie. *Imagine such a thing!* he thought. *Me! Charlie McCree, with my own personal chef!* Truly, the blessings and surprises of this world never cease.

But Charlie especially loved the hustle and bustle of the dining room at dinnertime. He loved watching the rich and beautiful people at their feed. He loved the smells, the sights, the sounds. The seamless melding of art, business, and performance. He felt he could learn so much about art and life from Paolo and his staff. Charlie felt like he'd been blessed with a once-in-a-lifetime opportunity to witness genius from within, and he made the most of it. He had so many new ideas for the Bad Friday Disagreement's future direction that he felt it would only be fair to dedicate their breakthrough album to everyone at the restaurant. (Working title: *The Long Kesh Dirty Skanket Protest.*)

Sometimes Charlie got so carried away—by the odors, the pageantry, the precision—that he'd find himself suddenly wandering into the kitchen and taking food off of plates and out of bins. He'd eat it in a posture of holy rapture. No longer was he a man who ate the food of peasants. Now he ate only the finest meats and cheeses. He had even gained a few pounds! He was becoming substantial. He was becoming the best possible version of himself.

Charlie McCree was becoming a man.

Late one night, while eating an entire sour cherry tartine he'd found in a refrigerator, Charlie realized something about becoming a man. A man sought privileges, he reasoned. Not just sought them—a man took them. Charlie struggled to his feet and walked across the largely empty dining room. But this time he was not bound for the kitchen. He'd been spoken to about going into the kitchen the night previous. A very fit young woman had suggested that Charlie's charm and attractiveness were interfering with the cooks' ability to do their jobs—which made a lot of sense, when Charlie thought about it. He didn't want to be in the way of genius, after all, and he decided then and there that when he was seized with the desire to feel the heft and fresh coolness of the unprepared food in his hands and against his bare skin, he would do so after everyone else had gone home.

But Charlie was a powerfully curious man. Some might say the most curious. And the kitchen was not the only attraction in the French Restaurant with the French Name that drew his eye. There were other rooms. He'd spotted one during dinner service. He was lingering by the men's room, staring into the Bibliothèque bar, when all of a sudden a panel decorated with a picture of a beautiful woman slid open to reveal another room within.

"Secret room," Charlie whispered.

He moved swiftly across the Bibliothèque and managed to slip in behind two diners. Once inside, his heart filled with golden wonder. It was small and warm and there were beautiful people eating snacks and drinking tiny crimson drinks out of crystal glassware by candlelight, their faces lit up like Halloween lanterns. It was a sanctum. Charlie wanted to live there forever.

But wonders truly never cease, as Charlie was fond of saying. And as he was being dragged out of the secret room by two burly kitchen lads who gripped his arms and legs in a good-hearted embrace, he saw something even more miraculous: Paolo sliding open yet another secret door to yet another secret room. A bar within a bar within a bar. Instead of a beautiful woman guarding its entrance, this one was guarded by the beautiful game.

Charlie couldn't see what was in there, but it exerted a powerful hold over him, and he devoted the rest of that evening to getting through the barriers to that inner sanctum. He pretended Paolo was waiting for him in that special room. He pretended to be Paolo, offering Paolo's driver's license and a pair of his shoes as proof. He said his grandmother's cancer pills were in there. He said his grandmother herself was in there, choking on a vegetable roll.

Eventually he waited until everyone was gone, napping in a cart full of dirty tablecloths. He just wanted to get a wee peek, but not even the first door would yield, though he greased the lock with grapeseed oil and pried at it with a crowbar! *Only the finest for Chef Paolo Cabrini,* Charlie thought with admiration, *from meats to doors!*

Undeterred, Charlie returned to the dining room, put a chair on top of the bar, climbed up, and, since he was already greased with grapeseed oil, attempted to squeeze himself into the HVAC system in the hope that it would lead him to the special room.

It didn't, sad to say. But what an image for the lads back home! Ol' Smilin' Charlie stuck in a pipe at 3:44 in the morning and screaming until Paolo came down and rescued him. What would the lads say if they saw such a sight? They'd all have quite a laugh, he predicted. *What craic life was!*

19.

NIA GREENE

NEW YORK, NY

Saturday, August 3, 2019, 1:15 p.m.

Nia did not want to represent Katie Horatio.

If she was being honest, she didn't really want to represent anyone. She didn't really want to work anymore. She was tired and, more important, she was a little spoiled. Being in business with John Doe, while certainly challenging, and requiring smarts and shrewdness and opportunism, was comfortable. Their union was as natural as breathing. They flowed together, and the money flowed too. The gig made her a more fully realized human, but it unquestionably made her less of a killer. When she was young, she was a killer. She didn't enjoy it like some of her colleagues did, but the world she existed in required it, so a killer she became. And it worked for her. Being a killer helped her win the business of John Doe.

But she was hurtling toward fifty, and she was tired. She often thought of Hollywood as an ecosystem. While the beetles fought in the scrub grass all around her, she was the lion dozing in the sun. They lived in a state of perpetual readiness. Nia lived in a Fort Greene brownstone that had been featured by *The World of Interiors* magazine. Enough said.

She had some time. She didn't need to go back to work right away. Her commission for all proceeds of Doe's company—Hapless Sodden Wanderer Productions—was 35 percent on everything but his first book. Money would certainly keep flowing after Doe's death, especially if he remained so fondly remembered. It would spike over the next couple of months, quite likely. But after that, it would start to slide. She'd made $700,000 last year. Next year, her income would probably be down to $450,000, and it would drop more each passing year before drying up inside of a decade. If Nia's salary were to stay level, with her current lifestyle and her current savings, she was a solid fifteen years from retirement.

That lifestyle was expensive. Nia understood very well the absurd trajectory promised by the American dream. Her great-grandfather picked fruit. He fed people, and he made nothing. Her grandfather worked in construction. He built buildings that still stand today, and he made a little. Her father worked in computer sales. It was more trivial than what his forebears had done, but it had allowed him to crack the middle class. Nia did something even less consequential than that, and she cracked the top 1 percent of earners in the United States. Ever thus in America. Each generation makes exponentially more money doing something dumber than the previous one. If she had a child, it would no doubt make a billion dollars creating a smartphone app that turns fart sounds into cartoon characters.

Nia was still a decade away from paying off her brownstone. She had bought an Audi A8 and a nice house upstate. She loved nice stuff. She bought into the animist belief that things have souls. Her furniture was custom. Her clothes were bespoke. She still needed to fund her IRA, whatever the fuck that was. She acknowledged that it was ridiculous to be anything but completely free and clear after making this much for so many years. But it was what it was. The curious predicament of the American rich. Having money costs a fortune. She figured she needed $5 million to retire, and that meant going back to work, sometime.

There was the agency route. The offers were generous. Some offered to make her a partner, some didn't insist she move to Los Angeles. But the thought of being in a firm again filled her with dread.

By the time she'd gone into business for herself, she was sick of graciously deflecting questions about basketball and hip-hop without making the questioner feel bad about asking. She was sick of being praised by middling white colleagues for accomplishing rudimentary tasks. She was sick of people mentioning *The Wire* to her. One executive told her he hadn't understood Black people until he saw *The Wire*. When she told Doe about that he kept a straight face. "To be fair," he said, "I never *truly* understood Japanese people until I saw *Tora! Tora! Tora!*"

(He did not keep a straight face, however, after Nia pitched a show based on a memoir about a Black billiards prodigy at Eton College, and the exec described it approvingly as "*The Hustler* meets *The Wire* at Buckingham Palace." Doe roared at that one.)

She was sick of having to filter every utterance through three levels of cognitive approval before opening her mouth. Will they be hurt? Will they be freaked out? Will this play into a stereotype? If her coworker Parker Chatworth got mad, it was because Parker was mad. If Nia got mad, it was because she was Black. If Parker fucked up, it was because Parker fucked up. If Nia fucked up—which she did far less than Parker did—it was because she was Black. The only time they'd be regarded as equals was if someone were to cry. When that happened, it was because they were both women.

That's why she loved John. He trusted her and paid her what she was worth, in both money and respect. He also gave her about a thousand pounds of shit a day, but most of it was predicated on her being an individual and a human being in full. And she gave as good as she got.

If she did work with Katie, maybe she could do it with her own little shop and avoid agency life. That was the dream. Still, she remained deeply wary of this up-and-comer, and she resented being put in a corner by some little white girl. But she had time.

Meanwhile, she had gotten two calls about more urgent matters. One was from Paolo. The situation in his apartment had not been defused by an offer of $10,000 any more than it had been resolved by that three-hour crime against music that they'd never live down. Paolo seemed oddly hollowed out when they spoke. She thought he was giving up. But she was not. She just had to figure out what the hell Charlie wanted. Maybe it was more money. But maybe it wasn't money at all. Maybe he was after something else entirely. The fact that he hadn't actually demanded a thing might be a good sign. As long as his ask wasn't simply to live with Paolo forever, Nia was confident she could figure it out.

The second call was from John's estate attorney about settling his affairs. Some years prior, in a show of faith that had brought tears to her eyes, John had named her his executor. When she'd asked him if he was sure about it—there were whole thickets of conflicts around such an arrangement—he'd told her, "Of course I'm sure. I trust you. Besides, if you turn out to be a crook, what the fuck do I care? I'll be dead."

The estate attorney asked Nia to come in to his office. There, he told her that, for the most part, the will was simple. There was nothing left to family—the source of most headaches when it comes to these things. John never married, he had no children, and he sincerely did hate what little family he had—which included a brother who was a Notre Dame–educated corporate lawyer and a younger sister who had married a hedge fund guy. Nia recalled a story about the brother-in-law. Before John was famous, his sister had dragged him to a dinner party at their house in tony Wellesley, Massachusetts, where her husband stood before a long, elegant table rhapsodizing about a sublime bottle of wine he'd acquired for just $2,000. "It was an absolute steal," he told them. When he was finally ready to grace his guests with a glass, he absently handed it to John to open—because, of course, John was a bartender.

John, feigning excitement at the chance to put his grubby bartender hands on such an extraordinary vintage, took it into the kitchen. There, he dumped it into a bowl. He then grabbed the solid but inexpensive red he'd brought and carefully poured that into the expensive bottle—using a *Forbes* magazine he'd rolled into a funnel—and he poured the expensive wine into the cheap bottle, using the same method. Then, after rooting quickly and quietly through the cabinets, he added a pinch of cinnamon, a gob of ketchup, and a spritz of Windex, shook the whole thing up, and returned to the dining room, holding this treasure aloft. There was light applause. The wine was poured, and he gave the host and his guests a few minutes to fawn over it before he told them what it was. His sister demanded he leave the party at once, which he did, but not before grabbing what appeared to be the cheap wine he had brought with him.

God, she missed him.

Doe's will called for most of his money to be divided between charitable organizations. He funded a scholarship for disadvantaged high school students to study abroad, and another for gifted kids without means to attend culinary school. There were bequeathments to organizations that helped recovering addicts find work. There were gifts to orphanages in some of the countries where he'd shot the show. In all, he'd given money to two dozen groups amounting to about $6 million. All Nia would have to do, said the attorney, was oversee the dispensation of the assets—like selling his Tribeca apartment and his Land Rover—and write the checks. All his remaining personal effects went to her.

"But there's one other thing here, Nia," the attorney told her, studying the will. "The company: Hapless Sodden Wanderer Productions."

"Right, I'm guessing we have to liquidate his stake."

"No, we won't," he said, handing Nia the will. "It's yours. He left you his shares. You're now the sole proprietor."

And with that, her income for the year tripled, and the killer within her stirred. Instinct took over. She shook hands with the estate lawyer and walked out onto Fifth Avenue.

She thought of John's notebooks. There were boxes of them in Doe's office. She had gone through some when she was helping Paolo prepare his eulogy. Her initial plan was to hold on to the notebooks for a while, until she missed him less, and then arrange to have them donated to a university archive.

But Nia knew the noble archive plan was no longer operative; Doe's legacy remained intact but would require sustained protection from bad actors. There was the Katie Horatio problem in the near term, to be sure. But there was also the inevitable backlash stage of the celebrity death cycle. Like jackals circling a carcass, marginal people from Doe's life had begun emerging with their own stories to sell, each promising to reveal "the real John Doe." A former *Last Call* production assistant was currently shopping a memoir of his time with Doe, as was a barback who'd worked at The Pub. There was even talk of an unauthorized quasi-biographical book/film project produced by a former girlfriend and the author Ben Mezrich.

Fuck that, she thought. *If anyone was going to sully John's name, it was going to be John himself.*

The next moves were clear: she went back to the boxes and conducted a thorough examination. It wasn't just journals. There were inscribed cookbooks from friends, printouts of emails from writers he'd admired, yellowing newspaper clippings of reviews from his first book, some old passports, an unbound and unpublished manuscript called *Don't Eat Before Reading This* written by his old friend Tony Bourdain—with a note from Doe on the title page that said, "Dear Nia: read this or you're fired," and another from her replying, "Dear John: one of you is quite enough."

The journals, however, were the real find. They were illuminating, insightful, interesting, and funny. Reading them was like being with him. She called John's editor at Viking, which had published his previous six books, all of which were bestsellers. The editor was Australian, which always annoyed her for some reason. She found Australians disingenuous. They were like Canadians pretending to be Scottish.

"Toby," she said. "I have boxes of John's notebooks, and I've been reading them, and they're extraordinary. Revelatory. They're a major event. A masterwork. And I'm coming to you first."

"Nia," Toby said. "That's wonderful news. When can you send them over? We'd love to see them."

"You're not seeing shit."

"Nia, we can't rightly buy something that we haven't—"

"This is a courtesy call. Tomorrow morning, *Good Day* is devoting a whole hour to John. The notebooks will be prominently featured in the segment. Because they're fucking amazing. After that, I'm taking them right to auction. Bids are due at five p.m. Monday. Bidding starts at a million five. I'm telling you this now because I love you and I love your stupid Australian accent and want to give you a head start on stuffing cash into duffel bags."

"They're that good?"

"They're spectacular, Toby. It's like he's in the room. It's uncanny."

"Can I make a preemptive offer?"

"Sure. Five million."

Nia could hear Toby sighing morosely. He was always sighing morosely. You didn't expect to hear an Australian sighing morosely. It felt like a transgression of the supposed national character. It's probably why he had to come here.

"Give me a couple days?" he said.

"I'll give you a day."

"Okay."

"Have I ever led you astray?"

"No, you haven't."

"Then why would I now? Have a little faith. Take a breath. Go chew some eucalyptus."

"You're such an asshole."

"Au revoir, mon petit koala."

Toby hung up. Next, Nia called her contact at CBS, a producer. When the network had first approached Nia to ask for her blessing to devote a whole hour to Doe on the Sunday show, she'd given consent. Now she was retracting it. She wanted to try to shoehorn Katie in there to see what happened. Katie thought she was testing Nia. Well, Nia would test Katie right back. If the kid was good, then her star would keep rising. Maybe she'd be worth taking on as a client. If she imploded, that was fine too, because she'd be out of the way. Sink or swim, you little maggot. Either way, there would be national attention for John's notebooks.

It was a dicey move, but Nia kind of enjoyed trying it out. Predictably, the producer went berserk.

"Calm down," Nia said over the shouting. "I'm not taking something away. I come bearing a great gift." Nia told the producer about the notebooks, how they were an astonishing glimpse into the mind of John Doe, and that *Good Day* would have them before anyone else. This was real news.

"So then give them to us and we'll feature them."

"I have one condition."

"Nia, this shoot is tomorrow. *Tomorrow.*"

"I have one condition."

"Go ahead."

"You know Katie Horatio, right?"

"Not personally, but I read that essay, sure."

"We need a segment where Katie reads from the notebooks."

Two birds, one stone, she thought.

"Nia, we can't have her paging through random notebooks on camera."

"She won't be. You and I will agree on the passages and mark them ahead of time. Katie will pretend to just happen upon them. It'll be great."

"I don't like it."

Nia laughed, then sighed fondly.

"What?" the producer said.

"I was just remembering back to when a certain star of a certain one of your top shows got into a certain kind of situation involving a certain kind of prostitute and a certain kind of amphetamine, and I called you and offered to help clean it up gratis because your PR people suck and so did his, because I love and respect you and only want what's best. I remember thinking, *'Man, I really am busy, but if I can't do it for her, who can I do it for?'* "

"You fucker."

"Plus, if you don't do it, I'll pull out and have all of Doe's friends pull out too. They're doing it as a favor to me anyway. And unlike some people, I always make good on favors."

"So that's what you want? The notebooks and Katie Horatio?"

"Sure. That, and a $10,000 handling fee."

"Oh come on."

"Clerical fee! There are dozens of notebooks to go through!"

"You're such a dick," the producer said in a voice that, for all its bombast, telegraphed surrender. "Can we at least have exclusive rights to post excerpts on the website?"

"Of course."

Long pause.

"Okay," she finally said. "I hate you and I hate this job and I hate the world."

But Nia had already hung up.

20.

KATIE HORATIO

NEW YORK, NY

Sunday, August 4, 2019, 5:53 a.m.

No longer would Katie Horatio bother with crazy ideas of being taken over by someone else. This was *her.* In bloom. She was in control. Not New Katie or Old Katie, but just *Katie.* And Katie needed to be somewhere.

She had gotten a text from Nia the day before. She was getting her big shot. National TV. Sunday show. Special tribute to John Doe. There was also something about notebooks. Katie had to be at Lobio at seven a.m. to shoot a pretaped segment. Katie had still never been to Lobio. And she really *hated* beans. *But this was showbiz, so put on your fucking game face,* she said to herself in the mirror.

Katie Horatio strode from her suite, took the elevator down to the sumptuous lobby, and stepped out into the street. A black car was already waiting for her.

She slipped in, and the car drove off into a world that was ripe for the taking.

Katie Horatio was getting hers.

TWO HOURS LATER, Katie Horatio was shitting the bed.

She couldn't figure out what was wrong. She was sitting in a chair in a small, evil-smelling restaurant, facing a camera, which was rolling. The man beside the camera was some kind of television director. He was asking her questions she didn't know the answer to. They seemed simple, but when she heard them, they'd break into a thousand pieces, and she'd try to answer each piece individually. She was pouring sweat.

"Tell me about how you met John Doe," the director asked.

"That's a really great question. Like, so very good a question," Katie said, panic rising through her skin and into the follicles of her hair. "If I recall, I was walking on a street in New York, here, in New York. Not a street per se but the sidewalk that lines, that runs along the streets. And I was . . . sad."

"Um, let's try that again, Katie. We're in no hurry, just relax, have fun. Just like we're having a conversation."

"Conversations are scary!" Katie said, laughing nervously. But no one else laughed. They just watched. Paolo Cabrini, the great chef. Nia, who looked concerned and who was holding a notebook that she said Katie had to read. The QVC chef Patrick Whelan, pale, unshaven, and vacantly spooning a Serendipity frozen hot chocolate into his mouth as he gazed into the middle distance. Some fidgety man with a brogue who never seemed to blink and wouldn't stop smiling at Cabrini. They all just stared politely. Which was worse than mockery.

Katie tried again. "I was walking down the sidewalk, by the street, here, in New York City—sorry, around Jackson Heights, and I was sad."

"What were you sad about?" the director asked.

"People get sad," she explained, cheerfully, as though speaking to a child. "Sometimes people can just be sad."

"Right. So, you were walking down the street, and you were sad. And then what happened?"

"Then I met John Doe, who saw that I cried."

"And . . . what did he say?"

"He said he wanted to eat the beans with me here at Labia."

"Lobio."

"Sorry. I'm sorry. He said he wanted to eat beans with me here."

"Where?"

"Here."

"At . . . ?"

"In this place."

"Which is called?"

Silence.

"Katie?"

"Labia."

"Cut!"

People began moving around. The director shot a look at Nia, who gave her a look back that said, *I'll fix it.* Katie rose from her seat like a defendant who had been sentenced to death: her shock muted by incomprehension. She handed the notebook she had been holding on her lap to someone. The director ordered the PA to give her some water and the PA handed her a bottle. Katie noticed the PA seemed afraid of her, so Katie apologized twice to the girl.

She glanced around the room. They all seemed afraid of her. Not afraid of her hurting them, but afraid of her infecting them with whatever it was she had. Rather than look at them, Katie looked at the water bottle. She held the water bottle with two hands and emptied the entire thing into her throat. She was starving. Only Patrick Whelan approached her. His face was blank as he silently offered her the half-eaten frozen hot chocolate and his sticky spoon as some sort of gesture. She just apologized to him and drifted past him to go outside. She bumped into a street sign and apologized. She was startled by a car horn and apologized to that as well. She stood out there alone in agony, flooded with all those Old Katie emotions she thought she had destroyed: shame, embarrassment, indecisiveness, compulsive apologizing. Her expensive outfit, such a source of pleasure before, now struck her as dangerously inadequate. Even reckless. What was she doing with just a thin layer of increasingly sweat-soaked silk between her tender flesh and a speeding taxi or flying crowbar? She was in terrible danger.

Katie, it turned out, had been deeply mistaken. She wasn't just Katie. She wasn't a unified being undergoing a growth spurt. She wasn't coming into her own. No: New Katie was very real. As evidenced by the fact that New Katie could go away. And if New Katie was gone, it was catastrophic. Old Katie would be stuck with immense debt. She'd be publicly humiliated, hounded. She'd never work in media again. There would be nothing but wreck and ruin, and without New Katie to guide her, she didn't have the first clue how to deal with damage. "I'm sorry," she whispered to the air around her. "I'm sorry I ever doubted you were real. I was wrong to think that any of this was because of me. It was you all along. It was *only you*. Please forgive me."

Katie stood out on the street for several minutes, eyes closed, breathing, beseeching New Katie to return. "Just come back," she whispered. "Please come back. I'll do whatever you say. Don't make me go back to who I was."

"Katie," a voice said.

"New Katie, is that you?" she whispered.

"What? No. It's Nia."

Katie opened her eyes. Her fear was gone. Her head was clear. Her clothing felt appropriate and not at all an open invitation to the universe to kill or maim her. Katie felt a stirring, the tremor of leaves preceding a great wind. *You've come back!* she thought.

"So they're going to do Lad next," Nia said. "To give you a minute."

Nia was being gentle. Nia was handling her. New Katie hated being handled.

"I don't need a minute," she said.

"Take one anyway."

"No, I think I'll go back in now."

"Katie, they want you to stay out here and breathe until it's your turn again."

Katie looked at Nia, and a smirk formed at the corner of her mouth. Her hand went into her jacket pocket and found a fresh cigar and a lighter. "Yeah, well, I'd like Sophia Loren to put on a fucking nun's habit and sit on my face after riding a bicycle," she said, lighting the cigar. "But we don't always get what we want, do we?"

She blew a cloud of smoke at a passing man, who coughed, and walked back into Lobio.

KATIE RETURNED TO FIND a tense scene. Not dissimilar from the one she had caused. Lad was sitting in the chair, camera trained upon him, and he was answering a question. And while he did, everyone around him—the crew, the guests—were exchanging concerned glances. Lad, for his part, seemed like he couldn't understand why his answer was making everyone so uncomfortable.

"So," said the director, "you mean you didn't know him *well*."

"I mean I never knew him," Lad was saying. "I never seen him. I don't know this man!"

The director turned to Nia and Paolo. "But . . . the story says he was here all the time. He was a regular. This was one of his favorite restaurants."

Lad scoffed.

"Surely you must at least recognize him. Sandy, can you show Lad a photo of John Doe to jog his memory?"

The PA called up a photo on her phone and showed it to Lad. Lad shrugged. "This man is a stranger," he said.

Katie watched this, and the wheels began to turn. She looked at Lad, and at the director, and at Paolo Cabrini, and at Nia, and at this smiling idiot Irishman who was standing so close to Cabrini that it looked like he was trying to merge with him, and at what appeared to be a sentient tube of bronzer named Janni or something. She looked at these people and she could see the connections between them. She could see the emotions. She could feel the stakes. What was clear to her was that they were all invested in Lad saying something that he wasn't saying. And the fact that he wasn't saying it represented more than just a potential weak spot in a broadcast. It was a rupture in a grander plan. A plan built upon their lie and upon her lie.

Katie put the cigar between her teeth and picked up a chair. She walked over to Lad, who was looking at the director like he was a simpleton. Something told her to check to see if the camera was rolling. It was.

"Move over," she said to Lad. The request baffled him, but he complied. She turned to the director. "Keep that thing running. I want to explain something." She sat down and threw her arm around Lad, and with a winning smile and tendrils of smoke curling cinematically out of her cigar, Katie began to lie.

"Here's what people don't get: the fact that a famous man came into this little restaurant—multiple times—and the owner doesn't remember tells you everything you need to know about my dear friend Lad, and about Lobio," she said. "Lobio would not be what Lobio is if Lad gave a shit about celebrities or wanted to be famous. Lobio is what it is precisely because he *doesn't* care about them, and he doesn't want to be one. And this is what I love about him."

"But you're famous now, Lad," said the director. "How does that feel?"

"The same. But with more mess outside," Lad said.

"Of course he's going to say that," Katie laughed. "Because Lad knows—unlike every other upstart Instagram chef in this city who wants to be famous when they should be cooking—that fame kills greatness. Lad is pure. As pure as any chef I've ever met. But you can't be pure and care about fame.

"John Doe told me that in this very spot. He said it was the great struggle of his life—apart from depression, of course. He said you cannot stay yourself and be famous. Because for every rung you climb on that ladder, you generate duplicate selves. There is your *self*, whatever that is, but there is also this persona you have to adopt in order to be famous, and then there are all the perceptions that people have of you, which, let's be honest, may as well be real too. And the more famous you are, the more doubles there are, and the more they come into conflict and vie with one another. Maybe the persona eats the self. Maybe you start suppressing who you are in order to be more like the perception people have of you. But whatever happens, you—the real you—is gone. And when you're gone, you can't come back, you can't go home, and you sure as hell can't cook."

Katie took a puff of her cigar. "No one knows this better than this man. With Lad, there are no so-called famous people, because there is no fame. There is only the bean." Katie turned in her seat and looked lovingly at Lad. "I'm not worried that you don't remember John Doe," she said. "I'd be worried if you did."

She kissed him on the head, apologized for interrupting, and stood up and walked away, leaving Lad to sit in his chair silently, watching her go, while the camera zoomed in on a single tear in his eye, which had been caused by all the cigar smoke.

"Cut!"

Katie walked across the room to where Nia and Patrick Whelan were standing. All the guests shot her looks of appreciation, except for Patrick. His eyes were welling up.

"What can I say? You're a star," Nia said.

"I'll take that ten large in a check," she told Nia. "Make it out to cash."

Then she turned to Patrick Whelan.

"Here, kid, make yourself useful," she said, handing him the cigar. "I gotta go take a squirt."

21.

CHEF PATRICK WHELAN

NEW YORK, NY

Sunday, August 4, 2019, 10:53 p.m.

Patrick Whelan was in trouble. After Gloria had fired him, he'd left the loft and tried to dump Jackie on the way out.

"Aw, Pat, definitely do whatever you need to do," she'd said, lying naked across the couch with her feet in that fucking Brazilian model guy's lap. "But, babe, we were never dating."

Since then he'd spent three days in a cocoon of dejection inside his suite at the Murser. Each morning, he'd given the bellhop $200 and asked him to pick up the same items: four Gray's Papaya franks with ketchup, mustard, sauerkraut, onions, relish, and a medium papaya tropical drink; a falafel sandwich from Mamoun's; banana pudding from Magnolia; three dollars' worth of pizza from a specific dollar-slice joint on Twenty-Third Street; a coffee-soda from the nearest deli; and two frozen hot chocolates from Serendipity.

While he binged New York nostalgia food and every John Grisham film adaptation, he felt shitty. Or, in the words of his old therapist, he gave himself permission to feel shitty.

But on the third day, something happened. In the middle of *The Firm*, just as the Quaker Oats guy tells Tom Cruise that the pictures he had of him were "not just screwing," but "kind of intimate acts, oral and whatnot," Patrick started to think about a conversation he'd recently had with his mother. She told him she'd run into that pretty girl from his high school, Alexis Lucente, at the Container Store by the Braintree mall, and how Alexis was divorced, had two kids, and was working there.

"Oh, that's too bad," he had remarked to his mother.

"Why is that bad?" she'd snapped. "She was one of the closet-organizer women, she was bossing people around and making jokes. She seemed happy."

Then his mother had added: "We can't all have owned restaurants, Patrick." He'd realized she had phrased it in the past tense, that she was already talking about his situation as over—because it was.

His bladder full from Gray's Papaya tropical drink, he went into the bathroom to take a piss and stood facing himself in the mirror. With his hotel bathrobe open, he had a full view of the entire Patrick Whelan Experience, and what he saw was this: a slightly overweight, pale, hairless Irish American in his fifties who hadn't really worked in more than a decade, who had tried to date a woman *thirty* years younger than him and didn't even succeed, who was a sellout and a tool, and who had no real friends except possibly his objectively terrifying Irish cousin whom he paid as an employee. He saw a man with no spark and no light, a man whose big play of the last ten years was to try to take a dead man's job by learning about Substacks. In other words, in the mirror of the skybox suite at the Murser Hotel in New York City, Patrick finally saw himself.

But once he did, and could self-assess and flagellate as needed, something strange happened: Patrick Whelan felt pretty fucking amazing.

He called Declan and told him to pack up his Vegas house, put it up for rent, and ship everything back to Weymouth (Declan included). Patrick scanned the room. He was done feeling shitty and eating shitty. He wanted real food. Good food. The best fucking food in the world. And so he called Paolo Cabrini and asked if he could dine with him at the French Restaurant with the French Name.

"JESUS FUCK."

Tasting the eighth course, Patrick saw God.

"Jesus fucking Christ."

He had been to the French Restaurant with the French Name multiple times, but before tonight, he couldn't have told you a single thing about the food. In times past he had been with multiple chefs, and they were definitely drunk and definitely on coke, and the food was just a prop for arguing and jousting their cocks at one another.

People seemed to think that no one enjoyed food more than chefs, but that was a fucking lie. In fact, it was much harder for chefs to enjoy other chefs' great dishes. There was too much to think about. It was like comedians watching other comedians on stage. You don't enjoy the jokes. Especially the ones that kill. You see them as a puzzle to be solved. But tonight, Patrick had no ulterior motive. He wanted only to enjoy the food. He could tell Paolo was surprised when he'd called. They'd just seen each other at the Doe memorial and that morning at Lobio. And, of course, as any of the famous chefs of the world might, they'd run into each other many times before at awards ceremonies, and *Bon Appétit* and *Saveur* and *Food & Wine* magazine shoots, and all the various bougie food festivals (Aspen, Pebble Beach, Charleston, Feast Portland), and Patrick had remembered Paolo from his days in Boston, but he'd mostly just known him through Doe. They would never be mistaken for friends. Patrick's "friends" had tended to be D-list celebrities. Older reality stars. Middling ex-athletes. E from *Entourage*.

Paolo's close friends were almost exclusively in the food world. Doe, of course. But other chefs. Farmers. Journalists. If Patrick was being cynical, he might've said that Paolo constructed and cultivated his friend circles as meticulously as his dishes. But fuck, were those dishes good.

Every single thing Patrick had tasted so far had been as perfect as he'd imagined. Waiters with deep knowledge of France's oyster history and clever limericks about Dijon flitted in and out confidently, and then disappeared. A white-haired Belgian sommelier showed up with wine, and a strikingly blonde Brazilian cicerone with beer, and a beautiful chestnut-haired Italian woman with kombucha, for some reason.

After taking a bite of the eighth course, Patrick stared at the thinly sliced, deep-crimson meat wrapped around a piece of crackling skin glazed with honey and placed on top of what tasted and looked to him like the innards of a lightly toasted croissant.

"Paolo," he said, his voice conveying genuine awe. "What in the fuck is this glorious dish?"

During the meal, Paolo hadn't eaten or drunk anything except a roll of Tums and four 500 milliliter bottles of Petrópolis Paulista sparkling water. The only food that was put in front of him was a small bowl of pistachios, but as of Patrick's eighth course, Paolo hadn't eaten a single one. His sport coat was wrinkled and so was his dress shirt, and he had what looked to Patrick like four days' worth of stubble. Considering this was a man who was known to have a tailor and a dry cleaner on retainer, this struck Patrick as extremely unusual.

As he waited for Paolo to respond, Patrick watched a group of men, all of them redheads, save for one with jet-black hair, walk confidently past their table and through the back of the restaurant. As he sauntered past, the non-ginger in the clan made eye contact with Patrick and gave him a wink and a grin. Patrick struggled to remember where he'd seen him before.

Staring at the group out of the corner of his eye, Paolo spoke.

"You are Irish, right, Patrick?"

His voice seemed different. Paolo had always spoken with a sort of nondenominational accent (Patrick remembered Doe calling it his "NATO voice"), but now it was hoarser and somehow—Patrick didn't know how else to put it—less European.

"Yeah, Irish on both sides, though my dad's parents moved to Boston from Ireland in the fifties. My mom moved from Ireland when she was nineteen."

"Did you know Celtic farmers were some of the first to crossbreed Phoenician pigs with Mediterranean wild boar? They would trade with the Iberians back around the sixth century. That's how they got their famous pata negra pigs."

As he told the story, he took pistachios out of the bowl and opened the shells with one hand, popping the meat onto the table. Then, without looking, he arranged all the shelled pistachios in a perfect line.

"There is a farmer I know in the south of France. I will call him Guy."

"Is his name not Guy?"

Paolo seemed perplexed by the question. "No, it is." He continued.

"I gave him Iberian black piglets to raise and told him to feed them a diet of French acorns dipped in manuka honey."

Patrick started to speak, but Paolo cut him off.

"I know, I know: manuka bushes are native to New Zealand. But I was fascinated by the idea that they retain all of their antibacterial, antifungal, and antimicrobial properties, and so I had the farmer feed them to the pigs. It was excessive, yes, but . . ."

Patrick had never heard of manuka honey.

"Anyway, we salt the legs of these animals, do a fifty-day desalination, then dry-cure them for ten months outside in the French countryside and age them for four years. So that is the meat you're eating. We then take the skins and cook them until they are crackling, thin, and crispy, and paint them with that same manuka honey. And my pastry chef, Laure, she has figured out how to extract the soft, glorious inside of a croissant"—Patrick silently felt satisfaction at guessing that—"and we crisp it just enough to hold the meat and skin and a single dollop of aioli."

Paolo was now putting the spent shells in a perfect line next to the pistachios.

"Do you know where I got the inspiration for this dish?" Paolo asked.

Patrick shook his head.

"The Honey Baked Ham store on Wolf Road in Albany." Paolo offered a slight smile.

"Shut the fuck up."

"I swear." Paolo was even laughing now a bit. "It was Doe's idea. We were driving through Albany on our way to film some stupid segment of the show, and Doe saw the store and made me stop. He came out with six whole Honey Baked Hams wrapped in foil that he ended up giving to the crew, and then went to a local grocery store, got white bread and mayonnaise, and we sat in a parking lot in Albany and ate Honey Baked Ham sandwiches."

For the first time since they sat down, Paolo took a pistachio and put it in his mouth.

"I remember seeing Doe break off pieces of that crispy sugar from the top of the ham and shove it in his sandwich. For a year and a half I thought about how I could re-create it. So I came up with this."

"Well, it's fucking brilliant."

Paolo smiled wistfully and popped another pistachio in his mouth. "You know, Doe thought you were a genius."

"Fuck you."

"No, I swear. He talked about you all the time. He said he'd never seen anyone's brain work like yours. The way you came up with dishes . . ." Paolo took a sip of his sparkling water. "You know, I was there in the beginning at Áise. I saw what you did. And I thought you were a genius as well. I used to go home after eating your food at the bar and try to break it down. Why did you use this ingredient? Why did you present it in this way? It used to drive me mad."

Patrick felt his face get warm. He could not believe this sort of praise was coming out of the mouth of Paolo Cabrini.

"I don't . . . I don't even really know where any of it came from, if I'm being honest," Patrick said. "Sometimes when I dream, I dream in finished dishes. And I can see the dish in such spectacular detail, it's crazy. But I have no idea what the ingredients are, or how I got there. And so the rest of my cooking life was working backward to figure that out, to try to interpret my dreams."

Paolo gave him an incredulous look. "Surely not all dishes."

"All dishes you've heard of." Patrick shrugged. "But then, as Áise started to become more famous and began winning awards, the dreams stopped. I tried everything to get them back. I hired sleep consultants, I bought dream catchers, I started ingesting ayahuasca. But they didn't come. So I took the deal in Vegas and the TV money. I thought I had to grab as much fruit off the vine before people knew I was a fraud."

Paolo's eyes were wide-open. He was eating pistachios by the handful now, and his staff, ever attentive, saw this and began replacing the bowls just as quickly as he could eat the nuts.

"But why didn't you just develop recipes? Test things? Get ideas from your staff?"

"Because I didn't know how to develop recipes. I was self-taught. As for taking ideas from my staff—fuck that. I was a thirty-year-old poor kid who became the biggest chef in America. My ego was four times the size of the Green Monster."

Paolo looked confused, but Patrick ignored it and moved on.

"I looked at someone like you and, if I'm being honest, I fucking hated your guts." He smiled, sadly. "You think I didn't notice you in Áise back in the day? I knew every fucking time you came in. I didn't know who you were, but I knew *what* you were. I could see you examining the dishes, trying to figure out the logic behind them. And you know how I felt? Like a first-timer sitting at a table with Doyle Brunson, getting dealt a shit hand, and going all in anyway."

Again, Paolo looked confused.

"Who is Doyle?"

"He was a pro poker player, one of the best ever. And because he was a pro, he was used to playing pros. What they did made sense. The scariest thing to him would be some dipshit amateur making an off-the-cuff move with no logic behind it. And that was me."

Patrick took a sip of his kombucha.

"You were trained. You knew the rules. You had the chops. I mean, the shit you just told me about this one dish? You think I know anything remotely close about any of the dishes I've ever made? I'm literally famous for jacking Asian culture, smashing it into Irish culture, and pretending there was a point."

Paolo continued to shell pistachios one-handed with uncanny speed as Patrick kept talking.

"Do you want to know why I decided to 'blow up the paradigm of food culture as we knew it'? Because I went to bed stoned after eating shitty Chinese food I bought in Quincy and had one of those fucking dreams."

He drained his kombucha and put the glass down on the table.

"You're fucking Doyle Brunson, Chef. And I'm just a cooking tourist from Weymouth who accidentally went all in at the high rollers' table with a three and an eight."

Paolo shoveled a dozen pistachios into his mouth. "Yes, but . . . you still made the recipes. You had to work backward from a picture in your mind, and somehow you managed to create dishes that no one else in America could even understand. We were all jealous of you, Patrick. You are a true creative talent. I am just a man who grinds and grinds—"

"Grinds his way into having the number one restaurant in the fucking world. Fuck you, Paolo. This fake modesty bullshit does not suit you. Now please, would you pause your weird squirrel diet for one second and have a proper drink with me?"

Paolo smiled and nodded, and, thanks to some sort of hand signal Patrick could not decipher, a 1978 bottle of Havana cachaça and two glasses suddenly appeared on the table.

As Paolo poured the cachaça, he asked, "So what will you do now?"

"I'm shutting down Áise Vegas," Patrick said. "I'm going home."

Behind Paolo, Patrick saw the young men with the orange hair all walking quickly to exit the restaurant, some of them holding bottles of Brazilian beer.

"To Boston?" Paolo asked, and started to raise his glass to toast.

"Nah, to Weymouth. My ma says—"

But just as Patrick was finishing his sentence, Fred appeared tableside.

"I'm so sorry to interrupt, Chef Whelan, but Chef Cabrini is needed in the back." Fred looked as if he'd just inhaled anthrax. "There's been an incident."

22.

CHEF PAOLO CABRINI

NEW YORK, NY

Sunday, August 4, 2019, 11:03 p.m.

Paolo Cabrini didn't want to die.

Paolo Cabrini didn't want to die partly because, though raised Catholic, he had since come to rest somewhere between agnostic and atheist. He sort of believed there was some higher power who had a hand in controlling the miracle of human existence, of thoughts and emotions and feelings, of the soul and the body. Though he also thought science made a pretty compelling case that humans were just evolved apes who told themselves stories of beings more powerful and mysterious than themselves to quell the despair of knowing that what awaited them after death was no more than a black nothingness.

But more importantly, Paolo Cabrini didn't want to die because he needed to know about the incident. And he couldn't know about the incident if he choked to death on pistachios, which he was in the process of doing, as Fred's news had caused the nuts he had been shoveling into his mouth to become lodged in his windpipe.

Fred, ever the professional, recognized the situation and immediately performed the American Red Cross–preferred "five and five" first aid approach, with five back blows to the space between Paolo's shoulder blades, followed by five abdominal thrusts with Paolo tipped forward slightly. The abdominal thrusts dislodged the pistachios onto the floor.

The few guests who remained at the French Restaurant with the French Name looked on in genuine terror as Paolo took a few deep breaths while on his hands and knees. When he stood again, he looked around the silent room and gave a small wave and a smile.

"If you liked that, you should've seen the seven thirty show."

The patrons, thrilled that the owner of the restaurant they were all dining at had not died as they were enjoying their pata negra with manuka honey, all laughed nervously and applauded.

Patrick was now standing next to Paolo, his eyes wide. "Jesus fuck, man. You scared the shit out of me."

Paolo patted him on the arm. "I'm fine." Then he turned to Fred. "Show me."

As Paolo entered the Bibliothèque, he kept his head on a swivel looking for discrepancies. To the average guest of the French Restaurant with the French Name, everything likely seemed fine. In fact, three tables in the Bibliothèque still included guests, all of whom seemed to be enjoying their brandy, oblivious to any concerns. But as Paolo looked around, he could see evidence of misdeeds everywhere, and so he needed these people to leave.

"Please tell Lydia to excuse our guests as quickly as possible," he hissed to Fred. "Issue them each $300 gift cards and give them the number to the private line so they know they have a guaranteed reservation to come back. If they want an extra gibassier or to take the brandy home, gift wrap it for them, but get them out of here in the next ten minutes."

Fred nodded and went to speak to Lydia. Patrick, who had been following silently, approached Paolo's side.

"They've broken it," Paolo said softly. In the corner, he spotted two cracked cyan-blue robin's eggs oozing on the floor close to the washroom. He walked in. On the giant painting of Claudia Cardinale, close to her mouth, someone had drawn a penis using the robin's egg yolk.

"The way the yolk drips down kinda makes it look like—"

"Patrick." Paolo cut him off.

"I don't understand. Who the fuck would do this?"

Paolo slid the door open. When he walked in, he thought no one was in the bar centrale, but then he heard soft crying. His server Matteo was there, sitting on the floor in the corner, his head between his legs.

"Matteo, what happened? Did they hurt you?"

Matteo shook his head. "I'm sorry, Chef. They were like a tornado. I didn't know what to do. The black-haired one kissed me on my mouth and took all the potato chips off every table and put them in the pockets of his jacket. Justin Timberlake was here, and they took his hat. And then they started to sing, Chef. The song was bad." He started to cry again. "So, so bad."

Broken glass and spilled Cardinale cocktails lined the floor. Paolo saw a partially eaten simmered veal shank mondeghili sitting in one cocktail glass, and baccalà mantecato lying across a series of lit candles. Briefly, Paolo wondered what the candle heat did to the flavor of the salty cod.

Despite the chaos and the crying, Paolo began to calm down. This really wasn't that bad. It was a mess to be cleaned. And guests would no doubt be put off. Plus, he'd have to deal with the Justin Timberlake hat situation. But he felt like he could handle all of that. Those were fires he could put out. He looked for Patrick and saw him in the back of the room, examining the soccer painting.

The painting captured a moment in a match between Brazil and Italy in the early 1990s. The original photo featuring the legendary Italian defender Paolo Maldini and the equally famous Brazilian striker Romário was a classic, even used for a Nike ad campaign in the mid-nineties. Paolo loved that image, and Doe had one of his famous artist friends paint it in black and white as a gift for Paolo's forty-fifth birthday. It was also Doe's idea to use the painting as the clue to the hidden entrance to Paolo's little boteco.

"It's Italy and Brazil fighting each other for possession," Doe had said. "Just like in your soul. Plus, one of them is named Paolo."

He was going to explain the backstory of the painting to Patrick when he noticed something. There was a faint, tiny glow emanating from a crack just above Paolo Maldini's flowing hair. For a second, he didn't quite understand what he was looking at, and then it hit him: the light in the boteco was on.

"No," he said simply. They couldn't. You needed a key. As he got closer to the door, he searched in his pocket for his keys, but they weren't there. Patrick was still looking at the painting.

"You know, there's a cock on here too," he said, gesturing to a tiny drawing right next to Romário's mouth, but Paolo was beyond worrying about phallic art. He tried the door to the boteco and it pushed open.

"No," he said again, softly.

The ipe wood table, handcrafted for Paolo in his hometown, was broken in half and overturned, its legs thrust out in different angles like a grotesque deer carcass. The frames of almost all the pictures on the walls, most of them from Paolo's personal collection, were broken, with doodles on the actual photos. Many of these were just those same penises, but on the one of Paolo's grandmother holding his mom as a baby, someone had also drawn new, bigger breasts on the outside of his grandmother's blouse, complete with nipples leaking what appeared to be milk, and a thought bubble coming from his mother, which read, "Don't mind if I do!"

The Brazilian cowhide rug was missing. Three of the four hand-painted, mismatched chairs, each purchased from a different Brazilian boteco, were smashed, and the fourth had muddy footprints all over the seat. Snacks like his bolinhos de abóbora com carne seca lay on the ground half eaten but thoroughly stomped, intermixed with partially smoked vanilla cigarillos and two unwrapped sheepskin condoms. Each corner of the room smelled of either urine or vomit or both. And in the antique icebox in the middle of the room, in lieu of bottled Brazilian beers, sat a single, perfect Ecuadorian banana–size piece of human feces.

As Paolo stood staring at the shit inside his icebox, he saw a series of faces. His cousin's embarrassed, darting eyes when Paolo had first kicked a soccer ball in front of other kids in a Canasvieiras field. The flared nostrils of a French chef, even younger than he, making fun of his accent to the others as they chopped carrots in a Bordeaux kitchen. His ex-wife's mouth as she read his bad review in the *Times*, her lip curled into a sadistic smirk. An old chef colleague's look of disappointment and sadness when he ran into him in Boston's Public Garden and Paolo told him where he was working. But when his brain got to Charlie's face, he just saw a pulsating splash of red.

He turned to Patrick, who had picked up one of the sheepskin condoms with a fork and was inspecting it with a genuinely curious look on his face.

"Do you know how I could have someone killed?"

A FEW WEEKS LATER, Paolo was sitting on a bench in Boston's Public Garden for a ten a.m. meeting with someone who knew someone who could have someone killed.

As Paolo watched a teen wearing a Winthrop High School football letterman jacket throw a full Dunkin' Donuts iced coffee cup at a duck, a smaller, well-dressed man wearing a charcoal linen shirt sat down next to him. Immediately, he began leafing through a tattered Gerald Seymour paperback and, without looking up, said, "Chef Cabrini. I just wanted to say I've had your food and it's dead-on."

Paolo was surprised by the man's accent. After the incident at the boteco, Patrick had pulled him aside. "Look," he'd said, speaking softly. "I don't know anything, you didn't tell me anything, but if you're serious about the thing you asked me, I'll set up a meeting with my cousin. This is his world. But if I do, you can't fuck around."

Patrick hadn't told him anything else about his cousin, but now hearing the lilt-less, staccato, rapid-fire Belfast version of the language made him tense up. The Northern accent sounded to Paolo like someone had taken the beauty and lyrical quality of the Irish voice and stuffed it into a vise grip. It was rougher, faster, dirtier. And it was all he'd heard inside his head and out for the last couple of months.

The man continued.

"I've made you an appointment with a woman called Lara Bates."

"Today?"

"Aye. She's an interior designer. Her office is that way." He pointed back behind the ducks. "She can help you with your situation. But you need to follow the script. No mistakes."

Patrick's cousin sought out Paolo's eyes. "Pat vouched for you, so I've vouched for you. D'you know what that means?"

He nodded. Paolo knew people like this man back in Brazil. It reminded him of something his father used to say about a florist in their town who was connected to the underworld in ways Paolo didn't understand. "He may look light, but that's a heavy man."

Paolo noticed Patrick's cousin looking down at his feet. Paolo had put on one of his bespoke Boglioli suits—white shirt, no tie—and a pair of shoes he'd been forced to buy off the rack for the first time in a decade, because every pair of his bespoke John Lobb loafers had inexplicably gone missing.

"You've got the money?"

"Yes."

"Before you go see Ms. Bates you need to go to a store called J.McLaughlin on Charles Street, purchase their navy sailcloth weekender bag, and put the money in there. Leave the tags on the bag and keep the receipt. She's gonna want to see you made the purchase in the last hour."

"What if they don't have the bag?"

"They have the bag."

Paolo nodded. "What else do I need to do?"

"You got the folder?"

"Yes."

"You good at memorizing?"

Paolo shrugged.

"Well, see if you can memorize this."

Over the course of the next twenty minutes, Patrick's cousin explained exactly what Paolo was to do and say when he met Lara Bates. An hour later, Paolo was walking down Charles Street carrying a navy J.McLaughlin sailcloth weekender bag filled with $100,000 in cash.

BATES'S OFFICE WAS UP three flights of stairs on a small cobblestone lane off Willow Street in Boston's Beacon Hill neighborhood. As Paolo walked upstairs, he could feel his feet starting to blister in his store-bought shoes. It would be months before replacements for his missing bespoke John Lobbs would arrive from the U.K., and these new ones—"size 10.5D," a crude affront to the dazzling variety of human foot shapes—were choking the blood out of his feet.

When he got to the top, he saw a woman waiting for him, dressed in an impossibly crisp white long-sleeve shirt and olive-green twill pants rolled up past her ankles. She held out her hand, which Paolo noticed contained zero jewelry save a tasteful Cartier watch.

"Chef Cabrini. A pleasure to meet you. I'm Lara Bates. Welcome to Bates Design."

With her blonde hair, blue eyes, and splash of freckles, Bates reminded Paolo of something Doe had once said when they lived in Boston and found themselves surrounded by young old-money blue bloods at a place called 75 Chestnut: "They all look like they were created by the descendants of William Bradford in a John Kerry–endowed St. Paul's science lab specifically for a Skull and Bones recruitment video."

Patrick's cousin had told him Lara was considered one of the most coveted high-end designers in Boston. He said her client list was a tightly guarded secret, but it contained low-key celebrities and other insanely rich people who wanted to be slightly subtle about that fact. She also arranged contract killings.

Her office took up the entire floor of the old building. She gave him a quick tour. On one side, there was her "boring old fabric room," featuring shelves and shelves of fabric books and baskets of swatches organized by color and manufacturer. In the middle of the room was an island with big drawers underneath it that held floor plans and cut sheets from furniture vendors. One of the walls was lined with bookshelves featuring resource books for pricing out custom furniture, every edition of *Miller's Antiques Handbook & Price Guide*, and giant coffee table books with names like *Twentieth Century Design* and *Villa*.

Lara pointed out her conference room with a big, old oak table, and beyond that, her personal office, which Paolo couldn't see into because the glass was frosted. On the walls of the "den," she explained as she led him to a spot with a couch and chairs, she rotated works from local artists she'd met through galleries. Using local artisans was incredibly important to her, she told Paolo, noting that the oak coffee table next to the crushed velvet couch was made by a custom mill workshop in Lowell, and the rug was a loaner from her favorite vintage rug dealer in Maine. She offered him wine, beer, tea, coffee, or water, but he declined.

"But enough of that," she said, settling into an upholstered chair across from Paolo and tucking her legs under her body. "I want to hear about you and the scope of your project."

He tried to remember exactly what Declan had told him.

"Well . . . it's a one-bedroom."

Lara began to write on a legal pad. "Uh-huh. And what did you want done? Furniture and accessories? Are we just giving it a face-lift or are we getting into the bones of the project?"

"Furniture and accessories, yes. But, um . . . also, removal of the . . ."

Inside Paolo's head, he could hear the sound of his heart beating. Lara cut in.

"You wish for us to also dispose of the old items in the space as well?"

"Yes, yes, please."

"That's not a problem, but of course it will factor into the cost." Lara looked at him and gave a friendly smile. "Now, did you bring any inspiration with you? Any designers or architects you like? Anything that has caught your eye in the past?"

Paolo nodded. He could feel his hand sweating as he fumbled through the weekender bag and found the folder Declan had asked him to put together. Inside, amid pictures of cabins and other inspirational items, there was a printed picture of Charlie. It was the only picture of Charlie that Paolo could find, a selfie Charlie had taken using Paolo's phone in a Hard Rock Cafe in Times Square. In it, Charlie was smearing some sort of creamy sauce on the glass case containing The Edge's guitar.

Lara examined the picture, nodded, then glanced up at Paolo. "This is the only inspirational material you have?"

He nodded. He could tell that wasn't exactly what she wanted to hear. She got up, walked over to the bar, took a waxed cotton Barbour Acorn jacket off one of the bar chairs, and put it on a hook. Then she grabbed a bottled beer labeled Whale's Tale Pale Ale. "You sure you wouldn't like a beer?" she asked him. Ever the host, Paolo realized it would be rude for him to make a person drink alone.

"Sure, a beer would be great."

Lara nodded, took another out, opened both, and brought them over. He noticed she was now barefoot. Paolo took the beer and they clinked them together. He choked down a sip, thankful, at least, that the liquid was cold on the back of his throat.

"Oh, that's right! I forgot to ask." Lara took another pull of her beer, crossed her legs, and leaned back in the chair. "Am I the first designer you've reached out to for the project? No contractors or anything beforehand?"

Paolo didn't remember this question from Declan's script, but he could see the intent.

"Yes, of course. You were my first choice."

"And you would feel comfortable with me verifying that?"

Paolo had no idea what she meant. He could feel a bead of sweat drip from his neck and run down his back like ice cream melting in a cone.

"Yes . . . yes, that would be fine."

"Great. It's just important to understand that the design world is a small, small circle of people. Especially on the high end. And taking on projects is as much about each side understanding and agreeing with one singular vision as it is about having the money to be able to afford the work in the first place." Lara stopped to take a sip. "I know I'm lucky to be in that position, but I only got here because I treat every project with a certain level of care. And I expect the same from my clients. As someone at the top of his field, you surely can relate."

"Absolutely."

This seemed to satisfy Lara. She put the beer on the table and clapped her hands together.

"Great! I just have a few more little questions and then you can be on your way. The first deals with timeline. When were you thinking of breaking ground?"

"As soon as possible."

She wrote something down on her pad.

"Okay, well, I will certainly try to accommodate that. The next is budget. As I'm sure you were told, I require a deposit so I can begin contacting vendors and implementing our vision."

Paolo picked up the bag and put it on the coffee table in front of Lara. She felt the weight and looked at the tags and receipt.

"You can count it if you like," Paolo said. This was not in the script. As soon as it was out of his mouth, he regretted it. Beads of sweat emerged along the edge of his forehead.

Lara smiled at him.

"In my experience, it's important to establish a certain level of trust with your clients. If you find yourself worried that the money is wrong . . . well, you never should've allowed yourself to get that far in the first place." She took another sip of beer while keeping her eyes on him. "Like I said, I expect my clients' professionalism to mirror mine. Final item, and then I'll let you get out of here: I didn't see an address for the project among the items in the folder. If you'd just provide that, we can get moving as soon as possible."

Paolo froze, his throat constricted. Charlie was staying at his place. It could not happen there.

"I don't . . . um, I don't . . ." English was suddenly becoming difficult. His mind was growing blurrier. He wasn't sure how to phrase what he wanted to say in the proper coded language. Lara tried to help a bit.

"Right, I'm guessing you haven't actually purchased the place yet, but know you want us to work on it when you do. That's not a problem. We just need the neighborhood or the city you're looking to buy in, so we can start the paperwork process for permitting and so on, to get things moving according to your expedited timeline."

His stomach began to sink past his intestines and slide down his legs. Paolo hadn't thought this through. He tried to think of the script, but English was no longer registering as a viable language in his brain. Each word he spoke, he was forced to translate in his mind.

"I am sure I want to purchase . . . somewhere in New York? I am sure of that. I am sure."

Lara nodded, her face sympathetic.

"Chef Cabrini, I would love to work with you, but I'm worried that, without more details, there isn't much for us to do at this juncture." Lara stood up, indicating that the conversation was over. "But honestly, it was so great to meet you and connect. May I suggest—"

Paolo's body began to shake. All of his years of cognitive, behavioral, cognitive-behavioral, psychodynamic, humanistic, interpersonal, and dialectical therapy, his flirtation with Quaker beliefs, the Buddhist meditation temple retreats, the yoga, the tai chi, the Medium essays on inner peace, all of it was out the fucking window.

"Não!"

English was gone. He stood up, his eyes hot and wet, sweat pouring from his hair into his face. When he spoke, he spoke loudly and in Portuguese.

"I NEED YOU TO GET SOMEONE TO KILL CHARLIE MCCREE! HE IS IN MY HOUSE BUT I DO NOT WANT YOU TO KILL HIM IN MY HOUSE!! I AM UNCLEAR ON HOW TO TELL YOU THAT! I HAVE DONE WHAT YOU ASKED!"

As he shouted, he took a step toward Lara. But before he could get out another word, she was pointing a pistol right between his eyes that she'd pulled from somewhere inside the couch cushions. He felt the small, cold metal circle of the gun's firing hole pressed against his forehead.

"Look at me," she said, calmly but firmly. It took Paolo's brain a second to process the fact that she was speaking in perfect Brazilian Portuguese. "Look at my eyes, Paolo."

Paolo forced himself to look into her eyes. They were a deep blue, a Maine blueberry blue, and for just the flash of a second, he remembered a moment from his past when he was standing over an open fire in the middle of a rocky beach in Falmouth, searing fresh salmon and pairing it with agrodolce blueberries.

She spoke calmly in Portuguese again.

"Listen to me. I need you to think very carefully about what you do or say in the next thirty seconds because it will be the most important decision of your life." She paused. "Do you believe me?"

Paolo nodded, the muzzle of the gun sliding up and down his forehead. His brain was empty, but Lara's words filled the void.

"We are going to walk to this door, then you are going to leave my office, walk down the stairs, walk down Willow and Chestnut to Charles Street, turn left, and go back to your car parked in space D8 in the lot under Boston Common. Then you are going to drive back to New York and go on with your life. If you ever say my name again, I will know. Do you believe me? Say yes, in English, if you understand."

He said yes, thankful that she had given him the word.

With the gun still pointed between his eyes, Lara smiled, nodded, and kissed him lightly on the cheek.

"Boa sorte, Chef Cabrini. Tchau."

Paolo thought of nothing but her directions. He was good at following directions. He walked backward to the door. He turned, left the office, and walked down the stairs. When he exited the building, he walked down Willow to Chestnut, then over to Charles Street, turned left, and went back to his car parked in space D8 in the lot under Boston Common. When he got in his car, Paolo took off his shoes, saw that his feet were bleeding, and realized he'd left the bag of money in Lara Bates's office. Then he began to weep.

PART IV

AFTERMATH

23.

VLADIMIR "LAD" BENSHVILI

HENDERSON, NV

Tuesday, December 24, 2019, 8:22 a.m.

The cab was ten minutes early, which was perfect because Lad had been ready for more than an hour. He'd said goodbye to Jann that morning around six, just as Jann got home.

"You smell like spoiled strawberries left in a women's gymnasium," Lad said as he hugged him, his son's nipple rings poking him through his Supima cotton nightshirt.

Jann laughed. They looked at each other and shook hands.

"მადლობთ," Jann said.

"You're welcome."

Before walking out to the cab, Lad opened his bag and took a last look inside. He didn't want to feel burdened by goods. Life was not about the items you accumulate, anyway. So he was only bringing thirteen nightshirts. The rest he left for Jann in the garage of the house his only son had rented in a gated community in Henderson,

Nevada, overlooking a golf course. It was too big for just the two of them, but Jann had been adamant.

"Dad, you'll love it," he'd told him when they first visited. "Frank Sinatra once owned it."

As he walked out of the large yellow house, the driver met him to take his bag.

"The airport?" he asked, in accented English. Lad nodded.

The driver started to put the airport address into his phone so the satellites would tell the robots to tell him how to drive, but Lad didn't want this. He asked if the driver would detour along Las Vegas Boulevard. The driver pointed at the red lines on his traffic map and explained that the satellites had told the robots that traffic would be bad, but Lad said it was okay.

"The flight does not take off for a long time."

Lad liked Las Vegas. He hadn't thought he would—he had heard rumors in New York City that Las Vegas was a cesspool of swindlers and snakes and prostitutes and underworld men who legally owned Komodo dragons. To some extent, they were right. The Strip was a towering display of capitalistic recklessness, a garish circus of wealth beyond absurdity. There was a fake Venice, a fake New York, a fake Paris, a fake Camelot, a fake pirate ship, and a fake Sphinx, and a hotel that looked like a combination of a real penis and a microphone. But the artifice was honest.

Much of America, Lad thought, masked its true intentions. Façades were supposed to blend in. Things were made to look old and historic, even or especially when they were not. The vilest example Lad could think of was in New York City, where Jann had taken him to a new bar that looked, to Lad, like it was two hundred years old. The ceiling was so old they bragged about it, claiming it was the original. The bartenders were dressed like soft versions of hard men, with their suspenders and beards and tattoos of devils and glassware. Everything, they pointed out proudly, was done by hand.

The drinks, Jann had explained, were all from a time before America had outlawed alcohol because Protestants and women thought it made Catholics noisy. Because Lad couldn't see the menu in the dim candlelight, Jann had ordered for both of them, and when the bartender finally brought the drinks back twenty minutes later, Lad had taken a sip and nearly spit. Upon explaining to the pretend man that he'd made a mistake and poured vinegar into his drink, he had been told it was actually something called a "shrub," from America's colonial era, and it tasted like vinegar because the recipe involved "drinking vinegar, which was popular at that time."

Lad had stared into his eyes for only a count of seven before the man looked down, then asked if he'd consider making him "an actually good drink, which is popular now."

Vegas didn't have this problem. It was not obsessed with recapturing its past because it had no past. There was no distinguishing between native and invasive in Las Vegas, because Las Vegas itself was an invasive entity. And he enjoyed that. He liked that you could drive into Chinatown and see Chinese restaurants, but also French and Filipino and Colombian and Russian. Even in what were supposed to be ethnic pockets, there were no real rules. It was commerce. It was transactional. It was America at its most honest.

And so he did not mind that Lobio Vegas featured a hundred-foot re-creation of the mural in the original Lobio. In this version, Tamar was even Greater and George V somehow more Brilliant (Zaza Pachulia remained the same). And he was impressed that the waters of the Black Sea shown in the mural actually morphed into real water, dyed deep-blue, and guests of the restaurant could choose to eat their meals lounging at swim-up tables from servers in red-and-white

Georgian flag bikini tops, or in the Caucasus Mountain VIP Mezzanine, which sat halfway up the mural, and featured cave-like private spaces that appeared to be built into the mural's mountain range.

He felt little shame that Lobio Vegas's signature dish/drink, created by Jann, was the Khachapuri Kocktail, a cheese boat featuring four sparklers stuck into the house-made mixture of imeruli and sulguni cheeses and butter, plus a bread funnel on the end. When someone ordered one, the bikini servers would bring out a bottle of chacha, a Georgian pomace grape brandy (Jann had it made exclusively for the Vegas restaurant) in a bottle painted with a lion shooting a tattoo-covered machine gun. Then, as the speakers all played "Tavisupleba," the Georgian national anthem (rerecorded in an American way by a disc jockey named Khaled), whoever ordered the cocktail would kneel in front of the khachapuri and drink the chacha out of the bread funnel before they could start eating the dish. Each Khachapuri Kocktail cost $149. By their second day in business, Jann told Lad that Lobio Vegas had gone through five hundred bottles of chacha.

The success had not surprised Lad. He was no longer shocked by the decisions Jann made. After the TV program about the dead man came out, Jann had brought several men to meet with Lad. With their greyhound-like features, tattoos, American accents, and Eastern European names, he'd recognized that they were the type of men Jann would know from his time involved with nightclubs in New Jersey. These were confident young men with lots of money, and they'd wanted to back an aggressive expansion of Lobio, starting with Vegas "but eventually moving on to Dubai and farther." He'd looked at the terms of the deal and even brought in a Hungarian lawyer he knew from his building in Queens, fully expecting this to be some sort of loan-sharking pyramid scheme that would eventually result in both of their deaths by Komodo dragon. But the lawyer had said it was real, and the terms were favorable. After a brief negotiation in which Lad secured final say on the design of any and all sleepwear-based promotional merchandise, he'd sold his shares in Lobio to his son and these men, and was bought out of the entire enterprise.

And though the success hadn't surprised him, Jann occasionally still did. The restaurant featured the original signature dish of lobio. When he saw it, Lad immediately thought of what his mother had said when he'd started his restaurant so many years before. He'd called her to ask about her lobio recipe. At the time, he'd been consumed by the idea of making the version she made, but he could not find pomegranate molasses or blue fenugreek. He searched all over. He was tortured. He wanted to make it "authentic," he'd told her. At this, she'd laughed.

"What is this *authentic*?" she'd said in a mocking tone. "You are thinking of a version of lobio I made when you were here. But my lobio was different from our neighbors and their neighbors. And the lobio I make today is different from that one. Is my new version not authentic? Was the neighbors'? It is all a story in your head. Use what you can use. That's your lobio."

On the Lobio Vegas menu, which was made to look like a weighty, seventeenth-century religious tome, Jann had put the dish directly in the center and, in a different color font from the other dishes, had named it Lad's Lobio.

In the description, it said it was "internationally famous deceased TV personality John Doe's favorite dish in the entire world (RIP)." Though it went on to describe the making of the beans with what Lad later noted were several inaccuracies, he had still teared up when Jann had first shown him the menu.

"This is all because of you, Dad," Jann had said, his voice breaking slightly. Lad had tried to meet his eyes, but seeing that they also seemed wet, he'd realized this was one of the few times when it was acceptable if they both looked away.

AS THEY INCHED their way up Las Vegas Boulevard through the Strip on the way to the airport, Lad learned about the man driving. He was from North Africa and had come to the United States just three months earlier. Lad asked this man what he'd done for work back home. Lad had heard stories of immigrants from that area coming over, professionals who had been doctors or engineers or lawyers who now had to start at the bottom of the American job ladder, and, upon meeting this man, figured this was his story. *A radiologist*, Lad thought. *Or perhaps something with architecture.*

"I drove a cab," the man said. He paused. "You came to America too, yes?"

"Yes."

"So you are an immigrant as well."

"Yes."

The driver looked in the rearview mirror. "And success now?"

Lad shrugged. They both watched a man on the corner dressed as Elvis advertising a buffet.

"But you are going on a trip? A vacation?"

"Mykonos."

"The beach!" The man seemed to light up. "I know Mykonos. It is beautiful. You are being . . ." He searched for the word but didn't come up with it. "You have success."

As they neared the turnoff for the airport, the cab driver spoke again.

"Do you have tips for me?"

"Maybe when you finish your drive."

The cab driver laughed good-naturedly.

"No, not tips," he said, searching for the word. "Advice . . . as someone who just came to America?"

Lad thought about this. If he had had someone to mentor him when he got to America, what guidance would he have wanted? That you had to work for decades in small, bad jobs until you'd saved enough to open a business, and then wait for someone to pretend a famous man who died liked your business? That the secret to America was not to try to understand it? What sort of advice was that?

Finally, as they pulled up to the drop-off point at the airport, Lad spoke.

"Albanians," he said, as he handed the man cash for the ride. "Do not trust them."

The cab driver nodded solemnly and wrote this down in a notebook.

"Well," he said, shaking Lad's hand. "Enjoy Mykonos. I will see you when you return."

Lad stared at the man for a count of eleven. To his credit, the man met his gaze the entire time.

"I'm never coming back," he said.

24.

CHEF PATRICK WHELAN

WEYMOUTH, MA

Tuesday, December 24, 2019, 2:33 p.m.

The first thing Patrick did when he'd arrived back in Weymouth in August was call Funeral Joe.

Funeral Joe owned zero funeral homes but had several buildings in Weymouth. One of them was a broken-down old bar, not far from the Fore River Bridge. Patrick wanted it.

"Fuck you want that for?" asked Joe. "It's a piece of shit."

"I want to make it a pub."

"A pub, huh? But not *The* Pub, right, Paddy?" Joe said, and laughed at his own joke for ten seconds before an explosive phlegmy coughing spell ended the fun. Patrick sighed. It was good to be home. They made the deal that day. Patrick and Declan, who always seemed to have extra money that Patrick couldn't account for, would be co-owners, with Patrick's mother, Siobhan, getting 10 percent just to keep the boys honest.

Upon stepping inside, Patrick realized the place was, in fact, a piece of shit, but it had a long mahogany bar and booths along the back wall, and that was good enough for him. He attacked it with a nearly religious fervor, sanding and sealing the bar, installing new hunter-green treated leather booths and bar seat covers, and ripping the floors up and reusing the original wood, which he finished with a dark stain.

One day, as Patrick and Declan were sanding the bar, Patrick made a crack about the rather pointy and shiny nature of Declan's shoes. Declan grabbed the back of Patrick's head and slammed his face against the bar, exploding his nose like a piñata. Then, in one quick motion, he took off the handle to the Guinness tap and smacked Patrick in the knee with it, causing him to buckle and crumple to the floor. Declan stood over him, holding the tap like a club, and sighed. His expression looked almost bored.

"All right, Patrick?"

As he sat up and tried to stop the bleeding using his Aerosmith *Get a Grip* tour T-shirt, Patrick tasted the metallic flavor of his blood.

"Honestly, this is a huge relief," he said, stretching out a hand to Declan, who took it and pulled him back up.

So much for the Krav Maga.

Once the bar, booths, and floors were done, they put an old-school jukebox in the back and filled it exclusively with records they could all agree on (which basically meant the Pogues and Motown), and Patrick created a dead-simple Irish food menu, with three rotating dishes as the meal of the day, depending on his whims and the farmers market. For those inclined, he also had his mother's three favorite bar snacks: Tayto cheese and onion crisps, Bolands custard creams, and Jacob's cream crackers with Irish butter.

They had Guinness on tap, good Irish whiskey behind the bar, and two natural wines, both of them selected by Jackie, with whom Patrick had gotten back in touch. To appease any crotchety townie bastards, they kept tall boys of Budweiser under the bar and basically served them at cost. *Doe always liked little quirks like that*, Patrick found himself thinking one day as he stocked the bar. *John would've liked this place.*

Befitting his personality, Declan preferred to remain a silent partner. Patrick decided, from the start, he would mainly just tend bar. He would cook whenever he wanted to and prep in the mornings with Caetano, the old Brazilian he'd hired from Framingham, but that was it. To help, he'd also hired a local girl named Kathy, who took classes at Massasoit, as his server. He offered his seventy-eight-year-old mom any job she wanted, but after decades of working in pubs, she declined a formal role. Because her name was on the door, she said, she preferred to just "walk around like she owned the place."

Siobhan's had opened on November 24, two weeks ahead of schedule.

There was no press release. No soft opening. No friends-and-family or media-preview nights. The pub had no social media accounts. To commemorate its grand opening, Patrick just wiped down the bar and tables with a wet rag and unlocked the door.

A MONTH LATER, Patrick saw him.

It was Christmas Eve. The pub hadn't yet opened but there was already someone waiting on the step, pacing back and forth, holding a bag. He didn't have a jacket on, and his hooded sweatshirt looked damp.

"Come on in," Patrick said. "Get out of the cold, for god's sake."

When he said that, the man smiled broadly and lowered his hood, revealing a head of obsidian hair.

"Howya, Patrick?"

His hair was longer and he was much thinner, with facial hair that gave his face a wet-wolf quality, but it was definitely him. The man Paolo knew from Belfast. Charlie held out his hand.

"I'm sorry," Patrick stammered, as he shook it. "I've forgotten your name."

"Charles Ulysses McCree," the man said. "But my friends call me Smilin' Charlie."

Charlie walked over to the bar and pulled up a stool by the cocktail garnishes. As Patrick offered him a pint and some food, his mind raced. *Why would this man be in his bar? What the fuck was happening?*

During the 119 seconds it took to finish pouring the Guinness, Patrick texted Declan: "Paolo's problem here. In bar."

Immediately, Declan called.

"What's he doing?"

"Nothing," said Patrick, glancing at the man. "Just eating and drinking, by himself."

"Okay, I'll get back as soon as I can. Going to be a wee bit, though."

"Why?"

"I'm north of Bangor."

"Maine? Why?"

Declan ignored the question.

"Don't leave the pub. Just keep him there. And Patrick . . ."

"Yeah?"

"There's a pistol behind the cash register, a bat under the ice chest, and a tire iron in the beer fridge."

"Jesus fuck!"

But Charlie clearly had no plans to go anywhere. For the next six hours, he didn't move. He told long, winding stories about his recent travels around New England, and tales of his uncles and their Republican heroism in Ireland, pausing only to repeatedly ask Patrick if he could crash at his place just for a wee bit. And he sang songs—some songs actually playing on the jukebox, but more often than not random ones sung in a spirit of competition. Though he seemed to have no cash or card, Charlie offered to buy rounds of drinks for others who came in, including a woman in her thirties, who had the poor luck to take a seat next to Charlie.

She was dressed in a denim jacket with curly brown hair and a pretty smile. Patrick took her for a Weymouth townie, and half expected—when Charlie started to talk to her—for her to tell him to fuck right off. But, shockingly, she seemed taken by the man, laughing at his stories and accepting his drinks (which Patrick knew were actually *his* drinks) and, as the evening wore on, she somehow didn't leave.

Around eight p.m., Declan finally appeared. Dressed in a charcoal peacoat with a plaid scarf, he walked in and, following Patrick's eyes, located Charlie and his woman friend at the bar. For the next few hours, Declan wiped down tables, emptied the trash, and brought out food. But for the most part, he just watched Charlie. The Irishman drank pint after pint, sang, misquoted poetry, and inquired as to whether Patrick's guest bedroom had "a proper door." Both Patrick and Declan were flummoxed. Charlie offered no tell, no tip-off as to his true intentions. Declan had known men who would laugh at your jokes, sing "The Patriot Game" with your mother, and then disappear your body in a field, but usually with them you could see the hard coils hidden beneath the soft layers if you looked. Charlie appeared to be soft all the way through. And that scared them even more.

A half hour before last call, as the bar emptied out, Declan walked over to Patrick.

"Enough of this," he told him. "I'm going to see about yer man."

And with that, Declan sat down on the other stool next to Charlie at the bar, ordered a shot of Jameson and a pint back, and waited for an opening.

When Charlie told the story of a flat he'd lived in with friends in New York being "totally banjaxed," Declan took the shot, saw his opportunity, and cut in.

"Banjaxed?" He let out a little whistle. "Haven't heard that in a while."

Patrick stood at the garnish station cutting lemons, keeping his eyes down. Declan turned his body toward Charlie and smiled.

"Both from Belfast?" he asked, nodding in their direction.

"Just me," Charlie said. He turned his head toward the woman. "She's too lovely. Was just telling her about growing up in Divis Flats there. It's mad."

Patrick set down a pint in front of Declan, who grabbed it and took a long pull. His eyes flashed.

"You're from the Flats?"

"Aye."

"Where?"

"Here and there, me ma moved us around," he said, turning his attention back to the woman. But Declan wasn't finished.

"When did you move out?"

Charlie didn't turn around.

"Never did! Had its problems, but it was home."

"Kinda hard to live there these days, though, isn't it?"

At this, Charlie finally turned back around.

"Is it?"

"They knocked the Flats down in 1993. So yeah, mate, I'd say living there'd be a bit complicated."

"Too true, sad to say," Charlie said. "Me ma used to say it's a foolish man who thinks he can impede the march of time . . ."

Once again, he turned around to face the girl. And once again, Declan went in.

"My family's from the Flats. Actually, before that, when it was Pound Loney. My da was on the Demolition Committee. But my point is this: if you were in the Flats, I'd know you." He paused to take a sip, then looked Charlie full in the face. "And I don't know you."

Patrick watched as Charlie, a wide smile on his face, stared back at Declan. For the first time since he'd entered Siobhan's, Charlie's body was perfectly still. Declan didn't move either. But Patrick saw a small smile make its way across Declan's face. Most of the talking in the bar seemed to have ceased. The only sound came from the jukebox as the Pogues' "Fairytale of New York" started up again for the fourth time in a row. Finally, after fifteen seconds, the woman sitting next to Charlie broke the silence.

"All right, you're both tough, we get it," she said, slapping forty dollars on the bar. She put her arm around Charlie and whispered something in his ear. Charlie's already improbably wide grin somehow got even wider. He turned and, with a dramatic flourish, removed the woman's coat from the back of her chair, holding it open as she slid her arms inside.

"Fantastic evening, lads," he said. He turned to Patrick, handed him his bag, and winked. "Don't wait up."

And with that, he and the woman walked out the door, Charlie loudly serenading:

> *I'm handsome*
> *You're pretty*
> *Queen of Weymouth City*

For a good thirty seconds, both Patrick and Declan stared back at the door, almost as if to be sure Charlie was really gone. As "Fairytale of New York" picked up again for the fifth consecutive time, Declan drained his pint, reached over the bar, and grabbed the bottle of Jameson.

"That man's not from Belfast," he said. He poured the shot. "I'm not even sure he's from Ireland."

25.

CHARLIE McCREE

WEYMOUTH, MA

Tuesday, December 24, 2019, 11:52 p.m.

Jesus fuck, what a ride, Charlie thought. He took the girl's hand and rose drunkenly to his feet like a newborn colt, clumsy now but he'd be riding soon enough—in more ways than one ha ha ha. *Wasn't life exciting?* he thought. *Wasn't life surprising?* Just months ago, all of his days and his weeks and his months were the same: carrying luggage and attending to the demands of spoiled foreigners during the week and raging on the weekends. And for a time, Charlie had convinced himself that that was enough. That it was all he really needed. But it wasn't. He now knew what life really had to offer. A chance meeting had led to a wondrous adventure, during which he'd carried the lemon with him like a talisman the whole way. That humble piece of citrus, grown in Bannfoot, a small village in the townland of Derryinver, delivered a world of riches unto him. It gave him variety, novelty, the world, a life.

At the same time, Charlie had noted a change in Chef Cabrini—his patron and best friend in all the world. He'd had some bad luck, sorry to say, and it had made Charlie sad. He had suspected the chef needed some time to himself. Charlie would take his leave. But before he kissed the beautiful man on his head and thanked him for all he'd done, he'd decided to leave the lucky lemon behind, as a gesture of thanks. But he didn't want to just hand it to Chef Cabrini. He wanted it to be a surprise. After considerable thought, he'd placed it in Chef Cabrini's medicine cabinet, right on top of his straight razor.

Charlie had been traveling ever since, looking for his next great adventure. Who knew what the world would have in store now for ol' Smilin' Charlie? He was alone—his bandmates and their associates had all gone home—but Charlie didn't mind. Maybe his future wasn't in music, after all. Sure, Charlie had felt adoration that night at the Pluto. He'd never forget the faces of the audience members who had made it such a special night. It was intoxicating, better than any drink or drug, and he could certainly see how people might get hooked on stardom. But not Charlie. Not anymore. He knew but one sup of the nectar of fame could change a man, make him a stranger to himself.

No thank you, Charlie thought. He was after something pure, something true.

That's not to say that he was done with music, though. Not by any stretch. Charlie loved music, maybe more than ever—now that it had been unshackled from the corruptions and obligations of fame and money. He'd never survive without music. He wouldn't want to. On the bus to Boston, he'd closed his eyes and imagined the next few decades of life—making a modest but lovely home with a beautiful wife and fourteen ruddy children—and music was always there. In his dream, he was always singing to them. Love songs and sad songs and fight songs to raise their spirits and ease their journey through this life. And when he finally died, his children, and their children, and *their* children would remember first and foremost the music, and they would sing to him at his bedside as he headed home at last. Home. Charlie was so moved by this image that he suddenly broke into song on the bus. For hours, he sang. The other passengers just went mad for it.

Charlie had been on the road for months, though it seemed like days. Hours. He couldn't even remember where he'd been, or what he'd been doing, or who with. There was only one thing he remembered, a scene that fell upon him like fate's hand. The day prior, he'd been busily availing himself of the free samples at a Starbucks in a place called Nashua, New Hampshire, when he was comforted by a familiar face. It was Patrick Whelan, the great chef and grand lad he'd had the pleasure of meeting in New York City. According to the story, Whelan, God love him, had opened a wee pub in a place with an impossibly poetic name, *Weymouth*. He was returning to his roots, the article said. Charlie had fallen into a state of wonder as he'd pondered this establishment. He'd wondered how it would smell, feel. He'd wondered who among the plain people of Weymouth might gather there. He'd wondered what Patrick's house was like. Charlie had gone out and bought a ticket to Boston straightaway, and soon boarded a bus that rode smooth and fast, as though ferried by the angels themselves.

His bus pulled into South Station around lunchtime. It was quiet in the bright, airy terminal. He spotted a woman standing under a great clock. She was wearing an inexpensive Timex watch, but her face had true character.

"Sorry," he said. "Can you tell me what day it is?" he asked.

"Why, it's Christmas Eve," she said, her eyes shining.

Christmas Eve, he thought. *Wasn't life a wonder?* He thanked her and followed the signs across the terminal, down the escalator to the subway, where he waited a long time for a train to arrive. But when it did, it was clean and pleasant. Charlie stretched his legs and wished a middle-aged man in an Adidas tracksuit and scally cap a happy Christmas. The man just stared at him, but in that hard stare danced a multitude of good wishes. The train was otherwise quiet. Charlie sat in contented silence until the train reached a place called Quincy Center. From there he caught a 220 bus through Quincy and into this town called Weymouth. The bus ran through humble neighborhoods, offering glimpses of the ocean. When it had arrived at Wessagusset Beach, the smell of the full sea came upon him.

Patrick Whelan's bar was a few blocks away from the bus stop. The air was cold and salty, the light hard and bright. Charlie had walked along the seawall by Wessagusset Beach, feeling the sun on his face and the cracked sandy pavement below his shoes. It felt like home. He tightened the hood of his sweatshirt against the cold and adjusted his pack. It only held the essentials: jeans, sneakers, T-shirts, all of Paolo's shoes. Not even a wallet or any form of identification. Just a wad of cash and a heart full of dreams. It was enough for a start.

Patrick's bar was as gorgeous a pub as Charlie had ever laid eyes on. The exterior was irresistible. You could see inside, and inside looked like heaven, even at this early hour—all dark wood and golden light. He had gripped the iron door handle and it felt substantial in his hand. There was a click, and suddenly the door was open, and your man Patrick Whelan was standing there in front of him.

"Come on in," Patrick said. "Get out of the cold, for god's sake."

Charlie stepped across the threshold and grinned.

"Howya, Patrick?" he said.

Only then did Patrick recognize him. His face lit up. He was beside himself with delight to see this humble, happy traveler again. This ghost from a previous life. Charlie offered his hand.

"I'm sorry," Patrick stammered as he shook it. "I've forgotten your name."

"Charles Ulysses McCree," he said. "But my friends call me Smilin' Charlie."

"Kitty, get our man here a drink," Patrick said. "And some food. Are you hungry, Charlie?"

"Always."

"Always. Kitty will take care of you."

Charlie had erupted into a compulsively sensual version of "Kitty" by the Pogues. He stayed for the whole day. It was bloody fantastic. There were songs, there were stories. The whole night was good craic. People came in, and people left, and everyone talked, and laughed, and sang, and all the while Charlie's conviction strengthened that this was his final destination. Charlie McCree was home at last.

HE HAD PLANNED to stay that night until closing and then try to follow Patrick back to his place and see about crashing there for a night, or a week, or maybe more. But then Charlie had met Heather. She'd come right up and sat down next to him. She was beautiful. She had curly brown hair and was wearing a denim jacket and Adidas Superstars, her cheeks ever so slightly flushed. She looked very familiar. *Was she an actress?* he wondered. *Had he seen her in the films? On the telly?* It was on the tip of his tongue. But then he placed her: she was on his bus this afternoon! Outrageous! Miraculous! What were the odds that they would wind up together in this same humble pub? It was as if their meeting were preordained by the angels. Charlie always considered himself a very lucky man, but this was almost too much.

He looked at her. She smiled. "Mind if I join you?" she asked.

"You were on the bus," he said, wide-eyed.

"What bus?" she said, coyly.

"The bus! The fuckin' bus! From Nashua," he said. "What on earth are ye doin' here?"

She looked at him with faux seriousness and arched an eyebrow.

"I guess I must be following you," she said, then winked and stole a sip of his beer.

He was hooked. In seconds. Sold. That was it. That was her, at last, in this little bar, in this humble town at the end of the world. He knew. He *knew*. Children would not be far off now.

As the night plowed on, with Heather at his side, Charlie only gathered force. He became magnetic, magnificent. He ascended to the rarified air. He became Prince Charlie of Weymouth, friend to man and woman, leader in song, and the world lined up behind him. Then, at 11:45 p.m. on that blessed Christmas Eve, Heather suggested they retire to the outdoors to perform an act of exuberant filth upon the beach. "I thought you'd never ask," Charlie said. He left his bag with Patrick, telling him not to wait up. He took his new love's hand, and they swept out into the cold night air, singing a devastatingly witty play on one of the auld songs.

Snow had begun to fall. Heather led him two dark blocks to the seawall, and then—looking both ways to make sure no one saw them—she hastened down some crumbling steps to the beach. Giggling like a couple of kids, they scrambled across the stony sand and nestled into a dark space against the seawall. He could see the moon in her eyes. He could smell the sea.

"I found you," he said. "At last, I found you."

But now there was another beautiful woman too. Charlie couldn't believe his luck! Two for one! *Oh beautiful, for spacious skies! For amber waves of grain!* This one was blonde, wearing a cable-knit cashmere sweater, fitted tweed pants, riding boots, and a Barbour Acorn waxed cotton jacket. He saw a glint on her wrist and identified it as a Cartier Pasha in yellow gold. Worth $10,000 if it's worth a penny. My goodness, the caliber of person Charlie continued to find himself in the company of! He looked to Heather for confirmation that this was all really happening, but Heather was already away, running up the steps in the seawall. *Oh well,* thought Charlie. *That's America for you. Easy come, easy go.*

The new woman pulled a silenced pistol out of her jacket and shot Charlie in the forehead. He felt his knees go out, and he crumpled to the cool, damp sand. She stood over him and shot him twice more. But he didn't feel those. He hardly felt the first one, if he was being honest. If one of his mates were to ask him, "Smilin' Charlie, what's it like to take a bullet to the forehead?" he'd say to them: "O, it's just a little bump. A love tap.

"A kiss," he'd say. "Why, you hardly feel it at all."

26.

NIA GREENE

JUDEAN DESERT, ISRAEL

Tuesday, March 10, 2020, 10:10 a.m.

Last Call had returned to production.

In place of a first episode, EEN planned to run a documentary, *Water Mud Blood Bone: The Life of John Doe*, executive produced by Nia Greene, which was already attracting Emmy buzz. After that, the network planned sixteen episodes, starting with a shoot in Israel and Palestine. After that: Uganda, Pakistan, the Central African Republic, Iraq, Afghanistan, Venezuela, Brazil, Laos, Haiti, and other troubled places. The selection—which would be complicated and expensive to shoot, and which required new crews that were trained to operate in combat zones—was pitched by the network as a tribute to John Doe. The idea was that *Last Call* would seek out grace and beauty at the tables of those who lived in places haunted by darkness and despair. It would show people who may themselves be struggling how people in even worse circumstances find comfort and community with family, friends, food, and drink.

Nia Greene sat on the hood of a white Range Rover gazing up at Masada, a fort atop a mountain at the edge of the Judaean Desert, overlooking the Dead Sea. On the side of the mountain there was an ancient ramp—barely recognizable as such—that reached the plateau at the top. It was supposedly built by the Roman army in the first Judaean Roman War, around AD 70. They were trying to get to the fortress, in which about a thousand Jewish holdouts sheltered. Rather than surrender to the Romans, the holdouts are said to have killed themselves and their families on this site.

Next to her, sitting on the Range Rover, was Paolo. He was smoking a lump of hash he'd scored in Tel Aviv. He had renewed his contract with EEN, partly because he cared about the show and wanted to make sure it stayed true to its founding spirit, and partly because he needed money. Nia had made it happen. He'd been in a bad way after the sacking of the boteco. While scouting locations for the show, she and Paolo had visited the Temple Mount in Jerusalem. The guide had told them that the destruction of the temple here by the Romans in AD 70 was an act that opened a permanent psychological wound. Paolo had nodded somberly. He knew how that was.

Perhaps more than Doe's death, that desecration had shaken Paolo's confidence and disrupted his focus. For the moment, he was done. The French Restaurant with the French Name had served its last meal in August. But Paolo came out looking good. Maybe even better. Nia had concocted a thoroughly fictitious story about an egg: how one day Paolo woke up, took an egg from its carton at home, and just froze. He couldn't recognize it; he didn't know what to do with it. The infinite possibilities presented by the item paralyzed him, obsessed him, and until he could figure out what to do with this egg, he would shut everything down. People loved that story. It was catching on as a metaphor in the culture, on entrepreneurship podcasts and self-help sites. It had even turned up in an essay by Malcolm Gladwell in *The New Yorker*, titled "Want to Be Great? Find Your Egg."

"You didn't want to go up?" Nia asked, nodding at Masada.

"No," Paolo said. "The boss wanted to do this one alone."

He handed her the pipe. Nia took a drag of the hash and nodded. They sat for a while.

"You happy doing this, Nia?" he said.

"It's a gig, man. What can I say?"

Nia looked over, cocked her head, and took him in.

"You doing all right?" she asked.

Paolo pondered the question. "Yeah," he said. "Yeah, I think I am."

"That's good."

"Better than I was."

"I'm glad."

Paolo swung his jaw a bit and squinted in the hard desert light.

"You ever think about the photo?" he asked.

Nia tried to follow his gaze.

"Yeah. I mean, I did," she said. "All the fucking time. But then he left, and at some point, I just kinda stopped."

"Yeah."

"I mean, look, we're all one hack away from being embarrassed on the internet. It's just the times." She spit on the ground. "Plus, I'm fucking tired."

Paulo nodded. Then a ghost of a smile appeared at the corner of his mouth. He chuckled.

"What?" Nia said.

He looked at her, as if to size her up, and nodded to himself. "If I tell you something, will you promise never to repeat it to anyone?"

"Sure."

"No, really. Not anyone. You're at the Pearly Gates and Saint Peter—"

"I can keep a secret, Paolo. You of all people should know that."

He nodded.

"I tried to get Charlie killed."

"What?"

"I was so fucked up last year that I actually went to a hit man. Or hit woman, actually. It was a woman."

"Bullshit."

"Oh no, Nia. I did. I really did. I had to get an introduction and go to Boston to meet her, and I had to bring this special bag with all this money in it. It was this whole thing. I had to do a spiel."

"Stop telling me this."

"But I didn't go through with it. I freaked out. I panicked in her office and started yelling at her in Portuguese. She put a gun to my head and stole the money. Fucking divine intervention."

"Holy shit, Paolo."

"So Charlie lives. That fucking sociopathic ska leprechaun. He walks among us because he got so far inside my head that I couldn't follow the simple instructions required to get him killed."

Nia could only stare.

"Anyway," he said, looking away. "I told you I was fucked up. That's how fucked up I was." Paolo took another drag. "But I remember, afterward, just bursting into tears in my car, and I was afraid, and I was sad, and I was lost, but mostly I was just *relieved*."

Nia nodded. They sat for a while longer.

"Sometimes I wonder what would have happened if I'd just told the truth," he said.

"You can't think that way, Paolo."

"Maybe. But I look at everything people wrote about him, and said about him, and the tributes, and the stories, and the suicide-prevention fundraisers, and even this show. I look at it all and I think, 'Man, John really would have hated this.'"

"Or he would have thought it was the funniest thing in the world."

Nia squinted at the top of the Roman ramp and handed back the hash. She stood up and stretched. "Here they come." There was a small band of crew members moving quickly back toward the trucks. Out in front, setting the pace, was Katie Horatio in a trim, flattering safari jacket and jean shorts. They were behind schedule. They had to get to a shakshuka place in Jaffa for dinner with a rabbi and an imam.

A minute later, she was upon them. Nia opened the door to the Range Rover.

"How'd it go?"

Katie strode past Nia and stepped into the car. Nia shut the door behind her and glanced over at Paolo.

"It's a gig," he mouthed. He went around the other side and opened the back door for Nia, and then got into the front.

Katie spoke up. "There was this guy up there in a cave doing a . . . what was it, Kevan?"

Kevan, the production assistant, said, "An illuminated Bible. He was a ninety-nine-year-old rabbi. He does these incredible—"

"Short answers, Kevan," Katie said. "So, this caveman was saying something about the Dead Sea. I don't remember what it was. We got it on tape. But we have to do a detour. I need to get some footage of me floating in it. Apparently, you float in it. You can't sink." She paused, and added idly, "Though maybe you could, Paolo."

Paolo looked in the rearview mirror at Nia.

"It's a gig," she mouthed.

"Katie, we're on a tight schedule here," Nia said. "We have to be setting up in Jaffa by two p.m."

"And if we're not, what happens, Nina? The fucking mook has to wait an hour before we tell millions of people to go eat in his egg restaurant?"

"He wants to get the shoot done before his dinner rush."

"And I want to fuck Donna Reed in the ass. We all want things."

Katie sat tensely—these pauses made everyone around her nervous, especially Paolo, who was her most frequent target due to what she claimed was his shaky on-screen presence. After ten seconds, she leaned forward and said sweetly to him: "Are you excited about the egg restaurant, Paolo? Or am I gonna have to stick a wooden spoon in your mouth to keep you from swallowing your fucking tongue on camera again?" She leaned back and chuckled. "You meatball."

She stared out the window at the passing desert.

"Wait a second," she added. "I have an idea. Stop the car, stop the car." The driver hit the brakes and pulled to the side of the road. "Kevan, get Vin in here with the handheld. I need this to look spontaneous."

"What should I tell him we're doing?" asked Kevan.

"We're going to make like we're gonna drive by the Dead Sea and I'm going to feel a sudden burning desire to wade into it. I'm thinking of John because of our little hike up suicide hill there, right, and I feel this irresistible urge to strip down to my underwear and go into that water and float, like I'm communing with him, or cleansing something. I don't know. But I need it to look spontaneous. Paolo, you sit back here with me. Nina, get out."

Nia got out of the car and back into the blast-furnace heat. Vin was already walking over with the handheld. "Kicked out again, huh?" He grinned and patted her on the back, or perhaps pushed her out of the way. Nia walked back to the other truck and got in. In seconds, the convoy was back on the road to the Dead Sea.

The trip had been a heavy one for her. Not just because it was the first episode of *Last Call* not featuring her friend, but because of the location. Jerusalem disturbed her. Some found it a place of quiet faith. She saw it as a wellspring of eternal war. The gates of hell. She was troubled by the men wandering around the streets of Old Jerusalem deluded into thinking they were Christ. But, really, was that so different from thinking some other guy was? The previous night, when they were shooting in Jerusalem, Katie had remarked, "We don't always believe because something is real. Something becomes real because we believe." She attributed it to Doe, which is to say, it was fake.

That irked Nia. "It might be worth remembering," she told Katie privately later, "if only every once in a while, that he didn't actually say any of this shit."

Nia would have loved it—really loved it—if Katie pointed out that, on the contrary, it actually was true. That Doe did say it, just not with his words. He said it with his being. He said it with his *life*. But instead Katie just looked at Nia blankly for a full five seconds, and then said, "Well, Nia, like W. C. Fields said to the goose: 'Shit green or get off my lawn.'"

THE MORNING KATIE had saved the TV segment—and gone on to read Doe's notebooks with an unsettlingly good imitation of being surprised and moved by what she found—they'd signed their deal. Katie had beaten the terms Doe had given Nia. Nia gave her the ten grand signing bonus but recouped it the next day when she sold Doe's notebooks for $2.5 million, paying off her two mortgages. Then Katie ordered Nia to get her the *Last Call* gig. Nia didn't appreciate being strong-armed, but it wasn't like she didn't have leverage herself. Either of the women could have destroyed the other, but in doing, so would have also been fatally damaged herself. They both knew it. There are worse things than mutually assured destruction. And the money was good.

Still, life with Katie wasn't easy. She was, as they say, complicated. She was brilliant but abusive and erratic. Nia had already had to talk a few of the crew members off the ledge and they weren't even done with episode one. She'd also had to cajole or sometimes pay off hotel workers and waiters who had found themselves the target of Katie's wrath. She had to endure a fair amount of abuse herself. Sometimes, early on in their partnership, Katie would call in the middle of the night and scream at her, and sometimes she'd call in tears and apologize, and then Venmo her $150 at three in the morning. After a few months, though, it was only the screaming.

More troubling, however, was a recent spike in what Paolo had taken to calling Katie's "episodes." These were more serious, and stranger. Katie spitting at a bartender. Katie throwing a full can of La-Croix at a flight attendant on a private jet. Katie getting caught shoplifting from Saks—twice. Katie having sex with a college student on the hood of a car around the corner from a nightclub that had photographers outside.

Nia had seen this sort of self-destructiveness before. The most charismatic people are often the messiest, the most careless. They always want to see how much more they can get away with, and sometimes it seems like they actually do want to be caught. In all her time with Doe, Nia had never made someone sign a nondisclosure agreement, but now she handed them out like flyers in Times Square. *Oh well*, she thought, *it's a gig. Worst case, I'm a well-paid flunky for a couple more years. Best case, the kid implodes and I skate away smelling like an only slightly shit-smelling rose. It wasn't impossible. No,* she thought, watching Katie grind her teeth in the front seat, *it wasn't impossible at all.*

THE LEAD TRUCK pulled over, and Nia watched as Katie stepped out, followed by Paolo and Vin the camera operator. She paused and said something to Paolo. Then she took off her shirt and shorts and walked toward the shimmering water. It was warm and oily from the minerals washed down from the surrounding hills. She undid her ponytail and her long hair poured down across her back. She wasn't trying to be sexy, and it didn't come off that way. It was meant to be profound, somber, a communion with an immensity. She waded into the water and turned. "It's warm!" she shouted back to the shore. When she got thigh deep, she pushed off and slipped below the surface. She came back up, turned over, and floated, her eyes shut, for thirty seconds. Then she flipped over and, with renewed purpose, she started back. She seemed clearheaded and focused as she took in the expanse of the desert beyond the shore of the Dead Sea. She reached the shallows and stood, smiling to herself as if at some private discovery. She stepped out of the water, her body glistening, and went to Paolo. The camera was maintaining a bit of distance, to give viewers the sense that it was eavesdropping on an intimate moment. Katie threw her arm around Paolo. He did the same.

"He's *here*," she said.

"I know."

"I really miss him," she said.

"Yeah," said Paolo.

They stood like that for a minute. She gave Paolo the sort of squeeze one brother gives another.

"Hey, buddy," she said. "Wanna get something to eat? I know a good place in Jaffa."

"Perfect," Paolo said, and smiled sadly.

She took his hand, and together they walked toward the truck.

The director called cut, and Kevan ran to pick up Katie's clothes.

"You get that?" Katie asked.

"We got it," said the director. "It's gonna look great, Katie."

"Great," Katie said, putting her shorts on. "Now can somebody throw me a towel or something? That water is fucking disgusting."

27.

KATIE HORATIO

TEL AVIV, ISRAEL

Tuesday, March 10, 2020, 2:21 p.m.

When they returned to Tel Aviv, the crew dropped Katie off at the Setai, a hotel built in a former Ottoman prison. She went up to her suite, popped a bottle of champagne, grabbed an apple out of a basket, and walked out onto the balcony overlooking the Mediterranean Sea. She took a bite out of the apple, but it didn't do anything for her. For some reason, she'd lost the ability to taste food. She reared back and threw it as hard as she could, hoping to reach the sea. Instead, it fell into the pool below, striking a child on the back with a great smack-thud. There was a commotion. A lot of shouting and running around and pointing. Katie was already back inside. She laughed and lit a cigar.

Katie took a hot shower and drank some more champagne. She got out, dried off, put on jeans and a navy-and-white gingham, Western-style button-down, tied her hair up with a green paisley kerchief, and threw on some boots. She looked sporty, fresh, young, optimistic, game. She looked great. *It's all been so easy,* she thought. *Talent and timing.* She felt fully in control of her destiny.

She picked up the phone and called Nia.

"Hi, Katie," Nia said. "We're almost set up over here."

"I'm in a limo mood tonight. Can you get me a limo?"

"Katie, it's like five blocks to the restaurant."

"We're in a fucking war zone, *Nina*. I'm not walking anywhere. I'm liable to end up with a rocket sticking out of my ass."

Nia sighed. "Katie . . ."

"Put that guy on the phone. What's his name? The fixer guy."

Nia sighed again. Katie heard her call over to the fixer.

"Hello, Ms. Horatio," Uri said.

"I need a limo for tonight. I'm in a limo mood. It's a limo night."

"But Ms. Horatio, it is only five blocks."

"What are you, a cartographer?" she snapped. "You think I hired you so you could dazzle me with your amazing fucking map skills? I hired you to get me what I want. And right now, I want a limo. A limo to the restaurant, and then a limo to fill with some tail from some of these clubs later."

"It is difficult to find a limousine on such short notice."

"You assholes can grow oranges in the desert, but you can't find me a limo? Fuck me! What is this, *The Twilight Zone*? Tell them to come get me in ten minutes."

"Yes, Ms. Horatio."

"Uli?"

"Yes, Ms. Horatio," sighed Uri.

"I'll also need a tarp."

. . .

THE SHOOT AT THE RESTAURANT went perfectly. It was a fifth-generation dump in Jaffa with a bunch of pans hanging from the ceiling. Katie was able to get her guests—the rabbi and the imam—to talk over shakshuka, which was something involving eggs in tomato sauce that everyone seemed really proud of but Katie found inedible.

The two men were uneasy at first, but Katie got them to talk about their families, their hobbies, and of course food. That fostered enough of a bond to allow them to move into more contentious matters. They got a little snippy from time to time, but Katie steered it expertly, being shrewd when she had to be shrewd and naive when she had to be naive. In the end, the men shook hands. It was fucking gold. The director called cut, and Katie leaned over and spit a mouthful of shakshuka into a bucket and left.

Watching the holy men eat eggs with their little hands had given her the willies. She wanted to get some air. She stepped outside into the ancient port city. A chauffeur opened the door to the limo parked on Beit Eshel Street, but Katie just walked by. She didn't want the limo anymore. There was something wrong about eating eggs and then getting in a limo. Not that she swallowed any of the eggs. Still, she told the limo to follow her on her walk because she didn't want to be kidnapped by Hamas or some other fucking thing. She came upon a main street and just walked across it, forcing cars to veer around her. She was jaywalking a lot more these days, she found. Why wait for other people to let you pass? Just fucking go, that was her motto.

The sun was setting. Katie stopped somewhere on HaYarkon Street by Independence Park, overlooking the sea. She had the sudden desire to swing by the Christian Louboutin store and steal some shoes. Maybe Burberry after that. Then the clubs. She'd seen an IDF soldier in a bikini on the beach and it had made her crazy. Maybe it was time for something new.

She turned to make sure the limo had been following her and waved it over. The chauffeur stepped out and held the door open as Katie got in. She felt the cool air on her face and the light but insistent pressure on her back as the limo pulled away. There was a little TV screen in front of her, playing clips from her own appearances. It was a nice touch, that TV, she had to admit. She looked closer. *There you are, you handsome son of a bitch,* she thought. Then she threw up all over it.

ACKNOWLEDGMENTS

When we excitedly told our literary agent/work-father David Granger we were working on a novel together, his response was, "Huh."

It wasn't that he didn't believe us—it was more that he figured that would be the one and only time he'd ever hear about this project. But a few months later, when we sent him a manuscript and—much to his relief—he actually liked it, he instantly became *The Lemon*'s first and best cheerleader, advocate, and reader. Having the best magazine editor in American history as our literary agent, friend, and dining companion is a luxury we hope we never take for granted, and we can't thank him enough. Here's to you, Granger. (Imagine we're all raising glasses of rare, expensive tequila we stole from your house.)

Our editor at Viking, Ibrahim Ahmad, was quite possibly the book's second-ever reader, and just as strong a champion. While his initial enthusiasm and understanding of the book augured well, it wasn't until the editing process got under way that we realized exactly what we were dealing with: Namely, one of the sharpest, funniest humans around, and the best book editor any of us have ever had. His intelligence and eye for details, character, and logic made this book 100 percent better. Plus, whenever the need to make fun of Kevin arose, he was both perfectly willing and positively unsparing. For that alone, he will forever be welcome at our table.

We're so grateful to the rest of the team at Viking for rallying behind us and the book, and for the expertise, encouragement, and unflagging energy they brought to the process. Thank you to Brian Tart, Andrea Schulz, Kate Stark, Lindsay Prevette, Rebecca Marsh, Lydia Hirt, Marissa Davis, Sara Leonard, LeBria Casher, Raven Ross, Bridget Gilleran, Colin Webber, Claire Vaccaro, and Jennifer Tait for being game.

ACKNOWLEDGMENTS

We want to thank Allison Warren at Aevitas for her steadfast belief in the book from the start, and her brilliant direction of the sale of the TV rights to *The Lemon*. Her drive, savvy, wit, strategic acumen, and patience in the face of our relentless malarkey made us feel like adult professionals, and not what we are. And thanks to Marios Rush for being the finest legal mind in the entertainment law game, while also possessing the best hats. We'll see you in Mykonos.

Thank you to Erica Brady for consulting on what an interior designer/assassin's Beacon Hill office might look like, and to our several other well-placed anonymous sources for informing us on the worlds of Hollywood and high-level crisis management. You know who you are.

And a special grazie to Mauro, Vilma, and Massimo Lusardi for their hospitality and generosity, and for being living examples of the unique combination of grit and grace it takes to flourish (for decades!) in the crushing world of New York restaurants. You've worked harder in the last two years alone than any of us ever will, and we are simply in awe of how good-looking you have remained. Grazie per il vostro amore, i vostri sacrifici, e le radici profonde che mi avete dato e sempre nutrito. VVTB.

The idea for this book was developed over a series of half-remembered afternoons and evenings at Swift Hibernian Lounge in New York City. It remains the finest literary bar in town, and we were both delighted and grateful when they agreed to let us shoot our author photos on the premises while John Slattery played cribbage at the bar.

We'd like to thank our spouses, Wendy, Jean, and Mike, for putting up with us, and our children, Annie, Peter, Cooper, June, Eva, and Marta, for doing everything we say, always. No questions asked.

Relatedly, we'd also like to apologize to our own parents for some of the contents of this book. While we are aware of the author J. P. Donleavy's dictum that the purpose of writing is to make your mother and father "drop dead with shame," please know that if there is something here you find objectionable, it was likely written by the other two, and not by your own darling child, who is probably just as appalled by it as you are but got outvoted.

Finally, a big shout-out to Marky, Ricky, Danny, Terry, Mikey, Davey, Timmy, Tommy, Joey, Robby, Johnny, and Brian, and all the other lads and ladies down at the Christmas. Save us a stool. We'll be back before you know it.